THE OCCUPATION OF ZAIMA

Georgeann Packard

THE
OCCUPATION OF
ZAIMA

THE PERMANENT PRESS
Sag Harbor, NY 11963

For information, address:
    The Permanent Press
    4170 Noyac Road
    Sag Harbor, NY 11963
    www.thepermanentpress.com

Library of Congress Cataloging-in-Publication Data

    Packard, Georgeann, author.
        The occupation of Zaima / Georgeann Packard.
        Sag Harbor, NY: The Permanent Press, [2018]
        ISBN: 978-1-57962-528-3
            1. Arab American women—Fiction. 2. Young men—Fiction.

    PS3616.A329 O23 2018
    813'.6—dc23   2018015649

Printed in the United States of America

FOR ALL OUR VETERANS, WITH GRATITUDE,

BECAUSE WE ASK OF THEM

WHAT SO FEW OF US WOULD DO

AND FOR DANA AND HANNAH,

TWO TOUGH COOKIES

I wish I could become
a stranger to myself
because I would love to meet again
the person I used to be

—ZAIMA AL-AZIZ

ZAIMA AL-AZIZ

LATE JANUARY 2006 • DEARBORN, MICHIGAN

dust
thick on the bookshelves
of my childhood room
coaxed by the open window
to fly like snow

snow I know well
but the dust of the desert better now
fine powder that flies like tiny stinging insects
upward from the cement pad of earth

nightmares when I sleep
terror when I wake
I never sleep more
than an hour at a time

everything frightens me
every noise loud or sharp
every hand reaching toward me
even holding only my change

I see dogs and cats
wandering the streets of Dearborn
and in Iraq I saw dogs and cats
feasting on human remains
and I cannot separate one from the other
so every pet becomes a pest
and every street unsafe

I may have killed innocents
which is as horrific
as not knowing for sure
we did not check
we moved on

dust
clouding my thoughts, my morality
igniting fires in my imagination
burying me in a slow dying
I will never again
be clean

I have become a stranger
to my father
will he ever stop distrusting the world?
and to my whimpering mother
will she ever stop her crying?
and to my sister who knows nothing
really
about the world outside hers

I wish I could become
a stranger to myself

because I would love to meet again
the person I used to be

tell her to choose differently
tell her to be more skeptical
not to trust so easily
and become inflamed by anger
or by pride

you leave the army
it does not leave you
you leave Iraq
Iraq does not leave you
the same

BRIGID BIRDSEY

FEBRUARY 2006 • EMPIRE, MICHIGAN

When Theodore Dash appears in the open door of Brigid's bar with snow flying behind him like feathers from a torn pillow, she immediately sees the boy. Not the tall, brooding, coatless man in the brown, hooded robe with a knotted rope around his waist. Not this man with the nearly shaven head and a tight, manicured beard.

Brigid sees only the boy he once had been, the fatherless boy with the kind and vulnerable heart. The boy who had been her gift every summer of their adolescence, blown north from Chicago. The boy at the top of a Sleeping Bear dune with the morning sun blazing behind him as he peered down at her, looking like Moses with God at his back.

His eyes now are not filled with the leaden pain of leaving on the last day of summer, but this evening with the pain of having been left.

It is a Saturday in the endless sameness of February in Empire, a tiny town on the Leelanau Peninsula. Nathaniel Jude Dash had died the day before and for Brigid and for all those fortunate enough to have known him, nothing feels normal. It's as if one soul departing has upset the earth's balanced orbit around the sun, makes the cold colder, the snowflakes uniform and bizarrely large. This loss will likely inspire even seasoned residents to reach for another blanket tonight or maybe just two fingers more whiskey to accommodate the change.

Brigid lays down her knife and wipes the stinging lemon juice from her chapped hands. She walks from behind the bar to cautiously approach the fragile man boy. She doesn't dare touch him but rather wills him into the room, and then closes the door behind him. Snow dusts the hood of his robe, his rounded defeated shoulders, and there is so much of the fluffy stuff in his short hair that he looks much older.

Theodore Jude Dash travels wordlessly to a barstool and sits there, his old man head in his hands.

The air in the bar is dense with two companionable aromas— one emanating from the woodstove, which holds no fire but reeks of ones past, and another wafting from the large brick of beef roasting upstairs. Brigid has been preparing all afternoon the offerings from the generous gentleman so recently deceased. Only Wednesday he had appeared (as he often did) bearing culinary goodies, this time a pudgy beef roast and a paper sack full of produce from his root cellar. So in order to squelch her frantic and unproductive grieving, she has prepared in hasty succession two apple ginger pies (Nathaniel's favorite); the roast dressed with dried thyme and rosemary and much garlic; roasted fennel, potatoes, and carrots; and a splendid condiment composed of sour cream, horseradish, and Dijon mustard.

Brigid Birdsey knows that her Bird's Eye View bar on Michigan Street just off M-22 will have a full house tonight. A good, solid meal will help many a mourner sop up the curative alcohol coursing through their veins. *Did Nathaniel perhaps foresee this need when supplying the comfort food?*

Brigid places an empty glass in front of Theodore. He pays her no mind but holds the glass in his hands as if perplexed about its purpose.

"I arrived too late," Theodore says, raising his head slowly with great effort. "Twelve hours too late."

This is a fact she cannot change or soften, so she says nothing. With all her preparations and sporadic emotional meltdowns, she looks overtired. Still, Brigid is a comely woman of twenty-six, with eyes the green of Irish hills, long auburn hair stacked randomly on her head, and possessing only nine fingers. Fortunately it was just a pinky that had been severed on a toboggan run when she was nine. But the loss has inspired the creation of several signature cocktails, such as the one she is now preparing in several pitchers, the Nine Finger Rum Slap. It features plenty of dark rum, locally produced cherry juice, fresh sliced ginger, and a generous squeeze of lime. It's quite sweet but "appropriate when your inner child wants to get sloshed," she likes to say. And for tomorrow's late-morning remedy, she might serve up Brigid's Bloody Pinky, a tomato juice and vodka treat with lots of horseradish (the snow) and a whole pickled jalapeño pepper (the finger). More likely she will mass produce The Cure, which involves beer, tomato juice, tabasco, a little lemon juice, and a smoky Slim Jim as a stirrer. Very popular.

"Too late." Again he speaks. "I wish Cooper would have called me directly instead of calling my mother. That wasted time." He paused to stare at the amount of rum she was dumping into the pitcher. "He asked for me. I guess he knew the Lord was calling his name.

"I had to rent a car," Theodore offers as an explanation for his failure to see his grandfather one last time, to hear the words the old man had only for him.

"You know he would understand," she manages. "The end came quickly. Cooper was with him."

He seems to ponder these bland niceties, but then shakes his head. His beard glistens with the melted snow and he wipes it with his sleeve. This simple gesture gets to Brigid in some vague maternal way so she quickly opens a bottle of Merlot and fills half his glass. It is what she knows to do to help.

"Do friars imbibe?" she asks innocently.

"We enjoy the occasional glass," Theodore admits. He takes a delicate, cautious sip. "The funeral is Monday at nine. At Saint Agnes's, of course. Will you come?"

She reaches through his detachment and touches his cheek just above the hard line of his beard. Then she leans across the bar and ever so sisterly kisses his forehead. He tastes like winter and incense and innocence. And she nods. She will be there. Fills the rest of his glass.

Outside his family, she believes she knows him as well as anyone. They grew up together. Were inseparable all summer long. Theodore was the first boy she ever kissed and she would sometimes fantasize about marrying him one day. She would move away with him to Chicago, away from the manure-dressed fields, and the annual cherry-mania, because Empire is all about the cherries. There's cherry wine and cherry salsa, cherry mustard, and chocolate cherries for the tourists. These are the same silly tourists who pay top dollar for T-shirts with the M-22 highway sign smacked on the back. No one who lives here would ever wear such a thing. But then Theodore had long worn one, even after it was ragged and obviously too small. But he was neither from here nor from away. Somewhere in the middle.

The boy went off to some Detroit university and then shockingly, to seminary. Brigid stayed in Empire where, unfortunately for her, the most common things talked about were the weather, someone's affair, or a surprise death.

This village is only a little more than one square mile with fewer than five hundred year-round residents, the majority being of German, English, and Irish ancestry. "A healthy mix of drinking cultures," Brigid has noted, "all plenty fond of a good pub." Many agree that the most magical thing about living there is the month of May. There are everywhere glorious orchards of cherries and apples, and even Brigid gets a little visually drunk when the whole Leelanau Peninsula is a blanket of delicate white and then pale pink blossoms.

The usual crowd starts filing into the bar just as the sun sets around five thirty. Brigid brings down the food and is then preoccupied with serving up shots, plenty of the Nine Finger Rum Slap, as well as plates of the roast and vegetables. Folks are a little quieter tonight and will be drinking a little deeper.

Brigid makes sure that Theodore's glass is never empty, and once the first wave has settled in with drink and food, she returns to him.

"You know your grandfather was no stranger here, though he never drank too much, even after Marie passed," she tells him.

"It's true. 'Always in moderation, except for love,' he'd tell me." And there on his sweet lips is the first hint of a smile.

But then he adds darkly, "I'll never be the man he was."

"You know what he told me?" Brigid chirps, bypassing his last comment. "Nathaniel told me he always preferred the company of women, and of animals, and, of course, his family and Cooper. He found most other men obsessed with sports, guns, some machine or another, or getting under some woman's skirt. And that's about it. He thought women were more tuned into the natural world, into food and people, and had a greater capacity to express love.

"Anyway, Teddy, you're a different kind of man. Of the cloth rather than the soil."

"He never owned a television, but had a radio in almost every room, and the barn as well," Theodore adds randomly. "Read newspapers, even poetry. Oh, yeah, and cookbooks, though he never cooked. Said it helped him grow the right vegetables and herbs."

"You know, Brigid, my lovely, Cooper and I proudly own a TV," a voice behind Theodore adds. "Idiot box, Nathaniel called it. But we love it and so did this guy as a boy when he was over. His grandfather deprived him of a lot of fine entertainment."

John Quimby takes the stool next to Theodore's and lays an arm across his shoulders, pulls him close.

"Rum Slap?" Brigid asks John.

"Absolutely," he answers, and to Theodore, "Glad you made it."

"I wish I could have seen him. What happened? I didn't even know he was ill."

"That's 'cause he wasn't. He wasn't ever sick." John thanks Brigid and takes a healthy sip of his cocktail, licks his upper lip. "God, I love these. Slaps a smile on my face every time, Brigid. But Nathaniel . . . well, this is what I got from Coop. He felt dizzy, overheated, had some chest pain. Drove himself to the hospital. Could have called us, you know. We could have had an ambulance there in minutes. For Christ's sake, it's what we do. No, he hops into his ancient truck and off he goes, Superman."

"C'mon John," Brigid interrupts as she tops off both their glasses. "He probably didn't feel all that bad. And you know how he is. Thinks he's indestructible."

"Well, he had himself a king-sized heart attack. They figured that out right quick. They ran some tests. Then he was doin' a little better and seemed stable. Nathaniel called Cooper himself and told him he was fine and not to come."

"But, of course, he did," Theodore says, knowing how good a friend Cooper had always been to his grandfather.

"When he got there, Nathaniel wasn't doing so well. He was giving the docs a hard time, very uncooperative. Wanted to leave. He asked for you, Teddy. The doctor wanted to put in a heart cath, but Nathaniel said no. He didn't even make it through the night. They worked on him but it was over. He was gone. That quick.

"Cooper drove home and woke me. He didn't have to say a word. I could tell by looking at him that he had just lost his best friend. We cried and cried. Then he called your mom. We were all blubbering like babies. She said she'd call you in the morning. There's no way you could have got here, Teddy. I'm really sorry."

"It's been years since I've been up here . . . been way too long," Theodore says, staring into his once again empty glass. "What did I think was more important?"

"Shit, Teddy, stop talking crazy," John says. "You're studying to do God's work. Being a friar is plenty important. We're all so proud of you. Especially your grandfather. Always said you were the closest thing he had to a son."

Brigid makes Theodore a plate of the meat and vegetables and brings it over with some more wine.

"You've got to eat something," she says. "Believe me, I know. You'll thank me tomorrow."

Theodore pushes the food around his plate, eats a little of the potato and carrots.

Brigid brings another plate for John. "Make me proud," she tells John. "It took a good chunk of the day to prepare. Hey, where is Cooper?"

"Oh, he's a mess. Wants to be alone. But, yeah, I could eat. And how about a slice of that pie over there? Looks like a work of art, my dear."

Once he's served, John hunches over both plates like he's afraid somebody is going to take them away. His long white hair almost touches the food as he swings his fork between the main course and the dessert. Theodore just watches him wolf it down, amazed at the force of his appetite. He looks so much like a wild animal feasting on its prey that Theodore has to look away. There are thirty or forty people joining them now, scraps of their conversations lilt and settle, some subdued laughter. Someone has prepared and lit a fire in the woodstove and many have drawn their chairs close.

"He had no fear of dying," John says, dotting his mouth with his napkin. "'Never suffer future pain,' that's what he said. Said it many times. Got to be a little predictable, but he's right. Why worry about something you can't control?"

"That is a luxury for those with normal lives," Theodore comments. "You don't know this, Uncle John, but for a short time I was living on the streets. I joined a wandering group of lost souls, all in a lot of pain. They had no direction and a dark future looming.

Some mentally ill, some veterans, addicts, drunks, all lost, rejected. You become so unimportant that you are invisible. And if someone does notice your existence, it's worse, having to bear their well-intentioned pity or disgust. I needed so much help."

John turns on his stool and grabs the young man by his shoulders. "Why didn't you come to us? At least call your family? When was this?"

Brigid leaves a group at the end of the bar and joins them. "What's going on?"

"We're fine," Theodore says, roughly pushing John's arms away. "I was just telling him about my work with the homeless in central Detroit. And, Uncle John, I did reach out to Nate. My brother came through for me. And the brothers at Saint Anthony's. They're my family now."

He seems agitated and a little hostile, so John pulls on his coat. "I've got to get back to Cooper. Thanks for the vittles, Brigid."

Theodore goes back to playing with his food. "You might want to cut him off," John whispers, shielding his mouth with his hand.

"I didn't mean to rile you, son," he says directly to Theodore. "Come by the house tomorrow. Any time is good. I know you've got things to take care of. And don't worry about the animals at Nathaniel's. We'll mind them.

"Take care of our boy, will you?" John then asks Brigid, slapping a twenty on the bar.

"Of course. I won't let him out of my sight," she says, but leaves the bottle of wine on the bar.

That is pretty much the night at the Bird's Eye. Near ten o'clock, anyone still there is sitting around the woodstove, eating pie or nursing the last of whatever they are drinking. Within thirty minutes, all are gone except for Theodore and the barkeep.

"I can't drive," he tells her.

"I wouldn't let you. I'm going to take you upstairs and tuck you in for the night. Now this will require stepping outside and climbing some stairs. Think you can handle that?"

Theodore gets up from his barstool and looks around the room. "Of course I can. Where is everybody?" He begins searching the floor around the stools. "I had a bag. Maybe it's still in the car." This strikes him as funny, but as soon as he breaks into a little laugh, he looks as if he will cry.

"How could I have done this?" he asks. "We are called to heal wounds, not create them."

"Don't be so hard on yourself," she consoles. "You can figure all that out in the morning. What you need now is a big glass of milk and some sleep. I'll look in your car for your bag."

Theodore is slight, but still over six feet tall, and in his heavy robe, a lot to handle for Brigid Birdsey. She functions as a walking stick he must rely on to negotiate the two flights of open wooden steps on the back of the building. Once on the top platform, he pulls away and spins around to take in the view. There's an empty road leading to Empire Beach, with many tall, dark, and frighteningly beautiful evergreens, a purply black sky, and the familiar dense scent of the unsalted lake.

"God, I love it here," he says, and wraps his arms around her. He rests his chin on her head, pulls her tight. "Just smell it. Even the cold has a fragrance. Do you know what Detroit smells like at night? Exhaust fumes. Exhaust fumes and urine."

"Very dramatic, Theodore. I'm sure that is not all Detroit smells like."

"How I've missed all this," he says dreamily, his arms opening and rising like the pope's. "How I've missed you."

"Yeah, missed you too. Now that's settled." She tugs him away by his sleeve and opens the door. "Bathroom's in the back on the left. Bedroom is on the right. Sorry, bed's not made. Not that you'll notice."

Brother Theodore zigzags down the hall, untying and dropping the rope around his waist as he goes. Brigid retrieves his bag from the only car left on the block. The bag looks like it's made of cardboard, very old, like a little boy's suitcase. *Could it be the one he traveled to Empire with over all those long-ago summers?* She takes it back up the steps and places it outside the bathroom door. Listens for sounds of life.

"Everything all right in there?"

No answer.

"I'm coming in, Teddy. Is that okay?"

Still nothing, so she eases the door open and there he is, sitting on the old tile floor, his back against the wall, a towel from the rack above falling to just above his eyes. He's been crying, that's clear.

He has neglected to lower the seat or flush the toilet, so she does. Then she sits next to him and removes the towel above him. Brigid gently strokes the surprisingly soft stubble on his head.

"This is about more than Nathaniel, isn't it?" she asks.

"I'm a little lost," he confesses and turns toward her. He lowers his head to her lap and nuzzles in a way that has nothing to do with grief.

"And now you're found? Oh no, we are not going there." She removes his thick head and stands. "If you are going to break a vow, it should at least be something you remember." She manages to get him upright and into her bedroom. He falls on the bed and together they free him from his robe. Theodore giggles through the entire process, making it all the more difficult, but reminding her so much of the boy she loved.

Once his cheek sinks into her pillow, his breathing slows and he appears to immediately plunge into unconsciousness. Brigid dims the lights and leaves to get a glass of wine, well-deserved for the trouble she both caused and averted. She returns to the bedroom and pulls a chair next to the bed to sit and observe this strange creature.

Theodore is not a conventionally handsome man. What comes to mind as she watches him sleep is a figure on a holy card, not Christ, but one of the saints. Darkly European, a little Middle Eastern or Jewish. His eyelids are gently tapered, his brows black and arching, as if always questioning. He has a small, sensuous mouth, a pointy chin. She strokes his cheek, not as she had touched him downstairs, but more leisurely, enjoying the softness of his tight beard on the downstroke.

She wants to protect him, but from what? Not from his grief; that's necessary. He seems so vulnerable, fragile, and as he himself said, lost. She remembers that one summer's end when he didn't go back to Chicago. He was fourteen, she sixteen, and things were starting to get more complicated for them. Sure, they did a lot of the same things that season, meeting up at South Bar Lake to swim or dune climb, or sitting in Brigid's small cottage on Front Street. There he would lodge himself in the kitchen and watch her cook everything from a ham to a pie. They would hang out at Empire Beach, sometimes smoking cigarettes when they had them. But there were awkward lulls when Brigid wished he was a little older and he probably did too.

When the summer was nearly gone, they both dreaded the looming separation. Theodore begged his mother to let him spend the entire year there in Empire. He could help his grandfather with the harvest and start ninth grade at Glen Lake High School in Maple City. She recalls how disappointed he was when his mother flat out refused. She insisted he attend Francis Parker with his brother, who would be a senior that year. Theodore complained about the teasing and hazing he would have to endure from his older sibling and his many friends. Still his mother refused to let him stay.

Theodore starts snoring now, his mouth agape. Brigid takes a sip from the wine glass she has forgotten is in her hand. She remembers how Theodore took charge in a surprisingly assertive way that early September a decade ago. He feigned a debilitating flu for days and assured his grandparents he could not abide the long bus trip back to Chicago. When day after day he refused to eat and professed to be too weak to leave his bed, Nathaniel called Isabelle. She was onto his pretense and insisted they put her son on the next bus, even if it had to be done forcibly. When Nathaniel explained this to Theodore and Marie, it was his grandmother who phoned her daughter to explain matter-of-factly that she would keep the boy until she felt he was well enough to travel on public transportation. This was going to be the case unless Isabelle was willing to drive up to retrieve her son. Everyone knew that wasn't going to happen. She was much too busy for an unnecessary trip like that.

Brigid sips her wine and smiles at the man of God in her bed. His refusal to leave was the beginning of what he came to call the best year of his life. He worked hard and seemed to grow into the height and build of the man he would become, lean, strong, tall, and with long hair to his shoulders that his mother never would have allowed. Brigid made sure he had easy passage into the social life at the high school. She concedes that she had the looks and big personality to ensure she was well liked and respected, and that year she joined both the football cheering squad and the girls' basketball team (not tall, but fast). She was unstoppable and always had some boy trying to win her over. So, though he was quiet, shy, an average student, and disinterested in sports, he got by just fine with her protection. Everyone thought he was mad for her, but she explained that they were merely the best of friends and didn't want to jeopardize that. Except for the time they were lying side by side on her parents' couch and she kissed him in a way that surprised them both, that's the story they stuck to. Just friends.

Much has happened in their lives since then. They became adults, a different, more complicated species. Even when he came back for a few months after Marie died, they felt awkward when they did see each other. Her life at that time was chaotic and in transition and she imagined his was as well. It felt to her like the best part of their relationship, all that easy intimacy and laughter, was past and irretrievable.

She's protective of him even now. And what else she feels is best left unsaid. It is late and her glass is empty.

She sleeps on the couch.

ZAIMA

I do remember
why I went to war

because Saddam tortured the Shi'a
our people
he gassed the Kurds
because my father hated Saddam
said he had stolen his country
so I also hated Saddam

because what Americans
were saying about us
was wrong
I too am an American
Michigan-born
and from a good Muslim family

and not a terrorist
just average really
but with a bad temper
as my mother has said
repeatedly

I went to war
because my father is a proud man
and I was proud
that he was proud of me
he had no objection to my going
my mother stopped talking to me
until the day I left
and then she spoke in tears

I was able to go to war
because I have no brother
and because I have a sister
back-up
this is important

because I am strong
in body and will
bones as dense as oak
and good with my hands
inclined to mathematics
and literature

but I don't speak Arabic
that would have been an asset

because I too believed the lies
that Saddam's hands
had American blood on them
that he came for us on 9/11
and would come back
we all did
and it was imperative to say so

because I was young
impulsive
idealistic
patriotic
and I offered the military my body
my peace of mind
my innocence

I also went to war
because I wanted to get away
a lot of that too

THEODORE DASH

THE NEXT DAY • EMPIRE

As requested the night before, Theodore arrives at Cooper and John's pristine farmhouse on Voice Road. He stops and takes in the way the apple orchards climb neatly up a large hill to the east and how the red barn sits just so behind the house.

"Where's your coat, boy?" John asks from the front door. "I know it's cold in Detroit too. They don't allow a coat over that dress?"

In Theodore's muddled, fermented mind, he wonders if it's John's advanced years that accounts for the annoying old man he seems to have become. "You know it's not a dress, Uncle John. And I've got some warm clothes underneath. I'm fine."

"Come on in, for goodness sake," Cooper shouts from inside the house. "Have a seat. John's made some apple and squash soup, but first I've got to read you this here thing of your grandpa's."

Once the three are all comfortably seated in the tidy living room, the official business begins.

"Last will and testament," Cooper announces, and then after pausing ceremoniously, he takes a sip of Jameson and unbuttons his shirt a tad. "Be it known that I, Nathaniel Jude Dash, residing at 117 LaCore Road, Empire, county of Leelanau, in the state of Michigan, being of sound mind, do make and declare this to be my last will and testament expressly revoking all my prior wills and codicils at any time made."

"Bunch of legal mumbo jumbo," John comments as he borrows Cooper's bottle and pours his own cup of consolation. "Does anybody even know what the hell a *codicil* is?"

"Hush up, John. This is important." Then Cooper continues. "He goes on to appoint me as the personal representative of his will, and if I'm not still around, then John."

"Nathaniel should have backed you up with a younger guy," John says. "As hard as we still work in the orchards, we could both fall like rotten apples any same time."

Theodore waits patiently, hands tucked into the rope around his waist. He has great affection for these two men he's known pretty much his whole life. Most folks prefer pretending that the two are brothers, but know they are not. They are accepted as kind and generous neighbors, longtime residents who still volunteer for the local fire department as EMTs. Theodore figures that losing Nathaniel is both heartbreaking and ominous for them as they are close to the same age.

"I direct that after payment of all my just debts," Cooper reads on, "my property be distributed in the manner following:

"I do hereby bequeath to my dutiful daughter, Isabelle Marie Dash, of Chicago, Illinois, all photographs and letters belonging to me and to my sweeter than her infamous sugar pie but too soon departed wife, my Marie, as well as any personal belongings of hers that I have stored in the northeastern corner of the attic in a box marked with her name. Also to Isabelle, all of her mother's china and sterling silverware, which belonged to Marie's own mother, as well as all her hair ornaments and jewelry, and her only indulgence, the bizarre and wonderful collection of hats that still graces the top shelf of our bedroom closet. You, Isabelle, I'm sure will not wear them as I do believe you no longer attend mass or would find them inappropriate for the busy, windy streets of Chicago, but keep them as a fond memory of your mother.

"I wish, however, that Isabelle should leave in the farmhouse, for reasons later revealed, all cooking utensils, pots, pans, everyday plates, cups and glasses, pie dishes, and the hodgepodge of stainless steel and silver eating utensils, as well as all cookbooks and her much coveted recipe box."

John stares at the top of Cooper's bent head, willing it to lift to meet his disapproving eyes. This small jab by Nathaniel is directed squarely at John; he coveted that wooden box he once was caught peering into and was duly reprimanded by Nathaniel himself. A huge embarrassment now noted *in his will*. Cooper, oblivious, continues.

"And to Isabelle's good-for-nothing partner of few but too many miserable years, a man who never did marry but did cruelly abandon Isabelle when she was encumbered with the myriad needs of two small boys, to him I bequeath my deepest resentment and hatred of his callous, selfish failures as a partner, father, and human being."

"Wow, tell us how you really feel, Nathaniel," John chimes in. "You know he had that bitter side to him, God rest his soul."

"These sentiments," Cooper reads, "are not indicative of my usual character and only the Lord knows my term in purgatory to pay for their utterance here."

"There's the God-fearing, backtracking Nathaniel we knew and loved," John says. "Teddy, can I get you a drink, a beer, some of that soup?"

Theodore pulls himself to the edge of the overstuffed chair and leans forward with his hands on his kneecaps. "I'm good. Please read on."

"To my first grandson and my namesake, Nathaniel Dash," Cooper reads, "who serves most bravely at the time of this writing in the defense of our country in Iraq, I do bequeath the sum of ten thousand dollars, which has been placed in his name, drawing interest, at the Empire National Bank. I also wish Nate to have my collection of firearms. Though they be painfully old and not in perfect repair, they may fetch a decent price as historical artifacts. Know that I am proud of you. I have not spent as much time with you as I often wished, but I know you well enough to anticipate that you will confidently master any challenges you may face. You will do this without much help from me or anyone else. You are your mother's boy.

"And now to Theodore."

Here in this room where as a boy he was allowed, even encouraged to stay up late, to watch television without supervision, eat as much heavily buttered popcorn and consume as much off-brand pop as he pleased before falling asleep on the huge, musty couch, here in this room with his grandfather's voice so strong and clear in his carefully chosen words, it all makes him weep in muffled cracks and whimpers. John rests his hand on Theodore's shoulder and the three simply wait until it is time to start again.

"I'm all right. I think I just got that he's gone," Theodore says, straightening his back. "You can go on, Uncle Cooper."

So Cooper does. "Over the course of more than a dozen perfect summers, this boy came to spend these precious months with us in our farmhouse, in our orchards, and in our close-knit community. He rolled down the dunes like a sugar donut into Silver Lake, fished from his rowboat in Glen Lake, cooked cherry pies with Marie, and played euchre on Saturday nights with me, Marie, Cooper, and John. And he got damn good and capable of all that, including taking care of the chickens and as much of the harvesting as he could before going back to the city in September. And we stole him for an entire year once, which was a blessing to us all. He always belonged here. Right here.

"This land became part of the man he has grown to be, a good and righteous man who has given his life to God. A dutiful grandson who helped me during that first year after Marie passed. And

I know, even now, that the sun-warmed sand, the sweet dark cherries, our well-tended soil, and the colors in the sky as the sun drops into Lake Michigan, all these inhabit him, have formed him. Though his devotion presently resides admirably elsewhere, I do nonetheless bequeath to Theodore Jude Dash the whole of my property, farmhouse, barn, fields, and orchards."

Cooper knew this was coming, but it visibly shocks Theodore. His hands fly to the top of his head, as though it needs securing. He looks from Cooper to John and back again. "What?"

Again, Cooper reads. "This includes all items not gifted to those family members already mentioned. For his use and pleasure are all tools, machinery, my Ford truck (which he operated at the age of nine), my tractor as is, livestock still present, and McIntosh, whose age in dog years surpasses mine, and yet he persists. Also, all the remaining funds at Empire National in accounts with both our names on them. This should carry you through whatever decisions you come to in whatever time you need to make them.

"Dear Theodore, you may be overwhelmed with this, even distraught. And I am sorry if this is the case. Still there is no other living soul who holds this land in the same high esteem as I have. Like your grandfather, you love it and so you shall have it. Do with it as you will. It is both valuable commercially and draining physically. But please know this, grandson, I could not have had anywhere on this earth a more blessed or happier life. I don't know what your new life holds for you, but so wish that I could know. You are a man of God, but please understand well what I write next. In tending this land on those long afternoons that stretched into twilight, when there was so much more to be done than time allowed, I did not lose faith or hope. There was always a divine presence accompanying my labor."

Theodore closes his eyes and sits erect with his hands cupped in his lap. He could be napping during a Sunday sermon, he looks that serene and distant.

"Then he signed the thing, and I and two nice ladies at the bank did as well," Cooper says. "It's all notarized and pretty much cut in stone, my friend. You should know that we've been tending to his horse and those crazy misbehaving chickens, and . . . well . . . come on out, Mac. Teddy's gonna take you back home."

The kitchen floor creaks in relief as the creature resting there rises to the mention of his name. The dog strolls into the living room, head lowered, tail pointing straight down.

"He's already stopped looking for Nathaniel. He knows," John says while rubbing the dog down. "Dogs can smell death before it hits the front door. The poor thing won't eat. He's grieving."

Theodore opens his arms and softly calls McIntosh to him, but the dog just winds himself up, and lies down, turning his head away. He looks like a puddle of rich caramel that someone has swirled dark chocolate into, his brindle broken only by a formal tuft of white on his chest. What breeds he might be is not known but he is the offspring of the dog of Theodore's childhood, a dog who looked much the same as Mac.

Theodore gets up to kneel by him. He lovingly takes the dog's heavy head into his hands. "It's okay, Mac. I understand. Let's go back to the farmhouse. This is just something we'll have to get used to."

John puts on Mac's collar and hands a plastic bag to Theodore on his way out. "It's the steak bone he's not interested in. Maybe later."

"Guess you've got some thinking to do," Cooper whispers to Theodore after an uncomfortably long embrace in the open doorway.

———————— • ————————

His grandfather's farmhouse is situated on the eastern side of LaCore Road, just south of Voice Road. The northern tip of South

Bar Lake is visible from the high point of the orchards, as is the great expanse of Lake Michigan beyond.

Theodore parks his rental on the roadside, even though the long driveway is clear with only shallow patches of snow. *Is he waiting for Nathaniel to return and occupy his spot next to the porch?* After sitting in the car for some time without any new arrivals, he climbs out and walks along the curving road's edge to the old birch. If his grandfather were a tree, he would be this one, an optimistic specimen, grand in stature, bent on survival. The main trunk extends a mere two feet from the soil and then, due to past injury, breaks into three separate trunks. Each is of equal girth and each curls skyward in elegant sweeps of pocked white bark. The old man of a tree easily held a boy in its crotch and provided a perfect spot to read or ponder.

As if to tamp down Theodore's emotional reverie, McIntosh solemnly approaches the tree, lifts his leg, and blesses it.

"Well, it's yours, too, Mac," Theodore says as he stoops to rough his fur. "C'mon in and show me around. It's been awhile."

There is no sidewalk to the house, only a worn path in the grass meandering from the driveway. Cedar and spruce trees close off all but a sliver of the view of the house from the road, but that narrow vision is the loveliest of the white, cedar-shingled two-story. Theodore passes through that opening and stands before his grandfather's well-tended home. There is a wide porch giving way to a heavy pine door and three narrow, ceiling-to-floor windows.

The porch has a rich, redbrick floor with three slate steps down at its center. On the bottom step are the two simple, white ceramic pots, which his grandmother loved, that are turned upside down. He wonders if they were still planted each late spring with red geraniums. Probably so.

Dropping to one knee, he admires the solid walls of rounded stones on each side of the porch steps. This was Nathaniel's masonry, constructed even before Isabelle's birth. It is still strong, still in perfect shape. And he thinks now that it would have been fitting to bury Nathaniel in front of one of the stone walls, if only he could have. It would be an appropriate headstone.

The front door has never been locked, but it does take a good shove to open it. The sun seems to have instantly set and his mind goes blank as he enters the living room. Perhaps this dim light affords protection from what could be an onslaught of memory and emotion. Theodore cannot remember the location of a single light switch and the objects that poke here and there could be strangers' heads in a darkened movie theater. In feeling around for a wall switch, his hands find the nubby surface of his grandfather's long, wool coat, his Sunday winter coat. *Was he well enough to wear the thing just last Sunday?* Theodore buries his face in it, then puts it on. The scents of winter and Old Spice still cling to it and it fits nicely over his robe, except for its hood. That he frees and slides over his head.

Eventually he finds the knob on a table lamp and the thermostat, which he adjusts fifteen degrees higher. Did Cooper turn it down? Or did Nathaniel do that one last practical thing before heading to the hospital? He's sure that his grandfather expected to return, had dropped off Mac just in case it wasn't right away. But he didn't return. He was a robust eighty-four and he has just disappeared. He wonders if there was a priest at his deathbed. *He would have wanted that, wouldn't he?*

Theodore lowers himself into his grandfather's favorite chair. He can't recall another soul ever sitting there, not even Marie. Marie rarely sat at all; she was always in motion. She hated knitting. She said nothing made a woman look more idiotic than sitting and twirling two sticks in her lap. Give her a shovel or a spoon and a bowl any day.

The room is kind of a mess, which surprises Theodore. Stacked near the bottom of the steps heading upstairs are piles of magazines and newspapers. The floor is littered with slippers and shoes, pieces of mail, even a few dirty plates and glasses. No one has dusted in quite some time and bits of McIntosh's fur spot the carpet. Everything smells old. The air dense with age. Old wood. Old habits. Old thoughts. Past meals. Past lives.

All of this is now, regretfully, his to deal with. All the booze in the pantry, the ancient family Bible, the Dickens and Kipling lining the bookshelves, the Wendell Berry always at his bedside. All the treasured remnants of his mother's childhood. The rotting food in the fridge and the dog shit in the yard. That dog and an old horse. Even the chickens and their future eggs belong to him.

His plan had been to bury the embers of his past, to simplify his life, to dedicate it to God and to helping others. His grandfather was correct; all of this baggage is overwhelming.

——————— • ———————

The next morning, few who knew the deceased well are surprised at the absence of a hearse. Nathaniel hated them. He found them to be as gaudy and sad as a heavy gold chain nestled in the graying chest hair of a middle-aged man. Marie had been carried in one because he was too broken up to break with tradition. He threatened to bury her on the farm, let the county be damned, but he caved. Just didn't have the energy to fight.

But for himself, he had told Cooper what he wanted and now his friend pulls up to Saint Agnes's in Nathaniel's 1966 Ford pickup named Celeste. Theodore thinks the truck is more than appropriate in its flawless, baby-blue and creamy-white finish. Stanley from the bank, the man who had arranged the loan to buy that truck, is leaning against the church doors, ready to open them on cue.

When Isabelle sees her father's coffin tucked into the bed of the truck, her lips pinch. The lurid funeral home bouquets on top are as stiff as the farmer inside. "Good Lord, Theodore! What century are these people living in? Honestly, are you hauling my father like bales of hay in an old farm truck?"

She clenches the collar of her thin, black coat and steers her pointy-toed boots up the steps. "I'll be inside. I won't be surprised if there's a witch doctor in there to conduct the service."

The assembled mourners are few in number and advanced in years, so Brigid offers to help remove the casket from the pickup. Stanley pats his lower back and shakes his head. That leaves Theodore, John, Cooper, a drinking companion of Nathaniel's, and the priest to join her in the task.

"He surely was a big man, so mind your backs," Father McGurley says, speaking with an Irish brogue he could have lost long ago. "A dear man he was, but not shy at the table."

Theodore hopes the priest has more substantial words for the service. He himself has not been asked to speak and has nothing prepared.

Once maneuvered to the sanctuary in front of the obsolete communion rail, the casket is draped by Brigid with what looks like a red-and-white checkered tablecloth. It seems as though a picnic lunch will be served there. Again from Isabelle a grimace. Even the priest frowns, but Brigid whispers to Theodore, "Goes with the truck theme, don't you think?"

Some are dismayed that the funeral is actually a funeral *mass*, which doubles the time in church. Some might even be thinking that it was too bad it wasn't yesterday, as it would have fulfilled the weekly obligation. But for Theodore, this was a comforting blessing. This feels if not like sacred, at least like neutral, ground. His mother sits next to him quietly, clutching not a rosary but a cell phone, hopefully on vibrate.

Cooper and John cry noisily during Father McGurley's eulogy, which touches on the obvious in Nathaniel's nature. Theodore thinks perhaps the priest did not know him well.

Then it is John who composes himself before he gets up and walks purposefully to the front and faces the congregation. He holds a single sheet of paper.

"This was Cooper's to read, but he ain't in any shape to do that right now. So I will. Nathaniel was a big fan of the poet Wendell Berry. He was the only poet he read and he usually had one of his books on his bedside table or even next to the john, more than likely. I looked at some of these poems sometimes and so did Cooper when we were over there. I know nothing about poetry, but Berry's poems were something I could get.

"Anyway, Nathaniel went and picked this poem for this occasion so give a careful listen, 'cause these are his words for you.

> "You will recognize the earth in me, as before
> I wished to know it in myself: my earth
> That has been my care and faithful charge from birth,
> And toward which all my sorrows were surely bound,
> And all my hopes. Say that I have found
> A good solution, and am on my way
> To the roots. And say I have left my native clay
> At last, to be a traveler; that too will be so.
> Traveler to where? Say you don't know.

"There you have it. I will add that if there is a heaven, and I do believe there is, then Nathaniel Dash is sitting pretty right there in the presence of his God. There you go."

On his way back to his seat, he folds the paper neatly and hands the poem to Theodore.

There is more sobbing and nose blowing now, but Theodore is dry-eyed. He tucks the paper into his robe and stares straight ahead. He knows his grandfather is not in that picnic casket and he has no sense of his presence, his soul, within the walls of this blessed space. He likely yearns to be back in his beloved soil away from all this silliness. Theodore prays silently for his grandfather, prays that his death was not horrible, and that he does indeed safely rest with God.

When they finally do lower the body into the ground, Theodore again is unmoved. He thinks only of the planting of this body. *What will the presence of such a man do to the composition of the soil once the pine box begins to rot?* Probably not much, he figures. Nathaniel spent so much of his life planting in that soil, reaping its gifts, breathing it in, rubbing it into his pores. Maybe this will feel like coming home for the old guy.

ZAIMA

AROUND THE SAME TIME • DEARBORN

there are many ways to die:

with purpose
for a just cause
or accidentally
without forewarning

emotionally
spiritually
morally

wrong place
wrong time
or just your time

giving birth
getting an abortion

at your own hands
with a weapon or a needle

or at the hands of others
even by someone you love

by freezing
bleeding out
or the rapid reproduction
of the wrong cells

at war with yourself
or at war with others

while saving someone
(a dead hero)
while running away
(a dead coward)

at the same moment
you kill someone else

alone
or in a mass shooting

as a mass shooter
or a suicide bomber

in your own country
in a foreign car
or at sea
or seeing someone you love
leave you

in humiliation
in obscurity

during intercourse
or an altercation

unknown, unidentifiable

loved or unloved

destined for heaven
bound for hell

forever or for a time

in your sleep like a dream

or while you're still
alive

THEODORE

AFTER THE FUNERAL • EMPIRE

Isabelle has her own car and tells Theodore to leave his rental behind and ride in the Lexus with her and her latest boyfriend, César. Theodore declines. His mother's lover is, for a change, closer to her age, and judging by the heft of his gold watch and inappropriate-for-a-funeral leather "motorcycle" jacket, either well off or well endowed. Theodore had not met the man before and likely will not see him again. Mom has a short attention span when it comes to dating.

Theodore would rather be with his own thoughts in his sub-compact than make small talk with the two of them. Then there is the matter of the will, about which he imagines the diligent Cooper has enlightened her.

This proves to be true once mother and son have removed their coats and sit with beverages in hand in the chilly farmhouse, somewhat apart from the others who have joined them there post-funeral.

"I swear this is the same air I breathed as a child," Isabelle says. "Smells like an old shoe in here." Then to poor McIntosh, curled up loyally at her feet, "And then there's you. I've never understood why people have animals living with them inside their houses."

"I tried to clean up a bit. Did all the dishes anyway," Theodore says. Then after a fidgety pause, "Guess you saw the will."

"Oh, joy," Isabelle quips. "Old lady hats and jewelry, yellowed photographs, and, best of all, china! Really, china? Did he know how I live? You know, like in the present. No one lays out china."

She places her glass on the end table's doily. "And this wine should be mixed with olive oil and dumped on some iceberg lettuce. It's undrinkable. Theodore, my love, could you find me something brown straight out of a recognizable bottle? It's been a long day and barely noon."

Without waiting for an answer, she grabs her wine glass carelessly, sweeping the offensive doily to the carpet. Her son takes the glass and returns the doily to its circle ringed with dust on the table.

"Always the good boy," she tells him, her tone bittersweet and verging on mocking. "And please check on César. I see the homosexuals have surrounded him. I worry for his safety."

The homosexuals are, of course, Cooper and John, partners since they served in Korea together as medics. To Theodore, they are more like uncles than merely the neighbors of his grandparents. The woman from the liberal city of Chicago should know that these two eighty-somethings are no more looking for a random hookup than is the old horse in the barn. This slam by his mother angers him. Should the good boy pour her a chunky glassful of the primordial ketchup he found stuck to the bottom of the fridge? Its contents are certainly brown and in a recognizable Heinz bottle.

Instead he interrupts Cooper and asks what he might have in his back pocket. "My mother needs a hit of something stronger than the local cherry wine."

"Excuse me," Cooper tells the other two men. "Duty calls."

In Nathaniel's pantry on the back wall behind the sacks of flour and sugar, Cooper exposes a sliding door. Behind it are more than a dozen bottles of liquor and aperitifs.

Theodore picks up the crème de menthe. "Mouthwash or shampoo?"

"That stuff is nasty. Marie drank it. It's old," Cooper says.

"Why is all this hidden?" Theodore asks.

"Bible on the coffee table. Liquor hidden in the pantry. One of the many laws of Nathaniel. You probably can't remember ever seeing him drink, I'll bet. He did enjoy the occasional nip. How about the Johnnie Walker for Izzy?"

"Hey, I'll bet nobody calls her that anymore," Theodore says.

"Too bad. It's a great name. What we always called her and still will."

"Pour my mother a good stiff one of that," the thoughtful son says. "Maybe it'll soften her up."

That is easily accomplished once she has finished her third glass and is holding court in the living room, her face damp with showy tears. The severe winter sun through the window serves as a dramatic spotlight on Izzy as she tells stories of her father's life. Most center on her and are quite ordinary and predictable. There are tales of the first day of school, ingenious tooth pulling, appendicitis, her academic prowess, and his pride in same.

The crowd is growing as the afternoon wanes, more locals, the crew from the Farm Bureau, the amiable veterinarian. Stories erupt from other sources, coaxed by the free-flowing alcohol. There's talk of Nathaniel's love for his land, for the whole Leelanau Peninsula, his wife. He has evidently been the go-to person in the community in times of trauma, rebuilding barns, visiting Lily LaCore weekly to read her the local paper after she went blind. Father McGurley recalls that it was Nathaniel who drove both Brigid Birdsey and her doomed pinky to Traverse City after the tobogganing accident.

Isabelle now lowers her head, shaking it slowly, either in great admiration for her father or because she is in the throes of a pronounced Johnnie Walker buzz. When she bravely stiffens her spine and throws back her shoulders, folks are rising from their chairs to greet Brigid Birdsey. They rush to help her unload and unpack all the fabulous food she's brought—a slow cooker of meaty, dark chili; cornbread; three roasted chickens; and two glass containers of oatmeal cookies, laced with dried cherries and coconut.

Theodore feels a tiny pang of pity for his mother and stays with her, sitting cross-legged before her on the floor. She seems so out of her element in this backwoods crowd and her buffer boyfriend has disappeared who knows where.

"Never get between the good people of Empire and free food," Isabelle comments.

"Mom, is there anything else you want to tell me about Granddad?" Theodore asks. "Maybe something more personal."

"Oh, it was just your basic childhood narrative . . . plays, pageants, predictable holidays, free child labor, fights over boyfriends. Nothing out of the ordinary. I couldn't wait to leave this boring little town. I was never cut out to swim in this pindling little fish bowl."

Theodore's pity is dissipating and he feels defensive. They'd spent little time there together. If she did drive him up for the summer, she rarely even spent the night. Those things should have tipped him off to the extent of her hatred for the place.

"Pray tell me, Theodore, that you have no intention of hanging around here or taking any of this on. I'm not wild about the priest thing, but at least you're still in Detroit where there's some evidence of culture and modern life."

He flashes back to the Institute of Art, the seedy clubs, his crowd, his spiraling downward life only two years ago. But she knows nothing of that.

"It's the Capuchins, Mom. I want to be a friar, not a priest. I've finished my postulancy. It feels right to me. Finally something feels right to me."

"So it's not official yet, the poverty and chastity thing?" She dabs carefully around her cosmetically enhanced eyes. "I had hoped that something would come out of Wayne State. Lord knows, the out-of-state tuition was killing me."

"I couldn't do it," Theodore admits. "I was just shooting in the dark." This is more honest than he intended, but she's eyeing the spread on the table and pays no mind.

"I would think long and hard on those vows, Theodore. A lifetime is a long time to go without your basic creature comforts and . . . well, female companionship."

"I have thought about it. This is exactly what I want. What God wants for me."

Isabelle looks away. "It's because your grandmother dragged you to church every Sunday up here. Put ideas in your head."

She can't actually believe that. He wonders just how naive she believes him to be.

"I would like to stay in Detroit once I make my permanent vows," he declares. "If they allow me. Parts of the central city are under attack by poverty, drugs, neglect. A lot of homeless. I can be of service. And don't worry about grandchildren. Nate, I'm sure, will give you a brood."

"Good God! Do I seem like the grandmotherly type? Nothing ages a woman like carting around her children's offspring. It's appalling how often I see this very thing. Free babysitters squandering what could be some of their best years. Once you've done the child-rearing thing, I think you should be onto something more, well, self-nurturing."

Theodore stands and straightens his robe. "The child-rearing thing?"

"I haven't hurt your feelings, have I, Theodore?" Isabelle teases. "Because you know I love you and Nate very much. But I have to admit I understand him a little better."

"Because he's more like you," he shoots back.

"I love you both equally. Anyway, what are you going to do with this godforsaken property? Sell it, I imagine. You could repay your brother. He said he's lent you a fair amount of money. God knows why you wouldn't come to me. But this place will fetch a good price, with all this land and the distant view of the lake. The house should be torn down . . ."

"There's nothing wrong with this house. I bet it's built better than anything they're putting up these days," Theodore says.

"Really? Is the wiring safe? Plumbing up-to-date? Efficient heating system? And all these small rooms! I can barely breathe, but I can actually feel the wind seeping in around the window behind me. It's old, honey. This kind of old isn't chic any longer."

Theodore looks around him. Beyond all the mold and clutter is something valuable to him. The best part of his youth was lived here.

"I can help you get it on the market. I can stay another day or two, get it appraised. Take some photos. Not the best time to sell, though. Might want to wait until spring."

She says it like it is already decided. "I need to spend some time here," he counters. "Talk to Cooper. Maybe he can help me out."

"He's too damn old to take on this place as well as his own."

"I just need him to help me get started. I want to sort out what's left behind here," Theodore says. "There may be other things you want."

"There's nothing here I need or want."

"I want to honor their life here, not tear it down," he says. "I've worked in the barn, the orchards. There's no shame in hard work. And John told me these are some of the finest apple trees around here."

"I know it means a lot to you," Isabelle says solemnly. "Certainly more than it ever meant to me. My father recognized that fact and I'm happy, really, that he gave it all to you. Nate'll be pissed it's all yours, given what it's worth. But if you do sell, wouldn't it be nice to help him out? His tour is almost over so I'm sure he could use it to get settled into civilian life. Your grandfather would like that."

"What he wanted is in his will," Theodore says. "You know I didn't ask for any of this. I don't want the land or the money."

"Such a problem, unwanted wealth. Listen, I'm hungry, aren't you? That Birdsey girl is a pretty thing, don't you think? That auburn hair and those green eyes, so deep and mysterious."

"What's your point, Mom?"

"Like any mother, I just want you to be happy."

"I am happy. The less I have the happier I am."

Isabelle stands and takes his hands in hers. "Where on earth did you come from? Nothing like your father. Even less like me. Must have been an immaculate conception."

"I'll let you know . . . in time . . . what I intend to do with this place. Until then, just pray for me."

"Said the God-fearing friar to the atheist," Isabelle concludes.

ZAIMA

you are like your father
in your looks, she says
in your temperament
as well
with fiery, cold eyes
always looking for fairness
restitution
as though the playing field were level
as though we had no history

you are like your father
your preference in foods
salty over sweet
fish over meat
and never finish what's on your plate, why?
Some shared superstition?
Some unconquerable fear of there
never being enough?

or pride that we have more than we need?
take mine, he says, if still

there is someone hungry for more
which neither you nor he would ever say
your needs
like his
so minimal, she says

and like him, to me
you always hold back
there is more to say
that is left unsaid

more to feel
than will be freed
from your hearts
so guarded
hearts neither locked nor open
but always left seductively ajar

if I had a son
my mother says
perhaps he would be like me

but there is no son
only another daughter
distant from indifference
and better things to do

only my father and me
to battle against her
two against one
unfair

you are like your father
in your looks

dark and brooding
in your looks at me
and then she looks away
walks from me
head bobbing low
whispering
you both love
what you call justice
and search endlessly for it
in love with war

but now mother
my love affair
with war
is over
done

THEODORE

Four apples had fallen to the ground and been deemed unworthy of retrieving last fall. How sad, he thinks, that their modest ambition after months of growth would produce nothing more than these shriveled, deflated, off-color failures.

Theodore sees beauty in them still. Their rusty orange color complements the bright green weeds that persist into February. Bits of delicate young snow leave a sugary coating on the apples, as well as on the brittle leaves surrounding them.

Early morning in the orchard, fifteen degrees and still this far into the winter, he's told there has been little snow. Odd for northern Michigan.

He flips up the collar of his grandfather's heavy wool jacket. He climbs to the top of a hill and looks beyond more orchards to a narrow crop of low evergreens. Beyond that, there's a flat view of icy South Bar Lake with Lake Michigan behind it. He loves how pared down the landscape is in winter, especially up here. It all seems so sterile, so neatly structured. Even the limbs of the apple trees are beautifully simple and cleanly delineated in their subtle rise toward the sky.

In Detroit, he often toured and yes, even slept in, some of the abandoned manufacturing relics. And these orchards do remind him of the rows of ruined columns that lined the barren open spaces of the Fisher Body Plant. Sure, there were hanging scraps of metal and debris, but there was also the stripped-down simplicity he admires. When the light was low and golden, the place had a cathedral-like ambience that felt quite calming to him. Rotten apples? Urban decay? There is always more to see if you looked past the obvious.

Theodore had experienced something similar in his mother's face. He hadn't seen her in years. Then, as the sun began to set and her profile was unflatteringly side lit, he noticed the extra skin poked by the corner of her mouth when she smiled. There were two extra folds of loose skin under her chin and her hands were starting to become her mother's. Her hair was flawlessly dyed but it looked thinner, flatter now. Was she considered beautiful? Yes, strikingly, but now he must add the disclaimer, *for her age.*

He continues down the hill and the water view is no more. *What is her age anyway?* He isn't sure. *Late fifties?*

What he does remember vividly right then is not his mother, but another woman. One morning before dawn, he had found himself at the abandoned Fisher Body Plant. He was mighty high, lying on a stained mattress, his head resting on a pile of he knew not what, possibly someone's discarded, soiled clothing. He was homeless and nearly broke. It was late August and unusually cool, like his miserable summer couldn't wait to be over and morph into autumn. He had taken to walking through the night and sleeping where he could during the day. Safer. As the sun began to pierce his eyes he sat up and found next to him a tattered paperback Bible. He started flipping through the New Testament when a woman appeared to him who had probably been standing there for some time. She was neatly dressed in a gray suit and black, practical shoes. She sat down on the wretched mattress in a ladylike way, with both knees together and to the side. She might as well have been his mother for all the mortification he felt.

He also remembers their conversation well. It all seemed so surreal. She asked why he was there, like she knew him and could guess why he was in that awful place. He told her he had nowhere else to go. She asked if he had money. He said he did, but not enough for a room.

Then she wanted to know if he was Christian, Jewish, or Muslim. He wanted to lie, but didn't. He answered with a question. "Would you help me if I said that I don't identify with any of them?"

She bent forward to stand and he saw a small silver cross escape from her blouse. "Jesus has taught us through his words and example to help those in need. The Torah is also clear on this instruction. And if you are a Muslim, then you likely know that Muslims are required to give a fixed portion of their income to the less fortunate," she explained. "Zakat, like a monetary commandment, and this is done regardless of the religion the less fortunate follow."

He wanted to leave and stood. She came uncomfortably close, then handed him a card. "Do you know how to get to this address and do you have the means to get there?" she asked.

He just nodded.

"If you are in danger, whatever that danger may be, and need help, come here. No one will force you to do anything you are not prepared to do. And you will be safe."

Safety, he thinks now. What a ridiculous assumption. Still, out of the rubble of a decaying city desperate for hope, and to a hopeless man, more broken and faithless than he would ever admit, a petite woman in drab clothing and in plain language had found him and reached out to him. He could have disappeared and no one would have noticed.

The wind dies completely and the winter stillness of the orchard is deafening. Hundreds of trees, naked but noble, surround him much like an orderly crowd, patiently queued up for spring. A few frozen rotten apples still cling pathetically to their branches, and whether they are a sign of hope or futility he is not certain.

All he is sure of at this moment is that he is warm enough in his borrowed heavy coat and boots. His head is clear and he mumbles a jumbled, disconnected message to his Creator. He questions the meaning and value of living without anything of one's own. How has he been afforded the property rights to this place of boundless beauty and responsibility, this place which may have been the only place he has ever been happy at all? What is he to do with this unwanted gift?

Theodore kneels on the frozen ground and bends to lay his bare hands on the patchy snow. He crawls like a curious infant to the nearest apple tree and runs his hands over its bark to the collar of a severed limb. The bark has hardened and healed around the injury, but the wound remains within its rimmed oval center. Time does not heal all wounds, he thinks. It only closes around them, making them smaller, but also darker, deeper.

He stands, brushes snow from his knees, and feels the need to urinate. He does so, but between the rows, free of the spreading roots.

As he walks back to the farmhouse, he remembers Nathaniel's words in his will, delivered so eloquently, but almost apologetically, by Cooper. Nathaniel referred to his grandson as a man of God, but said that in his own life, in his caring for the land over so many years, he felt a divine presence. Well, that may be, Theodore acknowledges. *But what good does that do for the rest of humanity? What does that give back but bushels of fruit?* This is not his calling.

His grandfather had been the primary caretaker of every seed, every apple, and every tree. He had cared for all the livestock, all the bills, and all the repairs to an aging orchard, farmhouse, and barn. It exhausts him just to think of it.

BRIGID

She knows that accomplishment often defines a person. That one has completed law school. This one has given her first major concert. Another makes the best apple pie on the whole Leelanau Peninsula. This one has saved money religiously and purchased a home. That one survived cancer.

Well, surmises Brigid, she needs no more sense of accomplishment than doing what she's doing right now, unlocking the sturdy oak door of the Bird's Eye View, her establishment, paid for and supplying adequate income and shelter for this girl, Empire born and raised. On guard in the large right window is the fake, stuffed growling bear climbing his fake rock. In the left window looms the traditional mounted deer head. This beloved space is where she labors, and on the second floor, where she lives.

The bar is the most beautiful to her when it's empty and quiet. The morning sun polishes the dark wood with light and the place seems holy and perfect. Just the best local bar on the peninsula, that's what the folks say who frequent this watering hole, even the seasonals. Similar to a church allegiance, she figures, and it is a home away from home for many who have otherwise solitary lives. Mostly men of all ages come here, although Jane McCleary is a regular and good for a few drafts and a plate of free food.

Nathaniel lectured her about not charging for the food, but she never has, although many slip a few bucks under their plates. She doesn't feel obligated to cook; she's nobody's wife or mother. She just enjoys it.

Brigid bought the abandoned bar and renovated it after she came into money and property under hard circumstances. Three days after her twenty-first birthday, both of her parents were killed in a spectacular collision with a tractor-trailer on M-55 in daylight and clear weather. It was decided that the trucker must have fallen asleep and the company settled out of court.

After finishing high school, she had taken a job as a barmaid at a snooty tap house in Glen Arbor. Craft beers and crappy food. She admits to being a little sexually hyperactive during those two or three years and found herself pregnant just weeks after the fatal accident.

Funny, she thought at the time, that two people have sex and only one gets pregnant. She was sure of the father's identity and positive she did not want a child with him or anybody else. With no family, no connection to her church, and no friend close enough to advise her, she turned to Nathaniel Dash. He always had been surprisingly kind to her. He too had been shaken by the tragic death of her parents and checked in on Brigid almost daily since.

Nathaniel was against the abortion. He promised to help her in raising the child, financially or whatever she needed. Brigid knew his wife would approve of none of that, especially the money. But for Brigid, money wasn't the issue. She felt she was emotionally unsuitable for motherhood and wanted to leave Empire for any-where else. She arranged for an abortion at a clinic in Traverse City. Nathaniel drove her there and back and stayed with her that night, rubbing her feet, warming soup for her, and reading calming words to her from his favorite poet. It seemed to Brigid that the whole thing was harder on him than her; he seemed so sad and broken. The poems he read to her were earthy and life-affirming, but his voice, deep and solemn, delivered something more akin to a eulogy, so full were they of longing and pain. Finally she was forced to send him home to his wife or his orchards or his dog or anything that could break his deeply depressed mood. It weighed her down far more than the aborted life of her child. That would come later.

Then, shortly after all this, Nathaniel's wife, Marie, died too. That became just one more thing they would feel deeply, but never talk about.

THEODORE

A FEW DAYS LATER

It becomes a game of meeting necessities, doing that next thing and then the one following that. After deciding to put his grandparents' home up for sale, it became clear that he must stay in Empire for a while and this is easily arranged with a quick call to the brothers at Saint Anthony's. Next he must relieve Cooper and John of their duties while he is here. McIntosh has been consistent if not cheerful company, but Theodore is now out of food for him. The chickens are easy, there's plenty of feed, but they aren't laying so he must ask Cooper about that. And the horse. Such a strange being, his eyes so sad, almost human in their depth of emotion. Theodore doesn't like being around him, but provides food and awkward affection. Levi doesn't want to leave the barn, but if coaxed, will stay in the paddock for brief spells. Theodore doesn't remember the horse's scent being so strong and unpleasant. Another question for Cooper.

An immediate issue for the seminarian is acquiring the appropriate clothing and footgear for this northern Michigan ice chest. He discovers he is just shy of his grandfather's foot size, so this affords him basic work boots, muck boots, and well-polished dress shoes should that unlikely need arise. He also finds six pairs of slippers littering the house and those he discards. Some things are too intimate, too personal, to be reused.

Except for a few flannel shirts, a couple of pairs of decent wool socks, and that comforting red-and-black wool hunting jacket, Nathaniel's wardrobe must be either donated or thrown away. Although close in height, his build is very different from what Nathaniel's was. Nathaniel was barrel-chested, broad-shouldered, with a round belly that hung over his belt. Theodore has never gained back the weight lost during his dark days after dropping out of Wayne State. His shoulder girth is average, but he is slender and unmuscular. If you saw him undressed, you might think he was a pianist or a professor. Should he stay on, he will need more than his robe and the odd pieces of clothing he has salvaged.

First he drives to the bank to speak with Stanley about his grandfather's financial health. Perhaps, he thinks, there are many more debts than assets. He learns that Nathaniel did very well. He was a practical and measured man and amassed in cash and certificates of deposit close to $75,000, beyond the $10,000 he set aside for Nate. Stanley will be happy to front him a portion of that, pending the final details in confirming the will. So Theodore withdraws two hundred dollars for his and the animals' needs and asks that two thousand be placed in a separate envelope.

"Is that all you need?" Stanley asks. "I am sure there are bills to be paid, funeral expenses, you know, or utilities. Do you need checks?"

"I'm not there yet. I haven't even touched his desk," Theodore says. "I've never owned anything, not even a car."

"Well, everything needs to be transferred to your name—truck, property, everything!" Stanley sounds shrill and foreboding. "With the farm and orchards, we are talking a tidy sum here. We don't want any confusion. The estate will likely have to go through probate. Do you have a lawyer?"

Theodore is confused by the *we* that Stanley refers to. "How about my mother? She could handle all this."

"She probably could. But wouldn't you like someone local . . . operating in your best interests?" Stanley asks.

"I'll talk to Cooper, but what I need is a real estate agent."

"Well, you can't sell the house as it is," Stanley adds. "It must be updated, made more neutral, less intimate a space. Cleaner. You'll get more."

"I'll just take that money I requested," Theodore says. "There's no big hurry on the rest."

———————   •   ———————

Theodore knows his rental car, courtesy of the seminary, should be returned to Traverse City, so he has asked Cooper Boyd to follow him to the airport there. Traverse City, like so many beautiful resort towns near water, has been pockmarked by the usual sprawl of big box stores and condos. He is happy to find, however, that the downtown area right on Grand Traverse Bay is still full of life, with restaurants, pubs, and public places abounding. Cooper offers to buy him lunch and Theodore accepts, as long as they keep it quick and inexpensive.

"Stanley says I need a lawyer," Theodore says after the fried perch sandwiches have been eaten. "You know, to figure out the will and money and property and all."

"You don't need no damn lawyer," Cooper snaps. "His son's a lawyer and that's what that's about."

"He also said I should clear out Grandpa's house, make it more neutral before I try to sell it," Theodore adds.

"Well, there's some truth to that. Not so it'll sell better, but because there are things in there you might find valuable. You can't just sell away their lives like that."

"Uncle Cooper, you know how much *stuff* is in there? I mean the barn alone would take me weeks."

"So?"

"So I have a life I'd like to return to."

"And that life," Cooper says quietly, "is that life going somewhere? I mean what's the difference if you're gone a week or a month? I bet they'll be happy to take you back anytime. Herd's thinning, if you know what I mean."

Theodore takes his finger and makes a *T* in the ketchup on the edge of his plate.

"That for Theodore or is it a cross?" Cooper asks.

"Neither. Just not answering your former question."

"About that life going somewhere? Or is the question, 'Will I lose my desire to return to that life?'"

"I've tried so many things," Theodore says. "I've quit or failed at them all."

"What are you, all of twenty-five years of age?"

"Twenty-four," Theodore corrects.

"Okay, twenty-four. Wow. Let me see, where was I at that age? Probably not even aware I was gay. Probably thinking the military would be a good place to be. Probably had my goddamned head up my goddamned ass. You know why? That's what being in your twenties is all about. Figuring out who you are. Messin' up. Refiguring."

"Nate knows who he is," Theodore points out.

A pretty blonde gently lays the check in front of Cooper. "Whenever you're ready," she says sweetly.

"Yeah, right. Your brother is the guy that chases that," Cooper says, flipping his thumb in the direction of the blonde. "And lots of other pointless things. I seriously doubt he's got it all figured out. He just acts like he does. I assume. Haven't seen him in a long time. But I'll tell you, going to war doesn't mean you found yourself."

"We should get going. I've got a list," Theodore says.

"Lists. See, that's a good start. John gives me lists. I throw them away. Which reminds me. Get a dumpster."

———— • ————

Once back in Empire, Theodore loads Mac into old Celeste and they head for the thrift store on Lake Street. There he selects the gently worn jeans, T-shirts, and sweaters he will need. A modest selection of underwear and socks he is surprised to find at Deering's Market, which primarily sells food (human, dog, cat, and bird), beer, and beach toys.

Once necessary supplies have been procured and daylight is disappearing, neither man nor dog is anxious to return to the nagging mess of the farmhouse.

"Can Mac come in with me?" Theodore shouts to Brigid from the door.

"He's welcome, as always, but not that frigid air behind you," she answers. "It's good to see you. I was afraid you'd disappeared back to Detroit."

"Not yet. Have to go through the house and the barn. It's all more than a little overwhelming."

"Can I get you something?" Brigid asks. "I've got some lentil stew in the slow cooker. Notice that I called it stew and not soup? This has everything in it from fresh apples and pork sausage to kale. Complete meal in a bowl."

"Brigid, how are you set . . . financially? Is that too personal a question?"

"How about a nice cold draft with that stew?" she asks.

"That sounds kind of wonderful. Yeah, sure."

Before she serves him, Brigid comes around the bar with water and a biscuit for McIntosh. "Sorry for your loss, buddy. Don't be a stranger, okay?"

"Well, since you're not going to answer my question, here—" Theodore says, slapping down the envelope containing twenty hundred-dollar bills.

She returns to her post and peers into the envelope. "The beer is three bucks and the stew is free." She shoves the money back at him.

"No, c'mon, Birdie, take it. This money is weighing me down."

She smiles at his use of her childhood name. Sitting there in his grandfather's flannel shirt and a pilly wool cap, he looks more like a local than a wannabe clergyman. She reaches over and strokes his beard just once. "Always the caretaker," she whispers.

"Nathaniel instructed me to take care of you . . . in his will," he says.

"He did not. Mustn't lie, young man."

"He implied it. Chickens, dog, horse, Brigid."

"In that order?" she asks.

"Those he cared about. I think he sort of adopted you after your folks died."

"I was an adult. A little old for adoption," Brigid points out. "But he was sweet to me then. And since."

"Take it," he snaps, seeming irritated. "What am I going to do with all this money? It's a burden. Once the farm is sold, there'll be even more of it."

Brigid turns her back and prepares two bowls of the lentil stew, draws two beers.

"It's not that I can't use it," she admits. "It's just that little money changed hands between your granddad and me. We bartered."

"Good. Take it. Name something in his honor," Theodore says after a slug of beer. "How about the Nathaniel Jude Dash Barstool? Pick the one he usually sat on. I bet he had a favorite."

"You're on it, pal," she says, smiling. "All right, I'll take it. I really do need a new roof."

They eat and drink in silence. Mac stretches out near the wood-stove and soon is dreaming and twitching away. A few folks drift in and Brigid puts on some music, the kind usually heard at the Bird's Eye, soul-infused rhythm and blues. It's her bar, she tells patrons that request anything else. She gets to pick. Whether old school like Ray Charles and Marvin Gaye, or newer artists such as Alicia Keys and India Arie, it's mostly R&B, most of the time. One particularly wet and stormy week last fall, Brigid got stuck on *The Miseducation of Lauryn Hill* and that's all she played, over and over. "Nothing Even Matters" filled her with a longing she felt in the skin of her soul, but couldn't name.

If anyone bitched then or ever about the music, she flatly suggested they drive over to any of a number of cocktail lounges in Glen Arbor and soak up some of that slow jazz, which she detests.

Patrons do tease her about her love for black artists. "What's wrong with Sting or the Stones?" they might ask. "They have a lot of soul too." And she'd explain that sounding like you have it and having it are two different things. She points out that black folks just have this one on white folks. It's a fact. If they still need to argue about it, she's been known to claim that her daddy's granddaddy was a black man from Mississippi, that her affection for this music is in her blood. It's a total lie, but it shuts them up.

A young couple comes in now and asks to see the wine list. She has one and it's fairly lengthy. They order a good bottle of Malbec and yes, would love a cup of the lentils.

"We haven't talked about what happened Saturday night," Theodore says as she clears away their dishes. "To be honest, there's a good chunk at the end I don't remember at all. I know I stayed over, but if you walked me up there right now, I'd swear I'd never been there."

"You know we haven't had a sleepover in too long a time," Brigid says evasively, then smiles. She brings him another draft, but adds, "Just one more and that's it."

"You're playing with me," Theodore says. "I need to know if anything happened between us."

"Of course you do, what with your vow of chastity on the line. Personally, I think chastity is overrated, but it is a vow I have recently honored, what with the dating pool being a little shallow up here. Most guys probably think I'm a lesbian because I show little interest in them. And the women in town, I'm sure they think I've just been jilted too often." Brigid did not mention that many of these women and probably some of the men know about her licentious former life and probably the pregnancy and subsequent abortion.

Theodore has a long face and seems lost in thought. She softens.

"Don't worry, Teddy. I think you were more mesmerized by the scents from the evergreens and the lake than me. Nostalgic, you were, but not romantic. It was hilarious getting you out of your robe. You conked out. I tucked you in. Slept on the couch. All night. Vows intact."

"It was a little unnerving waking up in your bed. I jumped out of it and got dressed. Went straight outside. I didn't even see you on the couch. I think I was terrified you'd come out of the bathroom and hop back into your bed."

"Terrified?" Brigid asks, but is pulled away by the demands of a suddenly packed bar.

When she breaks free again, Theodore is back in his grandfather's oversized jacket with Mac at his side. "Come by the house tomorrow. There may be things you want . . . kitchen stuff, tools, books. Like Dickens?"

"No thanks to Dickens, but I am a big reader. Have to be. Not enough happens in my own life."

"Well, maybe you want some of the pictures on the walls. I remember you liked that 3-D horse head popping out of a frame. Lots of murky seascapes and portraits of frozen ancient relatives too."

"Enticing," she jokes. "But I will come by and help you pack up all those relics. Late morning okay?"

ZAIMA

AROUND THE SAME TIME • DEARBORN

at a farm
near Tikrit
many months ago
the murderer Saddam
was dragged from a hole
filthy and disgraced
after decades of tyranny
people we knew
even family
in prison or worse
he will face justice
and you, dear parents
prayed that I
would come home

but you heard nothing
knowing I was near Tikrit
but no men in uniform
came to your door
so you didn't know

what to think
you loved me
your elder daughter
why did I not write
so you could be sure at least
that I was alive?

parents, now that I am with you
think about it
would you like to have heard
about the Highway of Death?
maybe a nice photo of your daughter
dressed for combat
squinting down the sights
of her machine gun
there on the guard tower, a high platform
which you would say
is like the stage where I danced at nine
also in costume

I stopped writing
because there was nothing to say
I lived mostly in the silence
in my head
my heart disconnected
my soul deeply hidden
mortar fire in the distance
harmless as wind chimes
to a tree
I was that lifeless
sleeping in a pool of sweat
in the daytime,
and at night

seeing convoys mortared
on Highway One
right outside the camp
being shot at and shooting back
not that interesting
for a letter home
only the spectacular sunrises
worth the telling

we too
we Americans
have dug a hole
just like Saddam
and we can't climb out
that hole is Iraq
your beloved homeland
where my maternal grandfather
had an orchard in Basrah
and there were palm trees
and reed houses on
shining rivers

no shining river in Dearborn
no orchards or palm trees
and I bring back home
nothing for you
or nothing you
would want

THEODORE

He builds a bench. A simple bench made from weathered scrap wood found behind the barn. Theodore uses his grandfather's tools, antique, well-made tools that last generations. A handsaw, a hammer with a worn oak handle, cement-coated nails, a rusty square—these are his tools now to fashion what he will.

He is not entirely sure why he undertook this odd project when there is so much else to be done. It's just that if he finds himself again contemplating his life's past and present in the frozen orchard, he would prefer to be comfortably seated. There's also the issue of the denuding of Nathaniel and Marie's home that he has undertaken. Disassembling their lives feels disrespectful and prying. A tarnished-silver serving spoon may mean nothing to him, but was it present at every Sunday dinner? What did it mean to his grandmother? The imperfect quilts, the doilies, the tidy boxes of black-and-white photographs, and reels of 8-mm film with projector and screen . . . does all that get tossed in with the rotting food, old socks, dingy underwear, and dust balls?

Already on the front porch are two armchairs, the couch, the glass-topped coffee table, the mahogany frame of his grandparents' bed and the matching bureau. Tomorrow the dumpster he ordered will arrive. Into that will land the mattress upon which his mother likely was conceived. Saint Vincent de Paul will send a box truck at week's end to clear the porch of usable donations, all to be sold at a price well below their material and sentimental value.

Soon Brigid will come to sort through all those items and much more, especially from the kitchen. With Theodore's blessing, she'll take whatever she can use or pass along. Less to disrespect. Less to weigh him down.

The bench, he concludes, is symbolic of construction rather than destruction and will be Theodore's contribution to the future occupants of 117 LaCore Road.

With McIntosh at his side, he takes the bench to the spot he occupied earlier, placing it so it faces the slice of water view.

He doesn't sit, but goes directly to his responsibilities—the chickens must be cared for, as well as the hebetudinous horse.

Later Theodore orders oil for the burner, feeds Mac, and makes fried eggs and toast for himself. Flips on the radio.

As he sits and eats at the kitchen table, which he will not remove from the farmhouse as it's as much a part of it as the roof, he finds he likes eating alone. He had grown accustomed to communal meals at seminary, but sometimes found the forced prayers and cozy banter mildly annoying. Lately, when he prays at mealtime, his words are brief and rote. He's not at all sure what to pray for, so he conjures up prayers of gratitude, short and simple, for the food on his plate, the adequate heat, the solitude.

When he has finished his meal, Theodore takes out the folded piece of paper that has always been in his pocket since John handed it to him at the funeral. That first line of Berry's poem, *You will recognize the earth in me, as before* . . . how many times has he read it? It echoes many of his grandfather's words to him in his will, how this land and soil had inhabited his grandson, formed him. He knows this is true, truer than the hard lines of Chicago or the remnants of Detroit. No, too simple. Detroit had been both a death and a resurrection for him. If he had squandered his mother's money and his own time at Wayne State, somehow the experience of that and what followed had delivered him to where he was right now. Even as brilliant as his mother is, she admitted to hating the banalities of academic life, joking that she had graduated from the same university *magna cum lucky*. And she had possessed the benefit of ambition, which he, as everyone knows, lacks.

He revises aloud that first line, speaking to Nathaniel, "You did recognize the earth in me." Through all the searching in his young life, no words seemed more accurate. "You saw that, didn't you? You saw how good this land and this life were for me. How good it could be. But I'm sorry. I've made a commitment elsewhere that I, for once in my life, plan to honor."

He clears the table and is washing the dishes when Brigid shouts from the front door, "Hide the good stuff because I'm here and I have a van!"

Without as much as a handshake, she shatters the quiet and removes the horse head emerging from the frame. "My stash and don't touch it," she says as she places it in an empty corner. "I have a spot above the bar just screaming for this thing."

Then she does hug him, whispering, "How are you? I love what you've done with the place."

The walls are now completely bare and the windows stripped of coverings. The old Persian rug is loosely rolled and leaning against a wall. The only remaining piece of furniture in the room is Nathaniel's throne.

"Lots of stuff on the porch, as you probably noticed," he says. "All up for grabs. I haven't touched the kitchen yet. Come take a look."

"I brought boxes. I can help you sort through it, but I don't need much for myself."

"Whatever you want, just take," Theodore says. "All I need are a few plates and bowls and some basic cooking stuff. You know I can't rely on you to feed me all the time. Oh, the kitchen table and chairs, they stay."

"All the times I've eaten here over the years, even as a kid, I ate outside or here in the kitchen," she says. "As many as eight people right around this table. So crowded that the serving platters were all on the counter. Not sure why they even had a dining room."

"The first time I ever saw food on the dining room table was when you laid it out after the funeral," Theodore says.

"And still, no one sat there and ate!"

"I know the table and the chairs and that monstrous sideboard have been in the family a long time, but what am I going to do with them?" he asks. "My mom is supposed to take the china and silver, but she doesn't want it. Not her style."

Brigid drags the empty liquor boxes into the kitchen. "Your mom looks amazing. Right out of a fashion magazine. She showed me pictures of her condo renovations. And where is that little abode of hers? Chicago's freakin' Gold Coast! She's probably the biggest success to come out of Empire. By the way, how's your brother?"

She didn't mean to upset him, but her reference to those two, jumbled with the word *success,* sours his mood.

"He's still over there, but I hear this is his last tour. Mom told me he lost a really close buddy in a roadside attack. But you know Nate. He's incredibly resilient. He was born to be a soldier. He'll survive this. At least I pray he will."

"Oh my God, Teddy. It's the infamous recipe box. Man, look at this. The Library of Congress couldn't organize it any better."

He takes the open wooden box and flips through it. "Pretty cool. These go way back. Irene's Baked Beans. That's her mother's recipe."

"You can't toss that."

"No, I won't. It probably goes to my mom. I can't remember what the will said about her recipe box. If Mom doesn't want it, I'll take it. The brothers would get a kick out of it."

"And I can make some of these at the Bird's Eye," Brigid says. "Nice way to remember them. You know, I can't recall the last time I saw Nate up here. Must have been when your grandmother died. Oh yeah, I remember him decked out in his suit."

"His suit? You remember what he wore? I always thought you had a little crush on my brother."

Brigid is sorting through canned goods in the cupboard. "Sell by November 2001. But really, can tomato soup go bad? Remember that tomato soup cake your grandma made? Had raisins in it. Not a big fan of that one."

"Into the dumpster with the soup and all bad memories of it!" Theodore quips. "Seriously, Birdie, you could go for Nate, right?"

"There's a certain type of girl, or probably many types of girls, who would go for Nate. I'm not one of them. I barely know him. And, Theodore Dash, I remember what you wore to the funeral too."

"Seriously?" he repeats.

"A preppy, navy V-neck, white button-down, gray pants, and an awful tie that I suspect was Nathaniel's. And sneakers."

"Now I know you're crazy. My mother would never let me wear sneakers to a funeral," Theodore comments as he wraps in newspaper a ceramic cow that pours milk from its mouth. "My granddad hated this thing, said it looked like she was upchucking. But grandma never would get rid of it. My mom gave it to her when she was a little girl. Bought it with her own money at a yard sale, according to Grandma. Sorry, Marie. Off to Saint Vincent's she goes."

"You wore sneakers, I'm telling you." Brigid won't move on. "Bright white sneakers."

"And you wore a bikini," he says. "Maybe my mom didn't notice what I had on my feet. She was a wreck. I think that was the first time I ever saw her cry. Wailed and whimpered through the whole service and at the cemetery too. I cried too. But not Nate. Nate doesn't cry."

"I'm attacking this big old pantry," Brigid announces. "I know where he kept the booze. Any you want to keep?"

"Dump it all. We'll recycle the bottles."

"I'll use my professional judgment," she says. "Never throw out jewelry or alcohol without an appraisal. Some stuff gets better with time."

Theodore sits at the table and watches her as she unscrews bottles and sniffs the contents. Eventually she turns abruptly and smiles at him. "I'm leaving you this one. It was made by monks." She laughs and winks in a flirtatious way he remembers from their adolescence. With that combination, she could coax him into just about anything.

"Tell me about the seminary," she says, returning to her work. "Tell me why you chose that life."

"I was lost and then I was found."

"Vague answer. Does sound familiar though. When will you return to Detroit? You seem unsettled to me."

"I worry that I've replaced one obsession with another," Theodore says.

"There are as many paths to God as there are souls on earth." She's making great progress; three entire shelves are empty. "Don't ask me where I read that, but it stuck."

He joins her in the pantry and sits on a stool that is tucked into a corner. Just being in this room with her is a comfort. They move on to more inconsequential chatter, memories of this and that. He watches her sweater and slacks twist, gather, and cling as she works. He is asked to retrieve a box of spices from a high shelf and as he reaches above her, he can smell her shampoo, her meaty breakfast, the wool of her sweater, her perfume. He knows little about perfumes, knows only that his mother's smells like wealth and Brigid's like the wild, pervasive sweetness of honeysuckle. "Help me drag down Nathaniel's mattress to the porch," he says abruptly. "I hate to ask you but it'll be much easier with two of us."

"I thought you'd never ask," she answers. Showing him her box of alcohol selections, she adds, "I'm taking these six. The Benedictine is appropriate for you on your next frigid night. The rest can be turfed.

"Don't worry so much, Teddy. It's not like the rest of us have this whole thing figured out."

"I built a bench."

"That's a good start, sweetie."

JOHN QUIMBY

EARLY MARCH

Why it pops into his head as he stretches skyward on his three-legged ladder, he has no clue. Maybe it's because the wars festering in Iraq and Afghanistan are on the television daily. As awful as those conflicts are, most folks up here are unaffected. It might as well be another reality show, entertainment at another's peril. At seventy-six, John can remember World War II and how it shattered their lives even up in Marquette. Everybody supported the troops, sacrificed a little or a lot. He thinks Korea changed that and Vietnam, too, although a lot of people did care enough to oppose that war, himself included.

But all that is not what's on his mind out here in the cutting wind, pruning apple trees. It's this crazy policy in the military of "Don't Ask, Don't Tell." If ever anyone came up with a more ridiculous, head-in-the-sand way of handling a problem, he can't recall it. *C'mon now.* If a guy in your platoon is gay, it ain't that big a secret and most everybody has an inkling that this is the case. How they all deal with it is another matter. What it will never be is, "Gee, I'm not going to ask and I pray he won't just come out and tell me." John would prefer you just let the faggot do his job. That's just how he feels and he should know. He was once that guy.

Still he must focus on the work at hand. The initial objective in pruning an apple tree this time of year is to create the overall perfectly pyramidal shape. Then he must prune away broken or diseased branches, any crossing limbs, and anything poking straight up or down. Last year some of the trees had too many puny apples, crowding each other out. He tagged them last November so he would remember to thin the spurs to only a few per branch.

John considers all this to be an art. He creates form and brings light into each tree's interior, working slowly, efficiently, methodically. Other than his early years selling trucks all over the Upper Peninsula, caring for these trees has been his life's work, a gift from Cooper, whose family has held this land for generations.

It is Cooper who will follow behind John through the orchard to prune out the suckers that push from the root ball. They disagree on when these suckers should be removed. Cooper argues that winter pruning only stimulates regrowth, but John insists it be done then and again in midsummer. Cooper acquiesces, but makes John do the second pass mostly on his own. Cooper also is permitted to tackle the lowest branches in winter. John is over six foot and has greater strength, stability, and range to handle work on the ladder, and even climbing within the tree. Cooper is shorter, rounder, and six years older, thus confined to the ground by John.

John Quimby climbs down the ladder and appraises his efforts. It's hard to see the whole sculpture when one is in the middle of it. Satisfied, he moves on. Cooper gives him a hard time about how slow this process is, but it's the only way John can do it. A good month will pass before it's finished, unless he finds some help.

Last March his grandson, Laban, came down to help for a spell, now that he was old enough to be free from the influence of his mother. John left his wife in 1963 when his only daughter was just ten. Neither ever forgave him, and every year of his absence deepened the wound. John wants to start fresh with Laban and encourages his rare visits, but has to admit his work in the orchard was sloppy and his cuts ill-advised, no matter how much instruction was offered. Laban obviously had no interest in this or any work really and complained of the cold. He told John he was a journalist and preferred indoor work. Whether there were any published articles, John didn't know or ask. He paid his grandson for a full week after only three days and sent him back north to Marquette, undoubtedly the birthplace of many a famous writer and why not another? John wished he liked the boy more, but as Cooper put it, the twenty-six-year-old's personality was poisoned by the women in his life.

As John begins the shaping of the next tree in the row, he returns his thoughts to "Don't Ask, Don't Tell." It is actually the method his neighbors use in dealing with the two gay men on Voice Road. Whether or not the men share a sex life (and honestly at this stage of the game, they don't really) or a loving relationship (which they do), most people in town would rather not ask or be told. The couple sits together on most Sundays at the very Catholic Saint Agnes's with no chitchat other than warm banalities. When they step into a local restaurant, even in Cedar or Maple City, no one greets them asking, "Just the two of you?" (as though wives were in tow). It's clear that they are together and will probably tip decently.

There are three exceptions to this pleasant avoidance of too much information. Brigid Birdsey always lovingly acknowledges their relationship, as does Theodore. The last exception is the six-teen-year-old boy who delivers their paper and on collection days may say something to whomever answers the door like "How's the Mrs.?" If he's mocking them, it's done subtly and they are not offended, and answer him in short, witty quips.

Perhaps, John thinks, "Don't Ask, Don't Tell" isn't such a bad approach to domestic life. It may be understood by some as "Live and Let Live," which is more magnanimous and right-wing friendly.

There are competing leaders on the next tree so he must climb down to fetch the handsaw that is somewhere in the shallow snow. He locates it and as he expertly executes his cuts, he thinks of

Nathaniel. He was Cooper's closest friend, but always seemed to hold back a bit from John. He knows it's quite common for people in Nathaniel's position to be jealous of their best friend's spouse as they compete for attention and affection. This is true with men as well, even straight men. What was John to do? It's not like he could cozy up to Marie and quilt together or make jam (he did both of those things, she only the latter). *And they couldn't double date, could they?* So it was always Cooper off with Nathaniel to do this hunting or that calf-birthing, or something of that nature, and poor John was only included if his muscle was needed.

Then there's the matter of the will.

He and Cooper want for nothing, but . . . Cooper would never mention it or even think that Nathaniel should have remembered him in some small but meaningful way. In every couple, there is one who must be the petty one and keep track of all injustices and inequities. John is that one. There was not so much as a hammer and nail or even that gorgeous Persian rug that Nathaniel knew John greatly admired. Not even that silly old horse that Cooper loves and values more than Nathaniel ever did, the animal that Nathaniel, *the saint,* wanted to put down because of his age. It was Cooper who convinced him not to.

And another thoughtful bequest to John himself might have been something as insignificant as Marie's wooden recipe box which was chock-a-block with French-Canadian treasures collected over multiple lifetimes. Delicacies served at holidays or special Sunday dinners that they shared where recipes, no matter the praise thickly ladled, would never be divulged. There was the tourtière, a pork pie that he knew contained onions, mushrooms, celery, cinnamon, cloves, and savory, which Marie said was merely ground pork, vegetables, and some spices. What it was was divine and irreplicable, no matter how he tried. Her pea soup was sanctified with sage and some other mystery spice he couldn't name. There was bold ragout and a sugar pie topped with a tart cherry glaze. And

something as tired as baked beans was made a meal with the addition of bacon, maple syrup, bay leaf (he found one), and Keen's dry
mustard (spotted on the countertop). Quantities, other ingredients,
and time baked (he knew it was more than six hours) were tucked
back into the wooden box away from prying eyes (his, because who
else cared?).

Zilch. No rug. No old horse. No recipes. Nothing. That was
Nathaniel's thank you to his best friend.

Regardless of whether Theodore sells the property or not, the
apple trees as well as the few cherries should be tended to. John
will instruct Theodore and help out, too, once theirs are done. Even
though Theodore spent a couple winters in Empire, he was mostly
spared the bulk of the winter pruning. The little he did was under
the guidance of Nathaniel, which will need unlearning. It is not to be
done with a heavy hand, and although Nathaniel almost always had a
good harvest, he seemed to attack the pruning as merely something
to be gotten through, not as a true orchardist. An orchardist loves
his work, becomes one with his tools, and links the vision in his
mind to a unique reality in nature. John had tried to explain this to
Laban, but his grandson wisecracked about him smoking something
that altered his reality, and if so, would he please share.

Theodore would be different. John can sense the artist in him
and he must convince him to stay through the winter in that barren
house. Would it be gauche to ask him for that Persian rug he saw
still leaning by the front door? Most of the furniture is gone and
the windows are unwisely bare. Poor Mac with nothing to sleep on
but a hard floor.

He will talk to Theodore. He'll call their reliable hand, Hector,
and see if he can help out when there's no plowing to be done. He
has a good eye and decent technique. They could all work through
this orchard and then move on to Theodore's.

The afternoon warms into the high thirties and John works until
near dusk. More than twenty trees have been pruned. Tomorrow's

forecast is for even higher temperatures, and he will be out there by seven to take advantage of that.

It. is a lovely walk back home along Voice Road. He soaks in another classic sunset as the fireball slips into the big blue bowl of Lake Michigan. John Quimby vows to let go of his resentment over the will. Walking up to their farmhouse with all its luscious yellow light spilling from the windows, he affirms, yes, they do want for nothing. Both still in decent health, doing the work they always have, he and Cooper are most certainly blessed, but wouldn't that rug be just perfect in their bedroom? No harm in asking.

ZAIMA

SOON AFTER, LATE AT NIGHT • DEARBORN

seared in memory
blotting out sleep
this scene

I lower my M-16
into the coarse sand
drop it
remove my helmet
my flak jacket
utility vest
seven magazines of bullets
possibly intended for her

I discard half my weight
unwisely
as women and even children
could be concealing
my own death

I stand before this veiled woman
who I imagine is
afraid to leave her home

if she still has one
for fear of murder
rape
refusing to collaborate
with us
or insurgents
any of the insanity
that has wrecked
her once simple life

our eyes lock
is she Sunni or
is she Shi'a
as my own family
safe but filled with worry
for me
for their homeland

there is no compassion in her stare
only contempt
or worse, betrayal
because if any American
could help her
her fatherless children
rise above Mr. Bush's folly
Mr. Cheney's profits
or Mr. Rumsfeld's bluster
it would be me
there
at that moment
a woman with one foot
in each culture

but she doesn't know those men
or me

and if she had
we would be indistinguishable
all enemy
once rescuers,
now occupiers

I wish I could explain my intentions
why I was here in the 120-degree
white morning
what oath I have taken
to support and defend
the constitution
so help me God
to understand
why Iraqi children
stand by the side of the road
pretending to shoot at us
the righteous defenders
of this constitution

I push her arms up
I pat down her body
her breasts
her hips
between her legs
and then declare her worthy of travel
through the checkpoint
because I
another woman
even if I am weaponless
have this authority
over her
in her own country

THEODORE

EMPIRE

As he drags a large cardboard box across the near empty bedroom of his grandparents, the box gets snagged and won't budge. It's filled with cologne bottles, framed pictures of stiff strangers from another century, books, old cameras. The old box is bulky and heavy, but Theodore gives it another forceful tug. It moves but dislodges a section of flooring.

Where the bed had formerly been are three connected floorboards, staggered but of fairly equal length, pulled from the rest of the floor like a puzzle piece. On the center board is a rusted flathead nail that pokes up a fraction of an inch, about a butter knife's thickness, evidently enough to get caught up in the box's sagging bottom. An easy repair, but as he lifts the boards cleanly away, he finds they are meant to be removed, and probably often were, by Nathaniel, who from the looks of the tidy four-by-four-foot box now visible, was a horny old coot. Two stacks of *Playboys* stare back at Theodore, and as he removes them he finds they date back to the sixties and seventies, but are still in pretty good shape. How odd, he thinks, that a grown man would feel the need to hide this pretty mild pornography from his wife. Marie's mop must have passed over this treasure trove thousands of times. He tries to imagine

Nathaniel on his stomach, shimmying under the bed, knocking his huge head on the box springs, just to peek at something that should have been on his bedstand.

Theodore drags them all out, and there are probably three dozen. He flips through a few. The women are often in these weird, prayerlike, half-sitting positions, their water-balloon breasts perky and aggressive. Their expressions are mixed, sometimes naughty and unrepenting, other times almost schoolgirlish. These are not the women he has slept with, as must be the case for most men. He had always aimed low. Less chance he'd disappoint. Depression had tamped down his libido so much that sex felt more like an implosion than an explosion, and was usually followed by feelings of loss or self-loathing. The vow of chastity he will take one day seems to him a blessing.

Theodore knows that this is not what a normal young man should feel. His grandfather must have held the whole idea of sex to lusty heights. He thinks of his slight, well-proportioned grandmother in her aprons and Sunday clothes. No vixen, but who can tell?

He leaves the magazines in a neat stack by the bedroom door and is about to replace the floorboards when he spots something else at the bottom of the cavity. It's a pudgy manila envelope tucked into a corner. This worries him. He prays they aren't nude photos of Marie. Besides being innately repellent, they could shatter his childish image of the woman, who, of course, was more than simply his grandmother.

He could take the envelope directly to the plastic garbage bag in the hall. He could ceremonially burn the thing in the fireplace that he has yet to use. He could ask Brigid to look at the contents first and decide for him how best to proceed. Or he could write his mother's address on the envelope and drop it in the mail. Or send it all the way to Iraq for his brother to deal with.

Theodore sits on the cold floor and watches the last bit of sunlight leave the room. He pulls a table lamp to him, switches it on, and sits a bit longer.

He wonders how much oil is left in the tank. Wonders what Brigid is cooking down at the bar. Wonders when he will make any serious plans to return to his former serious life.

Then he opens the envelope. It contains several crinkly letters, folded in thirds, each only a page or two. He reads the one on top.

M

IN THE UNKNOWN PAST

Dearest Nathaniel,

It was such a joy spending time with you the other day. We get so little time together. Often it's just the back of your head I see at church or your truck as it races out of town. So when your hands, as rough and work-weary as they are, are upon my face or stroking the nape of my neck, well . . .

I shall not go on. Suffice it to say that these thoughts of you keep me going. Even the simplest task becomes quite the labor of love.

M

ZAIMA

walking on West Warren
behold the artifacts of our
imperfect assimilation
into where we are
from where we came
signs in windows for shakrlama
and ChickenSub
and french fries
preparing masgouf over an open firepit
behind the Nike store

men dance in the street
women shop

where the mosque is just down
Ford Road
the home of Henry Ford
is also the home of the largest mosque
in America

the number of workers
at the Rouge Plant
always shrinking
but cars are everywhere
expensive cars
for the few
with expansive wealth

on West Warren you buy
the foods of your country
the clothing of your country
cell phones and
televisions
on which you watch
a tiny sliver of
your country's destruction
wearing your soccer jerseys
the Iraqi flag tattooed on your chest

my family is a proud Muslim family
shopping through the Five Pillars
like good Catholic women
on birth control

I do not cover
or wear the hijab
I only prayed regularly
while in uniform
I don't read the Qur'an
but I have
I don't drink alcohol
eat pork

I believe there is no God but God
that Muhammad is His prophet

and my parents practice
much the same with the addition of wine
and charitable contributions
as their means allow

Islam, it is
practicing to give your life
to God
in a way pleasing
to Him

how is that at all
radical?

COOPER BOYD

He isn't tending to Levi anymore, but he finds himself there in his stall in the middle of the afternoon. No one else seems to be around and this is a relief to him. Empire is thawing, but not his heart.

After Nathaniel went and died out of the blue, Cooper cried hard twice and that was enough. He then constructed from routine and the precise amount of Jack Daniel's an impregnable wall around his heart. He felt little. His patience with John grew as thin as the patchy ice on South Bar Lake. Everything about the man seemed to annoy Cooper, like his constant throat-clearing all morning and the way he hums without melody as he does his chores. Then John went and asked him to see if Teddy wanted to sell Nathaniel's living room rug to them. Like he's a grave robber, like he'd ever do such a thing. John can be so materialistic at times, yet one more annoying trait.

Other than that, not much else rises to the surface in terms of Cooper's moods. Even Teddy, whom he knows he loves dearly, only reminds him on a near daily basis of Nathaniel's absence.

Nathaniel's absence. It is right now as nebulous as the air around him and as concrete as the compacted earth in Levi's stall. He feels it in his throat, this absence that creeps up acidic as bile.

"You need to get outta here, don't you, old boy?" he asks the horse. "A ride would do us both good."

Levi is less than enthusiastic, but does not resist the brush down or reject the saddle, the cinch, the bridle.

"Where you wanna go?" Cooper asks the indifferent animal. "How about we make our way over to the beach?"

Cooper leads Levi out of the paddock and through the gate. He hasn't been on a horse in years. He drags over Nathaniel's mounting block and puts one foot in the stirrup. Without grace or elegance, he manages to get himself up into the saddle. "I'm an old, old man, Levi," he whispers, "but let's pretend we just did this yesterday."

And off they go, crossing open land and up Bar Lake Road to the edge of the dunes. They ride in and out of the lazy surf as the wind dies completely. There's real warmth in the late afternoon sun and a tiny seed of optimism is planted in them both. Maybe an early spring is on the way.

When they return to the barn, their steps are lighter and their lungs have been washed with fresh lake air. "I loved that man too," Cooper tells Levi as he removes his tack. "He was a damn good man, a damn good friend."

Then he sits down heavily on a bench in the dusty stall. He thinks long and hard about his decades-long relationship with Nathaniel, their infrequent quarrels and all the time they spent together without a word being spoken, doing things they both loved, whether it was fishing or hunting or repairing some piece of machinery. Those were the best times, those quiet times together. Nathaniel did silence well.

"Why didn't God take me first?" he asks Levi's hindquarters. "I'd rather be missed than the one doing the awful missing. Damn you, Nathaniel Dash! You could have tried, but no, you had to fight the doctors, always invincible, always right."

"There you are!" John shouts into the stall so abruptly that Cooper leaps from his bench. "Why are you yelling at a horse's ass?"

"Jesus, John, you scared me half to death."

"I've had three phone calls from people telling me they've spotted you out riding Levi at a clip that's not safe. You or the horse could have been killed."

"Then we would have died happy," Cooper says sharply.

"When are you going to snap out of this?"

"When are you going to stop riding me?" Cooper asks. "He just died, for God's sake. Can't I mourn him? Can't I even have that? I mean, are you really jealous of a dead man?"

This hurts and it takes John a couple minutes to answer. "No. No, of course not. It's just that I feel like if I lose any more of you, there'll be nothing left."

"Oh, don't say that," Cooper says dismissively. "Let's go home. If you still want me to ask Teddy for the rug, I will. I know he doesn't want it."

"Forget the rug," John says. "I just want you. Alive."

ZAIMA

LATE MARCH • DEARBORN

you were easy to track
and find Brother Theodore

your own brother
Nate the fool
when pouring out his story
back in Iraq
painted you
sweet Theodore
as pure innocence
you a child again
shielded from the world's
harsh nature
by a cloth hood

Nate the fool
named the seminary
named all his kin
in sweet fairy tale fashion
offering each as proof
of his stellar past

his unblemished character
so loving and loved was he

but beneath his saccharine words
beneath the memories and holiday myths
(though father was missing
not revealed why or where)
lurked a darker creature
capable of the cold detachment
required by war
and capable of the violence
against me

you were easy to track
and find Brother Theodore
a simple search
and easy phone call
to the brothers at your seminary
to those who trust
in good intentions
anxious to provide news
of your grandfather's death
up north in Empire
and your prolonged absence
settling his estate
living in his home

so animated were the brothers
in their fierce longing for you
so happy to help me
an old friend
(you've yet to meet)
find you

FATHER MCGURLEY

EMPIRE

Theodore shows up on Sundays for the eight o'clock Mass. He sits near the back, always in his robe, reciting the usual prayers, singing the standard Lenten hymns with the rest of the parishioners. All that is fine, thinks Father McGurley, this surprisingly mild March Sunday. What bothers him is that Theodore also shares that same blank stare as most of the faithful during his sermons. And Father McGurley does not hold back in his words and delivery during this dark, holy season of doubt and loss. These are his most confrontational sermons, unlike the sweet, hopeful Advent messages as they await the birth of the Child. This time of year he likes to link his congregants with the sleepy, unfaithful, ineffectual disciples. He challenges their faith, calls out their insincerity, and demands attention be paid to these vital days in the church calendar.

Today he shouts. He pauses. He looks out over his flock and their expressionless faces awash with disinterest. They've heard it all before. He thinks of lazy, grazing cows turning their heads to look at you as you pass. You moo at them. They ignore you. You're not speaking their language.

Father McGurley focuses on Theodore, attempts to engage him. "Was it necessary for our salvation that Christ suffer and die on the cross?" he throws out there. "Did His excruciating death change what it means for all of us to die?"

They hope so. *Who wants this to be all there is?*

He decides to bring it closer to home. "Nathaniel Dash has just left us. You all knew him." A few nodding heads is all he gets. They would rather not go there. They would prefer thinking about whether or not there are any eggs in the fridge, whether they turned off the coffeepot.

"What did the gruesome death of Jesus Christ on a rustic, wooden cross have to do with the death of Nathaniel Dash?" he asks, more accusation than question.

Theodore wakes up now, crossing his arms high across his chest for protection. Others fidget in their seats.

"I'll bet Brother Theodore has an inkling," the priest continues. "But I won't put him on the spot. He loved his grandfather and I'm sure misses him terribly. But he's not worried about him. He's not worried about his *soul*. Because he knows that death is an illusion. An illusion shattered by an empty tomb! Amen."

Everyone seems relieved that the sermon is over and that the familiar, repetitive rituals that round out their Sunday obligation can resume.

After Mass, Father McGurley grabs Theodore as he hurries out. "How are things going at the farm?" he asks.

"Fine, I guess. It's getting emptier," Theodore says, still walking toward his truck, Celeste.

"Hold on a minute, Teddy," the priest says, touching his shoulder. "Tell me how *you* are. Your mother asked me to check in on you."

"To tell you the truth, I'm anxious to get back to the seminary. I wasn't planning on hanging around more than a week, but how can I just walk away? My grandfather trusted me to take care of things and I will. Who else would do it if I didn't?"

"So you feel it's a burden?" Father McGurley asks.

"That's not what I meant. It's just . . . a lot."

"Pray on it, son. Not for an answer or a direction to take. Pray for self-knowledge. Unearth what's in your heart. Pray without words."

"Without words?" Theodore asks.

"Yes. For you I believe it may be better to pray in silence. Find that quiet place inside you. Rest there. Don't hurry through any of this, Teddy. Not the grief or any of this."

"This?"

"This process," the priest says. "I believe God will speak to you. Move slowly and listen carefully."

ZAIMA

sometimes you go
without knowing why
I must find this man
I can't fully say why

will he be the
mirror of his brother
or a broken, less confident man
a gentle, prayerful friar
giving not taking
humble not boastful
now grieving a man he
likely loved

although I was told
without elaboration
that the new friar has a dark side
well then good
better that he knows
the look and texture of darkness

to dull its allure
to demystify its power

I need to see Brother Theodore
in the flesh
this has forced me
to find him

I need to hide away
this place as good as any
any the same as here

always a stranger
this will feel familiar
what I have come to know
and expect

he's on a farm
there's an orchard
these things pieces
of my parents' far past
bits of beautiful Basrah
bits in me as well

if there is a farm
there will be a barn
and with the promise of spring
the thawing of the soil
I will bed down there
and make war
or peace
I don't care which
the war rages within

peace elusive
always more myth
than actuality

should a crime be committed
against you
some would say
kill the life within you
you have every right
considering the violence
of its conception

but there has been enough
killing of innocents
don't you think?

there's enough hatred in this world
to bloody every birth
to reason against the simple
gift of life
which none of us requested
and few of us deserve
or are even at all grateful
for the next breath
for the warmth of the clear sun
through a dirty bus window
for another spring

I have a blanket
no phone
the clothes I'm wearing
a warm jacket, good boots
a map of Michigan

two books
notebooks of lined paper
and my father's favorite pen
(a grain of guilt for the taking of it)
some food
more money than I'll need
a weak will to continue
a stronger need to survive

with my short hair
pudgy backpack
and plain clothing
I could be a tall and handsome boy
bored with school
off to build his body
in an orchard
for three seasons

maybe I am a boy
or a girl, a woman
or a man
maybe I am every person
who left a life behind
who knows a partially broken limb
need not die
but only change its pattern of growth
who leaves a lot or a little
bravely, blindly because
sometimes you go
without knowing why

sometimes you go because
staying is not
an option

ZAIMA

It's the magic hour when the bus pulls into Empire, no longer day, not yet evening, a pure, luminous magenta. There is no bus station or even a covered bench, the village being too small and inconsequential. As she steps down and away from the bus, the usual structures emerge, the bank, small stores, an ice cream shop not yet open for the season, a bar down the street. Only one traffic light dangles across M-22 and even that only flashes yellow.

Zaima had left Dearborn in the early morning and it wasn't any great distance that ate up most of the day. It had been all the changing of buses, the layovers, and the frequent stops that made a simple trip north and west so time-consuming.

She had stared out the window most of the trip, had written a little, and taken no interest in the freshly manured fields or the tidy, repetitive Grand Rapids neighborhoods. She had not slept, being too anxious about missing connecting buses. Fellow passengers were neither hostile nor friendly. They all seemed distracted by their own thoughts or their phones. There was one woman in the row ahead of her who spent the better part of an hour in a phone conversation that seemed to be about the infidelity of the person on the other end. There had been crying and cursing, hang ups, and redials. The high drama exhausted Zaima; and after the woman announced that she never wanted to see "his sorry ass" again, she threw herself into the empty seat next to Zaima. If she was looking for consolation, she got none. Zaima turned her head toward the window and never looked back until the woman huffed and left.

Finally in Empire, she walks away from the highway down the main street where most of the commercial real estate is located. There are a number of small galleries featuring carved loons and driftwood sculptures. One even features a six-foot horse made of wide, smooth driftwood for the larger muscle masses and delicate, thin pieces for the mane.

She finds only two businesses open—a bar at the end of the street and Deering's Market, the better option. She anticipates long and curious examination of the tall, foreign-looking woman with the boy's haircut, but this does not occur. The gaunt, middle-aged man at the cash register smiles shyly and bags her fruit, bread, hummus, and apricot juice, offering only the bland niceties and the efficiency of one ready to close up shop. She wants to ask him where the Dash property is located, but instead requests a phone book. There the recently deceased is still listed as residing at an address easily committed to memory.

Back on the street, she stuffs the food in her pack and realizes she forgot to ask just where LaCore Road is. She could inquire at the tavern but knows that is a place where rumors germinate and spread in a small town. What she needs most now is shelter for the night, but in her wanderings, finds no motel—not that she would spend good money on such an unnecessary luxury.

As she walks north on M-22 and looks west down Phillip Street, she spots an old, wooden church. The temperature is dropping and her options are few. In two short blocks she reaches the double pine doors of Saint Agnes's Roman Catholic Church and, as she expected, they are not locked. Although the sun has set, there is still enough light inside to make her way to the front pew. She has never been in a church, but the piney, sweet scent seems familiar and welcoming. The windows on two sides are stunning, with soaring panes of clear glass. There is none of the heavy elegance of their mosque, this country church as unassuming as the mosque is grand. The ornate altar at the front has been upstaged by a simple wooden table closer to the congregation. On its linen covering is a small, erect gold cross, a heavy cup, and a gold plate piled with flat, white disks. On the wall behind, a much larger cross with Jesus Christ mounted on it with bloody spikes is alarmingly real to her. Here he is the Messiah; for others, he is merely a prophet—a difference grand enough to provoke men to wage war.

Zaima walks over to investigate an alcove to her right where another figure lifts her ceramic eyes to heaven. The woman's eyes are widely set and her skin coloring is much like a woman from the Middle East which, of course, she probably was. There is a place to kneel in front of her, and Zaima does this for a short time. Unfortunately she finds she has little to say to this distant relative.

Flipping on a light, she locates a bathroom in the basement of the church, and then returns to the first pew and its rock-hard, horsehair cushion. She eats her provisions as the church fades to a dense, palpable darkness. *One would never sleep in the mosque; is it forbidden to do so here?* The dullness of the day demands it, however, and she rests her body on the narrow pew. This feels like a place of safety, this strange church in an unfamiliar village. She longs to experience something other than the familiar things that dog her, the anger, the sense of not belonging anywhere, the sleeplessness, the nausea. Maybe her soul is not buried in the rubble of Tikrit. Maybe she is more than the sum of what her life has been so far. There is something profound in this room. *A beginning?* Is it possible that what seemed like running away could be running toward?

Zaima pulls her blanket tight. She is then granted a mercifully numbing sleep.

———— • ————

Even with closed eyes she sees the early, golden light of the sun, feels its warmth. When she opens them, she sees that it is not dawn and that the air is clogged with smoke. Behind her the back of the church is a wall of creeping flames. Someone is clutching her arm to pull her upright, a bald, short, comical creature. His mouth is forming words she cannot decipher, the voraciously consuming fire is that loud. She's trained to respond quickly to imminent danger, so why is her body ignoring her mind's commands and the pleading of this odd little man? All he manages is to pull her from her sleeping position to one flat against the floor. In shaking him off, she sends random food from a small table flying. He's still pulling on her sleeve once she's standing. They inadvertently knock against the wooden altar and scatter the tiny rounds, empty the cup. He stamps his foot, shouts, "We must go. Now!" She is worried about the wafers, can't focus. Don't they signify Christ's body? *Will the Messiah suffer yet another death?*

Zaima grabs her blanket and pack, and the man with bare feet and plaid pajamas all but drags her to a side door to their right. It's like an ambitious little tugboat pulling a barge to safety. He pushes her toward the open door and then steps deftly left to rescue the statue of the Blessed Virgin.

Outside, Zaima runs to a tight grove of trees that separates the church from a neighboring house on Phillip Street. The fire is spreading to both side walls and is teasing the roofline. She watches the man foolishly return to the sanctuary and reappear carrying the small gold cross and the cup.

Soon the sound of sirens fills the air and the heat from the fire intensifies. The man returns to her side, places his fat hands on her shoulders. "I saw you go inside last night. I brought you food. Are you all right?"

"I didn't do this," Zaima blurts out. "I didn't cause the fire."

"I'm sure you didn't. I'm Father McGurley. This is my church."

"Just go. Save someone else," she says and retreats farther into the darkness, away from the priest and the accusing fire.

Father McGurley crosses the street and leans against a tree. Already the volunteer firefighters are connecting hoses to the hydrant and strategizing their approach. Cooper Boyd is quickly at his side.

"Are you all right? Was anyone in there?" he asks.

"No one," the priest lies. "Not a living soul."

Together, mesmerized, they watch Saint Agnes's burn. The scene is as spectacular as it is horrific. It is clear that the small-town fire department will do its best to contain the blaze and not be able to save the structure. The water gushing from the fat hoses will only slow its near total destruction.

The fire is so fast-moving that within minutes they can make out the distinct exterior of the iconic church, ablaze from front steps to steeple. The furnace within is roaring through the lovely window frames, and to Father McGurley it is like hell has visited this quiet street in Empire.

As the sun begins to rise in clear skies, it seems the entire town is gathering to watch the church burn. Hands reach out to the priest and pull him uncomfortably close. This is such an intimate loss, he would prefer to suffer alone. They are repeating all the right words, their bottomless and heart-wrenching condolences. But their words are all lost anyway, muffled and obliterated by the roar of the fire. Really, what can be said when God's house will be transformed into a pile of charred lumber, when the organ and all her pipes are silenced forever, when every page of every hymnal and Bible is a crispy collection of ash? For him, it is a great historical demise. Gone are the weddings, baptisms, funerals, and ordinary Sunday services spanning decades. Gone are all the official records of those events, the succession of priests serving there. Here were pleas made for funds, pleas for forgiveness made in the confession booth. And in the great openness and compassion that was Saint Agnes's, here were altar girls, and the unauthorized blessing of more than one same-sex coupling. This church was to Father McGurley a living, breathing thing. *Even if the funds to rebuild materialize, how can one re-create its past and the lives it touched?* If he were alone, he would cry.

They stare in awe as a community, their faces flush from the heat, and watch the church collapse. First the front falls forward on the scorched lawn, and then quickly, both sides and the back inward. The steeple and the last of the roof disappear. All that remains standing is a section of the west wall containing the tall frame of a single window. It will be many hours before the last breath of fire is extinguished in the church's basement, where only hours before Zaima had prepared for bed.

———————— • ————————

Zaima has been walking aimlessly, heading nowhere, wondering how her emotional chaos might have ignited this fiery disaster. Impossible, of course, but there is a shadow behind her she cannot shake and she knows that it had been dogging her well before she set foot on Iraqi soil. The war gave her a fresh target, a direction for her discontent. She returned to Dearborn and her family an emotional zombie, disconnected and distant, easily angered, refusing the food her mother prepared or any morsel of affection they offered. Every day she became more insular, so that when she did board the bus and leave, she wondered if she'd be missed at all. So little was left and what did remain soon would not be welcome.

She finds herself walking north on M-22. Cars file past traveling the opposite direction. Evidently word of the church fire has spread and who would want to miss it? She is cold and nauseous and vomits behind an empty farm stand. She covers the small mess with dried leaves and returns to the highway, which soon makes a soft turn to the east. At that point, another road heads due north. It is LaCore. In less than twenty minutes she is standing before the white clapboard farmhouse at number 117. The structure looks solid and proud, all the angles sharp, the porch level and unsettled. There's no car visible and the driveway winds to the well-weathered barn out back. Sanctuary. Sturdy with a solid stone foundation, it is as inviting and protective as any structure she has ever seen.

Zaima walks through the bristled tufts of grasses and weeds to a mowed circle around the west-facing barn. On the front is a large sliding door, and to the right, a worn, wooden door with a broken iron latch. A six-pane window is to its right, and the two smaller windows beyond that are set into the stone foundation. That last window is part of a one-room addition with a metal roof that slopes nearly to the ground.

She sees a chicken coop, a fenced yard, and some neglected raised garden beds, some made with wood frames and others formed with piles of rocks. She is reminded of her mother's urban vegetable beds that were situated in the backyard where every other family had a lawn. There is likely no shame in growing your own food here. She can make out the ruins of last year's plantings and splashes of green that are either weeds or hardy herbs. Well beyond all this and traveling eastward up the hill are row upon tidy row of small trees, their tangled branches reaching randomly skyward.

Zaima pushes open the door with the broken latch and inhales the fragrant, earthy air. There is a sweetness to it, blended with the pungent smell of livestock. She discovers only a single disinterested horse occupying one of the three stalls. Neatly carved into the stall's door is what must be his name, LEVI. Although his body is turned away from her, she sees that he is stocky and broad across the shoulders. His huge, noble head is positioned to gaze out his window, as if anticipating the arrival of another, more important someone. Finally he shifts his head to fix an eye on her. His coat is black but with just enough white to appear blue in this pale light. He quickly tires of her and returns to his waiting. His feed bucket of hay looks untouched as do the carrots and apples in another bucket nearby. This is likely a symptom of his grieving, so she opens the stall door to comfort him. Zaima has never been this close to a horse and is unsure of where to touch him. She strokes his neck and he doesn't bother to pull away. "Sorry, Levi. You must feel abandoned," she whispers. "Death can make you feel that way. Guess we're both in unfamiliar territory."

An old but handsome Farmall tractor is tucked near the back of the barn. The tractor seems to have the same utilitarian nobility as the horse, being no more or less than its purpose. There are ancient farm implements and a bulky press, likely for cider-making. She wanders below the hayloft to the far right corner where she finds a small, rustic door without a knob or handle, just a worn hunk of wood on a screw to secure it closed. The room inside has a rough wooden floor and two small east-facing windows. Below them is a long, raised platform with low sides, possibly for sorting or storage. The ceiling tapers down to the side opposite the door, but there's still plenty of standing room. There's also a chair and a few wooden crates. The intended use of this space is not clear to her, but it will be sufficient for her needs.

From the barn's well-organized work area, Zaima finds a square farm table, a broom, a bucket, a rutted piece of bar soap, a few clean rags. With water from an outside spigot, she cleans her room as best she can. She lays hay on the platform and covers it with her wool blanket. The crates are stacked for storage. She empties her pack and stows her two books, her map, paper, pen, and what's left of her food. She eats an apple and a chunk of bread. She has learned well to survive on little and this modest meal is way better than the MREs the army provided. She stretches out on the platform, which is narrow but of adequate length, and covers her upper body with her jacket. Then she sleeps.

———— • ————

The late afternoon sun is hitting the west side of the barn when she hears the tires popping gravel out front. There's a new chill in the barn so she gets up and pulls on her jacket. A door slams. She ventures out into the belly of the barn and looks out the larger window. She sees the front of an old truck, no more. Zaima hears another door slam and rushes back to her room. The chickens are making a ruckus and then the barn door screeches open, followed by a voice.

"Hey, Levi. Sorry I didn't turn you out today. Not that you even want to leave the barn, right, buddy? Oh, not hungry? That's okay. Brought you some more apples. See, I'm leaving them right here."

Then the crack in her doorway widens and in trots a big, brindled dog. "Shit," she whispers. He checks out the room, sniffing her, her empty pack, the platform, her boots. She runs her hand down his spine and he bolts when the voice calls him. His name is Mac and she now has two friends.

Zaima needs to see the man she has come to find, this complete stranger who is all that's keeping her focused, keeping her sane. She hopes but cannot promise to spare him the soul-suffocating choler that pants behind her like a rabid dog. *Does she want to harm him? Is that her purpose here?* She's not sure. She's working on impulse and has no grand plan.

She hears him close the barn door, then a few minutes later, hears him load up his truck with a series of soft thuds, boxes perhaps. She dares to look out that dusty front window and sees him standing by the truck's door momentarily and then climb in. He wears a pale blue turtleneck and jeans, and has hair as short as hers. The dog sits next to him like the loyal companion he most likely is. Once the truck pulls out and they reach LaCore, this stranger hits the gas hard and heads south. Although he doesn't look much like his brother, something about his gait, his height, and his age tells her this must be Theodore.

Zaima can't move for a few minutes. She wants the image of the truck and the man and the dog to be carved deeply into her memory, so she could close her eyes at any time and see every detail. This day began with a fast-moving fire and nears an end with a pickup tearing down a rural road, all happening without explanation in Empire, the small town with such a big name. But now, she acknowledges, the Dashes, with the stature and influence that flow from here to Chicago to northern Iraq, that family now has a thorn, a kink, an obstruction, something not anticipated in their dramatic, entitled lives. She is that thorn.

Zaima enters the farmhouse through the unlocked back door. This brings her first into a mudroom and then the clean but barren kitchen. One door leads into a large pantry and the other to a bathroom, which she utilizes.

In the pantry there's not much on the shelves, but she takes an unopened box of Saltines, a can of tuna, and a can of peaches. From the kitchen, she steals a couple of plates, a bowl, a mug, a paring knife, a spoon, and fork. There are two can openers in a jammed drawer that she has to pry open. She takes one, and then fills three mason jars with water from the tap.

There's nothing she needs in the empty adjacent room—probably the dining room—or in the living room. There she finds only one large chair, a small table beside it, and on that, a Bible. But upstairs in the narrow hall are two plastic bags neatly tied at the top. From these, Zaima extracts two blankets, a stained feather pillow, sheets, a pillowcase, and an oval braided rug. She fluffs up the remaining contents and reties the tops.

Safely back in the barn, she incorporates the stolen goods into her living quarters. Dinner is hummus, crackers, and peaches. Then she reads and writes until the room is dark. The truck returns shortly after that. All of this is one full day in Empire.

ZAIMA

INTO THE NEXT DAY

Zaima does not sleep well, but in a new way. There is a world of unfamiliar sounds, loud irregular creaking and banging of loose boards. Some animal howls mournfully in the distance. The wind is, however, the worst sleep wrecker as it penetrates the exterior walls and rattles the windows above her bed so forcefully she fears a shower of broken glass will fall upon her.

The moon is full and when she dares to venture out to pee the whole foreign landscape is ghostly lit, a black-and-white nightmare that sends her running back to her manger.

Theodore returns at dawn to check on Levi. Again the dog visits Zaima to sniff and nuzzle against her legs. The friar leaves the barn without calling him, so Mac stretches out on her small rug and seems intent on staying, but she nudges him out. "I seem to make everyone uncomfortable," she tells him, "except you."

She hears Theodore let the chickens out into the yard and then he's back in the barn. From a crack in the door she watches as he gathers paintbrushes, a roller, and a drop cloth from the tool area. From the back she sees he is lean, not like his broad-shouldered, sinewy sibling. He walks away from her in a meandering, shuffling way that looks like he's not sure where he wants to go. Soon he's off in his truck and she's back in the warmth of the farmhouse. There's a rotisserie chicken in the fridge and it seems he doesn't care for dark meat, so she picks at that and at a container of store-bought potato salad. There's a new loaf of white bread and some cherry jam. She brushes the jam on two slices and wraps them in a paper napkin for later.

Zaima washes up and goes back upstairs to see what else she can scavenge. She finds a half-dozen large plastic bags in an empty bedroom. In one are three usable white T-shirts that don't fit well, but will give her something clean to wear. Also reclaimed is a spiffy western-style denim shirt with pearly snap buttons that looks like it has never been worn. She immediately tries it on. It's long and loose, but she likes it. In it, she becomes a different person, one who has control over her life, over her decisions.

Back in the chilly barn, Zaima grabs her jacket and returns on foot to the only other place in Empire where she's spent any time at all.

FATHER MCGURLEY

THAT SAME DAY

There is an ugly chain-link fence imprisoning the blackened remains of his church. In the air is one of those early warm whispers of spring, the joyous season of renewal, but he's struggling to be in any way optimistic. *Why? Why, dear God, did you commit your house to Satan's flames?*

Of course, Father McGurley knows it was not God's hand that set the fire. Crappy, old wiring or the decrepit furnace, take your pick. There is insurance, but it will never be enough to replace the architectural gem that was Saint Agnes's, not the glorious, upward sweeping clear windows or the heavy oak pews. Not the beautiful, round stained-glass depictions of Saint Agnes. Even the iron rack for the votive candles was more than one hundred years old and irreplaceable. Maybe he'll find it in the debris, still functional.

It has been decided that Mass will be in the grange hall in Burdickville until it is warm enough and dry enough to be celebrated on Empire Beach. This is how it will be for a year, maybe longer. Two weddings are scheduled for the summer. They will no doubt be performed at another church and not in a vacant construction site.

Oh, these are indeed dark thoughts. Where is the hope that so often gushes from his lips to those in crisis? But wait, what does the priest see rolling toward him but a cloud darker yet. It's the wayfarer, the no-thanks-for-saving-my-life sad sack. *What had she said? Go save somebody else?*

He realizes that he's been clenching sections of the chain link for some time and has trouble freeing his arthritic fingers. "Hello there," he says with little enthusiasm. Not very priestlike, but so what? Rude begets rude.

"Did you forget something?" Father McGurley asks as he unlocks and opens the only gate. "Welcome to hell," he adds with a sweep of a hand.

Zaima passes by the perfectly intact wooden sign that lists Saturday and Sunday services and the hours of a thrift store. "You saved my life. I should thank you."

"*Should* implies obligation," he says. "But you're welcome. You allowed me to perform the last good deed in this building." He has thrown two cardboard boxes into the fenced area and now picks up a blackened hardcover book, which he drops into one of them.

"AA. The Big Book," he announces. "Shall we look for Bibles?"

"I'd like to help in any way I can," Zaima says.

"Well, thanks, but not even I should be in here. The bowels are likely still burning," the priest tells her. "But I guess we could poke around at the edges. We'll need gloves. There's a thrift store in the building behind the parsonage."

Father McGurley squints his eyes, examining the young woman. "That's a nice shirt you have on there, but it's not your size now, is it? Do you need clothing? Do you even have a home?"

"I have a place to stay . . . enough to wear."

"Even Christ relied on the kindness and generosity of others," he replies. "Come with me."

At the Helping Hand, the priest gives a cloth sack to Zaima and into it he throws T-shirts, a checked blouse she would never wear, a blue fleece jacket, two pairs of baggy jeans, and a baseball cap that reads *Lake Michigan. Unsalted.*

"Good. Now people will think you're a local," he says.

"More likely a tourist."

"What shoe size?" he asks.

"Nine."

He produces a pair of black-and-white Converse high-tops. "Here's a men's seven and a half. Try these."

Zaima does not want to remove her boots. Her one pair of socks smells like her one pair of socks. "They'll be fine."

Father McGurley wisely grabs a couple pairs of white athletic socks for her and then two pairs of heavy leather gloves. "Let's get to work, my dear. Do not climb over any of the debris and stay toward the outside. Use one of the rakes to pull things to you and if you see Cooper Boyd, play dumb. I've promised him not to get in there until the heavy machinery shows up."

An hour into the dig Zaima calls the priest over. By unearthing some blackened roofing and broken boards, she has uncovered the iron bell from the steeple.

The priest is ecstatic. "Good God, my dear. You have paid me back in full. The demolition crew can extricate it for us."

The *us* strikes her as oddly inclusive. She is neither Catholic nor even Christian and an old church bell means nothing to her. The last group she felt at all comfortable in was the handful of women who served with her in Tikrit. And even with them she kept her involvement minimal and superficial.

"I'm going to rest for a bit, but I'll keep you company," he says, lowering himself down to lean against the fence. He watches her comb through the debris methodically. He wonders if this is not new for her.

"What brings you to Empire?" he asks nonchalantly.

Zaima looks his way and shrugs off the question. "Just passing through."

"Where are you headed?"

"Not sure."

"Tell me your name again . . . or for the first time," he says.

"Zaima."

"Zaima, don't you think it's horrible that Saint Agnes's burned down during Holy Week?"

"Holy Week?" she asks as she retrieves three red glasses. They are larger and heavier than her parents' shot glasses, something used only for measuring alcohol, not downing it.

"Yes. Tomorrow is Good Friday. We'll have our Stations of the Cross at a nearby grange hall."

She has no interest in either these stations or a grange hall, so says nothing.

"Easter Sunday, we will greet the risen Lord at the beach here at six A.M., regardless of the weather. Why don't you join us?"

"I'm a Muslim," she says, still not looking at him. "That is how I was raised. My family is, how should I say this? Muslim light."

"Easter can mean different things to different people," he explains. "For you, it could simply be a celebration of new life, a vernal rebirth, if you will."

She has no desire to discuss that either. Some distance from the carcass of the building she lifts joined fragments of stained glass. They compose portions of the angelic face of a young woman. Her skin is pale and her clear eyes are directed upward. "Is this your Virgin?"

"Oh my!" exclaims the priest as he scurries over. "Perhaps the heat of the fire blew out the window." He runs his fingers over the glass. "It's not *the* Virgin. It's another virgin, Saint Agnes of Rome. She was a beautiful young woman, really just a girl of thirteen, who was devoted to her religious purity and rumored to be a Christian. It is believed that any man who attempted to rape her was struck blind. She was dragged naked through the streets and eventually beheaded."

"How can *your* God have allowed that?" Zaima asks angrily.

"Your God has allowed equal brutality. Anyway these things are not the work of any God. If we cover our eyes, we can't blame God for our not being able to see."

Zaima lowers the image of the murdered virgin to the ground. "I have to go now," she says. "Tell me, was the funeral for Nathaniel Dash here?"

"Yes. A couple months ago. His casket arrived in the back of his pickup. Unorthodox, but so was the man. Not a big churchgoer, but a good fellow, honest and generous. His wife was a lovely woman, very devout."

"And their daughter?"

"Driven, very. Quite successful, I hear. Lives in Chicago. Did you know Nathaniel?"

"Not personally," Zaima says. "I knew someone who did."

"See you Sunday?" Father McGurley asks.

"Thanks for the clothes," she says, her back already turned.

ZAIMA

A BIT LATER

it is written in the Qur'an
both the divinity of forgiveness
and the necessity to fight
against injustice
and vile acts

but my well of forgiveness
has become a dry and empty
pit. And my spring of anger
surges with the power
unleashed when what has been
plugged by fear
gushes forth without restraint

indeed, God should close
his eyes
again

THEODORE

A FEW DAYS LATER

And then he stops. He does no work in the orchard. He doesn't repair or paint anything. He does feed the chickens and then decides to spend some time with Mac and Levi in the horse's stall. He brings two books with him, Wendell Berry's collection of poems, *Farming: A Hand Book,* and the Bible.

Theodore sits there in the dirt surrounded by stinging scents of dog and horse and barn. The stall needs a good mucking out, but that's not happening now. He holds the two books in his lap and closes his eyes. He feels the hunger in his belly and the thickness in his head. Nothing at all happens for a while.

Then he stands and paces, waking the dog and worrying Levi. He reads first from Psalm 89, gesturing wildly as he shouts, "Bid men return to dust, and say, 'Return ye, children of men.' For a thousand years in thy sight are as yesterday, which has passed away, and as a watch in the night. Thou tearest them away: they become like a morning dream, like grass that shoots up. In the morning it flourishes and is green, in the evening it is mowed down and withers away."

Levi wanders out into the paddock, away from his ranting, but Mac stays. It's his job, that loyalty. "Scary stuff, right Mac?" Theodore asks, putting down the Bible and taking up the tattered paperback Berry. He flips it open and quietly reads aloud a poem about a farmer who feels the soil like a drug in his body. It is about life and death, about the light and the dung pile and the resulting corn. The words are puzzling, yet vaguely comforting.

Theodore closes the volume solemnly and walks out into the paddock. He leans against the fence and looks out into the orchard. Soon enough there will be abundance there, flower and then fruit.

"Where's our place in all of this, old boy?" Theodore asks the horse. "All this time passing, all this death and rebirth? Dung piles into corn, men into dust. What's the message in it all for us, Levi?"

No comment from the horse, but at least he's turned his head slightly, feigning interest. Theodore gets some carrots from a bucket and hand feeds them to Levi. "What's going to happen to you when I go? Do I just make it a package deal—house, land, barn, chickens, dog, and you? Do I just hand over my grandfather's life work to a stranger and hope for the best? You know I can't take you to Detroit. You'd hate it anyway. It's no place for a royal beast such as yourself."

It begins to rain. "When it rains, you go inside," he observes. "When someone dies, his whole life dies with him. When I get overwhelmed, I back down. I back away. I retreat in the face of adversity. Why is that, Levi? Why am I such a weak man? Nate's not like that. Nathaniel for sure wasn't. What happened to me?"

ZAIMA

SOON AFTER

How can he not notice that things are missing? Parts of the chicken in the fridge, the other half of his sandwich, most of a jar of pickles have disappeared. Garbage bags are lighter, less full. And how can he not pick up her scent, musky like a barn animal, acrid and sour like a vengeful creature? A few days ago, he was screaming in Levi's stall and she walked right past him and out of the barn. If he had turned his head only slightly, he would have seen her.

She has become more brazen in her trespassing and thievery. She takes all of the pricey strawberries and one of his flannel shirts. The shirt especially is valuable as it is rich with the clean, simple smell of him, the outdoors, and a mild soap.

Yesterday he never left the property. He was in the orchard for an hour or two doing what she couldn't say. She's taken to watching him from the slits between the boards in Levi's stall. The horse ignores her; and if Theodore starts walking toward the barn, she has adequate time to disappear into her room.

Today is different. Zaima leaves the barn before the sun has even broken upon the horizon. She's been invited only one place since arriving and that is where she goes, wearing the newly acquired flannel shirt, the one donated pair of jeans that fits, her jacket, boots, and clean socks. Her hair is oily and flat so she wets it down and rakes her fingers through it. It is their Easter, celebrating their back-from-the-dead martyred Jesus. It's the least she can do.

She walks south on LaCore until she hits Front Street and the heart of town. At the end of that street is a path curving slightly north, and signs lead her to the town beach on Lake Michigan Drive. A runny yoke of sun is leaking into the dunes to the east and it is there she parks herself, partially hidden, close enough to see and hear the Christian rituals.

Soon the faithful gather, wearing their special clothes, meaning they're not flannel and jeans like she's wearing. Then, sure enough, Brother Theodore arrives in his pickup, stepping out in a full, hooded robe. If he turns away from the water, he easily could see her, sitting right there in the cold sand. But he doesn't know her, is not looking for her, and goes directly to Father McGurley with arms open to embrace the priest. Theodore stands beside him facing the small gathering, ready to assist if needed.

The priest is dressed all in white with a large gold cross resting on his round belly. He blesses the assemblage with broad, theatrical strokes and then looks to the little choir, their hymnals cocked and ready. But he raises one hand to pause them and whispers into Theodore's ear. The brother looks to his feet at the black box between them and stoops to push a button. For a few seconds, there is only the sound of the gentle waves. Then what pours from the plastic rectangle is not a hymn, but a pure rising and falling of notes that call faithful Muslims to prayer, the Azan. The echoing, undulating voice vibrates through her, rich in meaning and tradition. She knows its content, that God is the greatest and none is worthy of worship except God. The voice seems to amplify, traveling west across the vast lake. Clouds that drift above her appear to tremble from the heady resonance and she feels on the verge of tears.

It seems as out of place as a gritty rap lyric on this essential Christian holy day, but no one appears the least bit perturbed.

Maybe Father McGurley often throws interdenominational curve balls at them. They all wait patiently, some even closing their eyes as if to focus more intently on the voice. The sun has fully risen, just like their savior, and there seems nothing to fear in this surprising addition to Mass.

The priest turns his head ever so slightly and smiles in Zaima's direction. This causes her to duck behind a cluster of low evergreens. It would be too intimate a moment for Theodore's eyes to rise from his folded hands to fall on her; she feels exposed and vulnerable. She knows that is not what the priest intended. It's not even five years since the Muslim thugs flattened the World Trade Center, and not one person on that beach seems to revile their misunderstood religion, her parents' religion. Of course, she knows it's entirely possible that these locals have no idea that this is the call to prayer. But he does, the good priest, and he has found it somewhere to include here, for her.

And that's enough. She leaves them. She's suddenly ravenous and needs to get back to the farmhouse before Theodore. On her way back, at the base of Front Street, she smells lamb, grilled lamb. She is standing in front of a bar that's closed and there is no restaurant nearby. She walks around the corner of the building and finds the aroma stronger there. Looking up, she sees a smoking open barbecue on a small deck outside a second-story entrance. Zaima sits on the steps and remembers her mother's kitchen, spacious and full of light. Outside, her father would be grilling the meats and the fish, but in the kitchen, that was where the magic occurred. Juice was squeezed out of cracked pomegranates; mangos were transformed by turmeric, lemon, and salt; and the ultimate treat, shakrlama, a cookie made of flour and sugar and oil, but rendered irresistible by the addition of pistachios, rose water, lemons, oranges, and cardamom. It had been shameful to be in Iraq, the land of her parents and all this incredible food, having to eat the most tasteless crap imaginable. She ate little there and lost weight.

"Bar's not open today," shouts a woman from an open door above her. Zaima turns and stands. They look each other over, as if trying to figure out how they know each other.

"Sorry," Zaima says. "That lamb . . ." She doesn't finish and walks away.

"Wait! Do I know you?" the woman calls, running down the steps. But she finds no one. Zaima has disappeared for a second time today.

BRIGID

HOURS LATER

She's not trying to win him over with food. She convinces herself that she's really trying to save him from a life as a friar. It's noble and righteous and all that, but for him, it's hiding, and hiding from so many things. She ticks them off in her head: his sexuality, his emotions, his pain, his past. There are many methods to achieve this hiding; alcohol is popular, religion works for some. Personally, she prefers busyness and noise.

Brigid remembers those childhood summers she and Theodore spent together. Nathaniel often would drop him off with Marie for Sunday Mass. Theodore always maneuvered his way to her family's pew, stepping past her mother or father to sit next to her. He would rest his hand between them, lightly touching her dress or her fingers. He seemed so innocent then, toward her and his own desires. Then later in the day, the Birdseys sometimes joined the Dashes for an early dinner, but only in those summer months. They often ate outside at a picnic table under the huge birch in the front yard. Marie was an amazing cook; she invited Cooper and John over as well, but only if they had fulfilled their Sunday obligation at Saint Agnes's. Marie was stern that way.

Brigid still goes to Mass occasionally, but describes herself as an agnostic, someone who says, *I would rather not think about it.*

But why become a friar? He was never even an altar boy. Something must have happened at Wayne State. She could ask him, but won't.

Late last night, she had carefully cut the leg of lamb along the four natural muscle separations and pulled them apart. It sat overnight in a marinade of olive oil, garlic, salt, fresh pepper, and rosemary. She partially grilled it this morning and will finish it off just before she leaves. She will also make tabbouleh fava beans, and the marinated beets.

Brigid bought a new green dress and she's not afraid to wear it. It's cut low in the front and the hem is plenty short. If he doesn't look twice, let him go back to the goddamned seminary. He's that far out of touch.

ZAIMA

AND HOURS AFTER THAT

How odd, she thinks. People are arriving at the farmhouse on a spring afternoon when inside there are only two chairs to sit on, only a kitchen table, no sofa, no armchairs, bare walls, naked floors. *Is this because it's Easter?* Will they sit on the floor and eat with their hands as Jesus might have?

Zaima isn't inside the barn, but observes these further rituals while tucked into the first trees of the orchard. No one thinks to look and her lean torso blends well with the craggy trunks. It's a mixed lot, these guests, and Theodore greets them still in his brown robe and with his saccharine smile. *What will he serve these people?* She knows the meager contents of his fridge and cupboards.

Then the answer arrives in a beat-up Ford van. It's the woman from the pub in town and she is dressed in a sexy green dress with no coat. She must bend and dip to remove her cargo and this is not easily done without exposing more than is already. But Theodore is quickly on the scene and he stares at the red-haired woman with eyes greener and more dazzling than the dress, evident even from the distance Zaima keeps. Theodore takes her hand and raises it above her head, then twirls her around once. Zaima is shocked at this playful, flirty, old school showmanship. But then he stiffens and looks apologetic and awkward. The woman simply smiles.

Together, they unload the van. There are folding tables and chairs, trays of food (no doubt that lamb is on one of them), linens, and plates. There are even fresh daffodils, bright and hopeful in the mostly barren landscape. Two old men show up in shirts and ties and old-man jackets. One of them carries two bottles of red wine and the other a covered pie plate. Suddenly the one with the pie looks up into the orchard, directly at her. A sly grin and then he turns away.

JOHN QUIMBY

MAY

He is a happy man. It is seventy-two degrees and the sky is vast and clear. He knows there is no better place to be than right here for those few magical days when the sweet cherries bloom. No matter the severity of the winter past, this will happen at pretty much the same time in May. He and Cooper don't grow these trees so he's been keeping an eye on Nathaniel's small orchard of them. Theodore doesn't seem to mind the intrusion and he's usually with Cooper anyway. The trees are in full bloom now, a heavenly display of white, fluffy blossoms. From a distance they seem tinged with pink, but he knows that's just the red twigs around the blooms that fool the eye.

A few days after these have finished, the tart cherries will explode with their own flowering. And then comes the best time of all, when the apple trees provoke delirium with their masses of light pink blossoms spread all over the Leelanau Peninsula. Cars will be pulling to the roadside so passengers can take it all in. Bicyclists will leave the rutted spring road and take long, slow sips from their fancy water bottles before continuing on. John Quimby has seen sun-saturated vineyards in the south of France and swaying fields of Nebraska corn, but nothing comes close to the sensual splendor of Empire in the middle of May.

If the intoxicating beauty surrounding him wasn't enough, he now clutches Marie's precious recipe box in his hands as he crosses through Nathaniel's orchards back to Voice Road. It was his for the asking. Theodore only requested copies of a few of his favorite recipes and invitations to Marie-inspired dinners before he returns to Detroit—whenever that might be. It has been weeks since Theodore mentioned his previous commitment and no one brings it up.

What John also doesn't know is that Zaima is following him from a safe distance. She is watching his meanderings and musings as he stops often to touch this delicate bloom or that cheery dandelion. He seems in a trance. Now he stops completely and sits on the damp ground in the middle of a row of trees. He opens his small wooden box as if he were a child with a stolen treasure. Out come small yellowed cards, and one by one, he reads them and runs his fingertips over them reverently. Eventually he uses his arms to push himself carefully upright on his two sticklike legs. It saddens her to watch him; he is so old.

Then on he marches down the row, now at a faster clip. He seems eager to get home and by the time he hits the road, his long legs are like scissors opening and closing as he travels stiffly onward. Once she's on the road as well, there's little cover so she hangs back a bit, praying he won't turn around.

John makes a sharp right and disappears down a driveway or side road. When she reaches the same spot, she sees the appealing house he likely shares with the other man, the barn beyond, and then their orchards climbing the hill.

"Would you like to come in or would you prefer to simply stalk me all day?" John says from behind.

She swings around and faces him. "You startled me." He's tall but only has a few inches on her. "But cleverly done. I'll give you that," she says.

"Wasn't difficult. I'm not in the habit of startling people on my own property. My apologies."

She just stands there examining him with feet planted, hands shoved in her pockets.

He walks past her. "I'm guessing you want something from me. Wanna come in and tell me? Or you're free to stand out here. Stay long enough though and I'll expect you to work. Always a lot to do."

When he gets to the door, he turns around to find her pretty much in the same spot. He smiles. "You hungry?"

"Yes."

"Thought as much. Saw you skulking around at Teddy's," John says. "Bet you got a story. Come on in and I'll get you something to eat."

He sits her down at the kitchen table and places the recipe box in front of her. "You know what that is?" he asks.

She pulls it toward her and shakes her head.

"That's history. A family's history. Friends too. What was lovingly prepared and appreciatively eaten over generations."

"I understand those traditions," Zaima says. "We share them."

"Then maybe you'll cook a bit of your history for me someday. Something you love."

"I don't think I could find the ingredients I need," she says.

"Well not in goddamned Empire, that's for sure. But this is not the sticks. In Traverse City, you should see the airplane hangars full of all kinds of food. We can find what you need."

"We? Like we're friends?" she asks rudely.

"Like we could become friends. That's if you start acting more human and less like a wild animal."

And that's more than enough conversation for a while. John makes her a ham sandwich on white bread with Miracle Whip and iceberg lettuce. Pours her a glass of milk.

"Don't fret. I won't give you Jell-O for dessert," he says as he places the food in front of her. He makes the same for himself and is pleased to see that she doesn't start eating until he sits down with her.

"The ham is the best around, butchered and cured right out-side of town," he says. "I baked it yesterday. You may detect hints of Dijon mustard, apple cider vinegar, and maple syrup. Maybe you don't eat ham, but there it is. The white bread is fresh this morning from the best bakery on the peninsula, right here on Front Street. Miracle Whip is what we've always used and prefer. Iceberg lettuce? Yes, that's crap, basically water, but it's damn good on a sandwich. Oh, and the milk, whole, local, unpasteurized. Just so you appreci-ate what you're consuming."

They eat in silence. She's probably not been eating regularly, he assumes. Her tall frame looks sturdy. She's lean, yes, but muscular. He's tempted to touch her black, glossy hair, cut short but curl-ing around her ears. *Has she bathed lately?* Her skin is like melting caramel and her face is dominated by her huge dark eyes, almond shaped and heavy lidded. She has a broad but well-proportioned nose that dips ever so gracefully at the tip, and below that, full and sensuous lips that she is now patting with her paper napkin. She rises and places her plate and glass in the sink. Sits back down.

"I'm an old man, but not so old . . . and not so gay either . . . that I can't appreciate what a beautiful young woman you are. What I want to know is why are you so angry? It rolls off you like an approaching storm. So?"

She says nothing. Lowers her head and stares at the checkered tablecloth.

"All right," John says calmly. "We'll leave it for another time."

"Iraq," she says, her eyes engaging his.

He screws up his mouth and lowers his dense, white eyebrows. "You're Iraqi?"

"The war."

"You're a vet?"

"Yes," she answers. "And Iraqi-American. My tour ended in Tikrit in January. I returned home to Dearborn."

He half-expected her to add *Sir* at the end of the last sentence. *Why hadn't he picked up on her military service?*

"How rude I am," John says. "I haven't even asked your name. It is . . . ?"

"Zaima. Zaima al-Aziz."

"Well, Zaima, I'm a vet too. Korea was a different type of war, but more conventional for sure. It was also unpopular. No homecoming parade for me. Or for you, I'm sure. I was a medic with the 119th Detachment in Inchon. That's where I met Cooper. I didn't even know I was homosexual . . . until I met him. Did you know that? That we're gay folk?"

"I didn't know it or not know it. Makes no difference to me. There was a lesbian in my barracks, but she never bothered me."

"It's certainly not a secret," he says. "I don't care what people think about me, about us."

"We have that in common," she says.

"When I came home I was in love with a man and married to a woman, a good, loving woman. And I had a young daughter. So as you can see, I came back changed . . . by the bloody mess of the war, all the lost limbs, lives we couldn't save, but also changed inside. I was not the man I thought I was. I didn't know how I was gonna fool anybody that I was the same."

"What did you do?" Zaima asks, neatly folding her cloth napkin.

"I stayed in Marquette. I sold trucks. I couldn't leave my family. I wrote to Cooper. Told him everything I was feeling. Tried to see him at least once a year. That went on for ten years."

"That's a long time to be living two lives," says Zaima.

"There are a lot of things in our lives that we don't choose. The things we do choose, we have to stand behind. Which brings me to Iraq. Tell me about it."

"Be more specific."

John realizes that having a conversation with this young woman is like extracting a long, rusty nail with the wrong tool. Progress is slow. "Start with why you enlisted."

"I was in high school on 9/11. We watched it on television during biology. Then it was on in every class, all morning. They wouldn't turn it off. All the scenes, the planes, the collapsing towers, they kept playing it over and over. It's like you needed to see it fifty times before it was real. A lot of us were from the Middle East, from Lebanon, from Iraq. Some Muslims, some Christians. Once the photos of the hijackers were on the front page of every newspaper, their Arab names, their Arab faces, we knew. There would be a war on us all. Subtly or overtly, we would all pay for those heinous acts."

John keeps quiet. The floodgates were opening all on their own.

"After high school everyone I knew wanted to get out of Dearborn. I was jumping out of my skin. I didn't want more school. The army was the quickest way out of town. And I hated Saddam. They had already found him in Tikrit in a hole, a coward. I wanted to go to Iraq. I was only nineteen, but they were happy to have me, even when I told them all the Arabic I knew had to do with food. My parents were against it, especially my mom. All the more reason to go. I was so naive."

"It wasn't how you thought it would be?" he asks.

"No. I thought we would be peacekeepers. I thought we were going to help rebuild the country, the schools, the hospitals. I wanted to help these people who had been so oppressed under Saddam."

"And?"

"We weren't liberators in their eyes," she says. "We were occupiers. We made their lives worse. Sometimes a gunner's reaction to a single sniper was to mow down everyone in sight. Thousands of rounds in a minute. Who were the insurgents and who were innocent civilians? It was impossible to tell."

"And you looked just like them."

Zaima runs her hands through her hair, over and over. "When they saw my face, even only my eyes . . . they saw a traitor. Working for what was now the enemy to many of them." She lays her hands flat on the table, regains her composure. "And a lot of the soldiers I served with agreed with them. They questioned my loyalty, called me what they called them, haji, rag-head, sand nigger. I didn't care. My shell just kept getting thicker and thicker. I had to shoot at Iraqis. We all did. We just hoped we got the right target."

"You killed . . ."

"That question seems to fascinate people back home," she interrupts angrily. "I'm a soldier. It's what we are trained to do."

John scrapes his chair closer to the table and stretches his arms toward her, but does not touch her. He just leaves his large, gnarly fingers flat against the table, palms up. Submissive, nonthreatening.

"You *were* a soldier. War breaks you in pieces. It's necessary. You must compartmentalize your feelings, your duties, your morality. Otherwise you'd go insane. In basic, did they instruct you in how to fight or how to feel? Feeling is a luxury left for later. But I'll tell you, Zaima, things I saw, things I did, things I didn't do in Korea still haunt me. You have to leave behind what you did or saw in Iraq, everything that happened to you . . ."

She interrupts. "I can't. I'm pregnant."

———— • ————

"Nathaniel was obsessive-compulsive, as you can see by the layout of his trees," John explains to Zaima as they walk through the orchards. "Each row in each section is a specific variety and that will not change unless broken by a cross road. These here, they're Northern Spy. He's got quite a few rows of them. Big favorite of his, you know, being a traditional variety. No Jonagolds for him. A real purist."

They walk slowly on. The flower buds are plump and he tells her they will burst soon into a complex blending of pale pink, rosy pink, and creamy white blossoms. Zaima touches one bud, rolling it between a thumb and finger. "What are these trees?"

"Them's Red Rome. Good pie apple. And up there all along that hillside, all Golden Delicious. Now that can be a mushy apple, but not Nathaniel's. They are always crisp and sugar sweet.

"Honey Crisp is the hot apple now. Coop and I planted a bunch of them in the early nineties. Big seller, but Nathaniel would have nothing to do with them. Too trendy. You know, being this close to the lake lets us grow pretty much what we want."

They're climbing uphill now so Zaima slows her pace. She can see he's getting winded, but still he doesn't stop talking for more than a minute or two at a time.

"What does the lake have to do with how things grow?" she asks, feigning interest.

"Being right here east of the great Lake Michigan has a warming effect. It helps prevent extreme temperatures in spring and autumn. You get a longer growing season. Makes for a crisper apple."

There's a bench ahead, placed randomly in the middle of a row. They sit side by side, facing west and the midafternoon sun.

"Two things," John announces. "First this question. You keepin' this baby?"

"I don't know. But maybe not making a decision is making a decision."

"You must have thought about this," John says impatiently. "You're living I don't know where or what you're doing for food. You do have options, although I don't know how far along you are. But listen to me, you need to pray on this one. Pray to God, yours, mine, anybody's, that you make the right decision. I urge you to choose life. Otherwise, I think, the only choice left is regret."

She has no answer for him, just stares straight ahead.

"Okay. I need to ask another question then. Is the father of this baby in the picture?"

"No. Definitely not."

"All right. That's fine. No more on that. I would like to share with you something about your service in Iraq, like I was saying, what you saw, what you did. You know how they say the only way to get over somebody is to fall in love with somebody else? I need you to be very present here for a minute. Look around you. You see how beautiful this spot is, this intimate piece of the orchard? Feel that sun all over your body? Smell the moist soil. Feel the water that's moving all around you, seeping into the soil, churning in the lake that is so close. Iraq was real but this is too. Take one horrific moment from Tikrit and replace it with this one here with me. You don't have to forget what happened there. You have to integrate it into what will become the rest of your life."

"If only it were that easy," she says.

"If it were easy, I wouldn't still be doing it. And it isn't just Korea. There's a whole mountain of remorse I have to chip away at for leaving my wife and girl. My wife remarried. Still hates me, but she's a happier woman."

"No regrets?" Zaima asks.

"Regret is like all forms of self-imposed misery. It hurts you but helps no one."

They walk back to Nathaniel's farmhouse in a comfortable silence.

"I'm curious why you've come here and why you were at Teddy's place," John says before leaving her. "But you're here and it's kinda in my nature to help. There's a clinic near the hospital in Traverse. For women in your condition."

"Pregnant is the word," she says.

"Yeah, I guess it's not a condition, like an ailment. I could make an appointment. Take you there next week. Get you checked out. You must have questions."

Silence.

"Are you makin' out all right? I could ask Teddy about you, but I'm betting you'd prefer I didn't. You can stay with us for a while, if you need a place."

"I'm fine."

"You might want to just talk to Teddy sometime," John says, walking away. "He's nothing like his brother."

"Why would you think I know his brother?" she asks.

"Didn't say you did."

ZAIMA

THAT EVENING

my mother, the shape of an eggplant
long flowing hair, small breasts, wide hips
and short thick legs
like an afterthought
but with purpose
she needed them to walk places
for us

most of our backyard
was for growing vegetables and herbs
Little Mecca, my father called it
I felt shame growing up
as if we were too poor
to buy our food

she bought apricots
placed them on the rooftop to dry
and yes there was
even a compost pile
in Dearborn

that no one else had
she said to fix the soil
make it rich
and she planted and watered
weeded and gathered
like a peasant

dragged me out there
to watch
to learn
to labor
without shame
if you eat, she said
you must help
but my father did not help,
only grilled in a leisurely way
preferred washing the dirt from his car
than putting his hands in it
my sister did nothing but comb her hair
eat for free and smirk her superiority
looking all American

no fair I cried
there is no fair, my mother said
where does this idea come from?
such silliness
you are stronger

and I was
I ate her magical foods
and got stronger yet
until I was like a boy
muscular

flat-chested
taller than my father

ran track
then ran away
to the army, to Iraq
and have run away again
to live in a dirty barn
sneaking around
stealing food
like a peasant

my mother is beautiful
like almond brik
hard crust outside
soft and sweet inside

it's not our fault that
we come from different planets
we cry for different reasons
we love differently

how I long for her
if only she could come for me
and just be
not judging
not ashamed
not asking ten million questions
not crying
please not that

mother
just hold me

wrap me in your fragrance
tell me how it will be
all of it
how it feels
the moment life emerges

and how it will feel
the moment she leaves
like I left you

THEODORE

A FEW DAYS LATER

He sits. Drinks his coffee alone at the ice cream shop. Thinks about the many ways to exist in this world with only a thin sheet of skin to protect us from all that is out there. He feels small and worries about God's elusive presence. He tries to pray but it feels like just words in his mouth. Time is passing and he has not returned to the seminary. No one has called to press him on this, not for many weeks. The earth is warming and there's new color in the landscape, but he's as lost and aimless as he was the day he arrived.

He occupies himself with now familiar tasks, caring for all the distracted animals, even Mac, who still looks for Nathaniel. He's done a little painting in the farmhouse, all a boring white as his mother had advised him. He turned over the beds in the vegetable garden and rebuilt three of the raised beds. He finds himself avoiding Brigid. Seeing her more might make his leaving more difficult, more drawn out. Only a few times has he dared to venture into her bar, yearning for her company and the deadening power of alcohol. *Why can't he leave?*

He watches a teenage boy walk past his window on the other side of the highway. His heavy backpack forces him to lean forward to offset it, his shaggy head down. He's thin and awkward with a funny gait. *Will there be any kindness offered in his world today?* Will there instead be ridicule or will they respect his insularity? The boy probably could have taken the bus to school. Bet he hates the bus, just as Theodore did. You're trapped there, vulnerable to attack.

He sips his cold coffee. He's already been here for close to an hour. Maybe he should offer the kid a lift. He'd likely get a kick out of riding in Celeste. But Theodore stays put, doesn't want to be the stranger the boy wisely says "no thanks" to.

Then he turns his attention to a middle-aged woman walking on the shoulder of the road. She's obese, red-faced, and puffing. *Is there any love out there for her?* She has strawberry-blonde hair and a pretty face. Her huge breasts under a flowery blouse project forward like the twin hulls of a catamaran, slicing boldly through the thin spring air. Theodore is sure there are many men who would enjoy that much woman. Hopefully there's one out there to love her as well.

Another woman who is a bit younger opens the door of the establishment, but only pokes her head in. Her eyes scan the room, assessing its potential for satisfying her needs. It's a cozy and comforting place, with lots of knotty pine and red-checked curtains. There are so many open windows this mild morning, it's almost as nice as being outside. She might also just be looking for someone.

The woman's gaze falls briefly on Theodore and she offers a small smile. She enters fully then and walks purposefully to the empty counter. The menu is painted on the pale blue wall in white lettering and probably never changes much. From behind, with her long black hair pulled severely back and her thin frame wrapped in a tight black tank top and shorts, she resembles a barren tree against a winter sky.

She reminds Theodore of his mother, not so much in appearance as demeanor. Sheer confidence and authority. If no one appears to wait on her, he's quite sure she'll lay a hard knock on the countertop or call out rudely. Thin people are more likely to be impatient, he generalizes. That fat woman probably knows how to wait, hang in the background. Prefers it there.

Since he's feeling shallow and not that Christlike, he predicts the twig's order—black coffee and a low-fat scone.

"Hello! I'd like to place an order!" As expected.

An old guy ambles out like a sea creature on land.

"Hi, Smith. Eggs over easy and bacon, please. No toast. Black coffee."

Oh, that diet, observes Theodore. *And can his first name be Smith?*

She turns to face the young man who has been appraising and judging her since she stuck her head in the door. "Theodore, is that you? How good to see you and all grown up so nicely. I am sorry to hear about your grandfather."

She knows him? "Thank you," he manages, preparing to stand.

"Oh, sit, Theodore. You have no clue who I am, do you? I'm surprised."

She walks over and takes the chair opposite his. "Physiology?"

High school! That year here. "I do now. I was sure a lost cause in your classroom," he says.

"You were so adorable. My little shadow, always staying after class to talk a bit."

He has absolutely no recollection of that. "I did?"

"Oh, I wasn't the only object of your affection . . . or should I just say attention. But in terms of science, you had no interest in it, not even reproduction." Another knowing smile here. "The aptitude, I think, yes. I'd guess school for you was just something to be endured. Are you in college now?"

Theodore feels as if he's been transported to someone else's past. "No. I was, but you're right, school's not for me."

"Oh, that's fine," she says, smiling at this Smith fellow as he places her meal before her. "So what are you up to then? Working?"

He can't remember her name. He can't give her satisfactory answers to her questions. It's science class all over again.

"I'm not sure of my plans."

She breaks up her overcooked bacon with her fork. "Will you be staying around for a while?" she asks, and then looking him straight in the eye, adds, "What is it, Theodore? You're suddenly as pale as a ghost."

He wipes an inexplicable amount of perspiration from his face with a paper napkin. Fidgets and looks out the window.

She lowers her fork next to her uneaten breakfast and places her hand on his. Theodore looks at this birdlike appendage and thinks of a hawk's claw encasing a robin's egg. It's a violation of personal space at the very least.

"I think I will stay here for a bit," he announces weakly, slipping his hand away and then around his empty coffee mug. "I just decided."

She waves off the awkward moment and digs into her food. "Well, good then," she says, and then coming up for air adds, "I was born in Cedar and came back after college. It's a terrific place to live up here. Good place to raise kids. Winter's a bitch, but you get through it."

"I don't know about raising any kids," he says, "but being up here as a boy was the happiest time of my life. My grandfather has given me his land, everything."

"Your grandfather would remind you that the land doesn't belong to you, Theodore Dash," she says. "You belong to the land. It will invade your soul, change you . . . if you allow it to."

There's a little pause here and she returns to her cold food. Then Theodore takes her hand. "Your name is Mrs. Aylsworth. I remember."

Now she is uncomfortable. "Call me Grace."

"Thank you, Grace."

"You're welcome, although I don't know what I've done to deserve your gratitude."

"I've been rolling a boulder up a hill over and over, and of course, it keeps rolling back down. I've just decided to leave it at the bottom of the hill."

"Well, you go ahead and get to the top of that hill. Fuck the boulder," Grace says. "You've been given a great gift by a wonderful, wise man. Enjoy it."

"You're brilliant, Mrs. Aylsworth, I mean really brilliant," Theodore says, standing to leave. "Breakfast is on me."

———— • ————

A newly energized version of Theodore Dash rips into the driveway off LaCore Road. As he throws one long leg from the truck he sees Mac bounce rambunctiously out of the small barn door and run toward him. The weedy grass seems perkier and greener, and the sky is a brilliant blue with perfect, spun-cotton clouds rimming the horizon. Paradise has been here right in front of his doubting eyes.

He squats to greet his happy mate, no longer lethargic and detached. Mac knocks into him hard and the two roughhouse a bit. The soil has a musty sweetness and there are everywhere bulging buds and fledgling leaves.

But something is not quite right. He sees that a screen door is flat against the house on this windless morning. Levi is out in the paddock, prancing about happily, which is new and wonderful, but he did not let him out. There are muddy boots by the barn door and they are not his.

Well, he thinks, *this is not Detroit.* Why would anyone rob a nearly empty house? Nothing in the barn seems worth the effort. But still, things are not as he left them. *What would his grandfather do?* He knows there is a rifle in a simple cloth sack in the back corner of the front hall closet. His grandfather was a hunter, never shooting anything he wasn't prepared to eat, but he surely would defend family and property. There are bound to be addicts out here as well as in the cities; they're everywhere and will steal gold from a mother's tooth to feed their habit. He's known enough of them.

"Okay, Mac, stick with me," he tells his companion. "Let's check this out." Theodore moves stealthily through the unlocked front door to the closet. He unveils the rifle; it is sleek and masculine. The stock is a smooth, worn wood and he clasps his hand around the barrel. He has no idea if it's loaded but the magazine is in place. He doesn't know how to release it, but since the thing is more prop than weapon, he decides to draw the rifle up against his shoulder and point it menacingly in front of him as he scans the house. He kicks the kitchen door open but is greeted with a mysterious dirty plate and fork on the counter and nothing else. He continues through the entire house and finds no one.

Mac has been following him, sometimes letting loose an unconvincing bark. But now he turns and heads for the back door, happily capering toward the barn.

"Of course! Good boy," Theodore says, following him. He pushes open the huge sliding door with the left side of his body. Light splashes into the open space. There's the pockmarked workbench and the tools hanging on the pegboard above it. There's Levi's empty stall, mucked out and tidy. In the rear is the magnificent tractor he will one day ride. Mac heads to the barn's far right corner and Theodore follows with the rifle leading. He can't remember ever being in this back room before. He could turn around right now and call the sheriff. Or Cooper. But that seems silly and premature.

He pushes the door open slowly with the weapon. The dog enters first. The glare of the midmorning light from a window makes the contents of the room hard to decipher, but soon he sees lying beneath the windows on a long narrow ledge, the body of a woman, sleeping on her side, facing him. She's so still, he's not sure she's even breathing. Mac lifts one paw to the edge of her makeshift bed, proudly panting over what he's found. She's wearing only a white T-shirt and jeans, her long feet bare. He looks quickly around the room and sees familiar dishes, cans of food, books, and a rug he remembers throwing out. He touches her cheek with the tip of his rifle. It's only when Mac barks that she opens her eyes.

"Who are you?" he demands to know. "Did you steal my chicken?" He immediately wishes he hadn't said that, but it was the first thing he saw go missing. Tried to tell himself it was just a stray animal which, of course, it couldn't have been.

The woman smiles. "Did they teach you how to handle a Winchester at seminary?"

"Who are you?" Theodore shouts, looking down the barrel.

"Please get that thing out of my face," she says calmly, holding her position. He does not; so in one smooth arc of her forearm, she pushes the rifle away. Then upright with feet planted, she easily takes charge of the weapon and releases the magazine.

"You might want to load a round or two if you're planning on using it," she says. Returning the rifle to him, she adds, "Needs cleaning."

She's only a couple inches shy of his height as they stand nearly eye to eye. The woman looks foreign, exotic, with hair as blue black as a grackle's. They examine each other for a full minute, then she leans toward him and taps her index finger on his chest.

"I'm not your foe," she says and stoops down. Mac comes immediately to her. "He'd let you know if I was."

Theodore feels suddenly drained and sits on her bed. He strokes the warm walnut of the rifle's stock as if it were a cat in his lap. "How did you know I'm in the seminary? Did we meet at Wayne State? I think I'd remember you. Have we met?"

"Not directly," she says.

"All right. You don't know me. You're not my enemy. My dog seems to like you." He's growing impatient, his voice rises in what he hopes is a commanding way. "But why are you here? How long have you been stowed away in this filthy barn?"

She sits in the room's only chair and pulls on her dirty socks. He's starting to feel like he's intruding on *her* space.

"I don't expect you to let me stay here for free," she finally says. "I'm happy to work. I think I could get that tractor going."

"Stay here? Don't you have a home? Something better than this?"

"You need help here," she says, taking the rifle back. "I'll clean this for you and show you how to use it if you like. I'd be happy to paint. You really should repair the walls first and maybe paint the rooms something other than that blinding white. I can help in the garden too. My mother taught me a few things about growing vegetables."

"Anything else?" he asks sarcastically.

"Yes. Your horse needs therapy or at least a good ride. That you'll have to do."

"I'm selling this place," he counters.

"No, you're not. If there was somewhere else you wanted to be, you'd already be there."

Theodore stares at this alien being with the oversized eyes and ego. Yet another woman explaining him to himself.

"Leaving doesn't take three months," she adds.

"You don't know me or what I will or will not do," he says, incensed. "Stay if you want. Just don't get in my way." Then he stands and stomps out. Mac seems unsure of his loyalties, but decides to trot out a minute or two after him.

COOPER BOYD

For Cooper, Theodore becomes the mechanism for handling the cutting grief he feels over the loss of his best friend. Nathaniel's absence is a constant presence. Seeing Theodore unconsciously mimic his grandfather's gestures in tackling the work of an orchardist fills some of the void. The hardest part will be teaching the boy to care like Nathaniel did, to take on the work with the same love and diligence.

Most every morning they walk through the orchards with Theodore taking notes as to what apple varieties are where, what insects and diseases threaten their health, and what to do about them. Cooper tells him what Marie had planted in the vegetable beds and how she had amended the soil. He explains how to care for the strawberry field. He goes on and on about the nature of Levi's moods and the attention he requires. Cooper tells him how to take care of the chickens, too, although he feels they are more work than they're worth. The two also discuss cooking and composting, and how to read the weather without John's looking it up online. In the course of these walks, they find themselves becoming friends, despite—and maybe because of—all the obvious differences.

At one point, Cooper even dared to ask Theodore if he was still planning on selling the place. All he answered was that he was putting a plan together. To accomplish exactly what wasn't divulged. Cooper took that as progress and asked nothing further. Instead he took Theodore to his favorite secondhand store in Traverse City where they purchased a couple of comfortable chairs for the nearly empty living room, and replacements for the towels and other necessities that Theodore had so recently discarded.

Besides the fact that he's still here, Cooper finds many favorable changes in this person who had arrived some three months earlier as a sullen, directionless young man. What happened at Wayne State he does not know, but certainly the whole friar thing baffles him. Living with a whole houseful of men is not enticing, even for him, and he does not think Theodore is either overly religious or homosexual. His greatest enthusiasm now seems to be for the tiniest scraps of information on producing healthy fruit.

Today Cooper is preparing bucket traps as Theodore pulls up and immediately starts firing questions.

"What's in the bucket?"

"Yeast, molasses, water."

"How much of each one?"

"One part yeast, two parts molasses, six parts water."

Theodore grabs his small spiral notebook and pen from his shirt pocket and notes the recipe. "What's it for?"

"I'm trapping codling moths. The hibernating worms pupate in late winter. Little buggers emerge as moths right after budbreak."

"Seems like a lot of work, putting out all these buckets."

"Well, if you don't, you could have a ruined harvest."

"Can't you just spray them?" Theodore asks.

"I will if this doesn't get rid of most of 'em."

"With what?"

"Phosmet."

"With an *f* or *ph*? Is that organic?" Theodore wants to know.

"*Ph,* and shit no, it's not organic. It's less damaging to the orchard than those organic sprays. Kills the worst of the pests, but it's easier on the beneficials."

"My grandfather do the same?"

"Not early on. Took a traditional approach. Spray, spray, spray. I turned him around . . . slowly. Teddy, write this down, the less you spray, the less you have to spray."

Then Cooper tells him about spraying dormant oil right after winter pruning in order to control overwintering mites, scale, and the like. As they work together placing the buckets in the orchard, Theodore asks about the soil, why certain varieties are placed on certain slopes. He asks why the trees don't grow taller than ten feet.

"Nearly all my trees and Nathaniel's, well, let's call them your trees, are dwarf above the ground. The rootstock is that of a standard tree. Anchors it into the ground and it needs less water. But the dwarf part makes it easier to prune, spray, and harvest."

"Really cool, Uncle Cooper. How did you learn all this?"

"Son, it's all I do. Don't ask me to explain electrical storms or what we're doing over in Iraq. I know apples. I know what works."

By early afternoon, Cooper calls it quits for the day, and Theodore is ready to apply what he's learned to his trees. But before he goes, there's one more thing to talk about.

"I found a woman living in my barn. Kind of a stray," he says.

"Yeah, I heard about her," Cooper says. "John's met her. Interesting woman."

"She's not dangerous or anything?" Theodore asks.

"No, I don't think so. More damaged than dangerous. Just let her be. She'll probably wander off on her own."

THEODORE

He lies on his back and stares at the sky, which is a surreal blue, intense and unnatural. The apple blossoms are so thick and heavy on the trees that most of the supporting branches are invisible. His grandfather knew him better than he knew himself, knew that he would love the beauty of the orchard in bloom. He is grateful, but the abundance of it all is hard to take. It's like being too hungry, and then overeating. It hurts. It hurts to feel this much.

He rolls over onto his stomach and places the side of his face against the new clover and the dandelion flowers, mammoth from this perspective. The smell of the earth, of the air, the richness and complexity, is somehow foreign to him, and creates a yearning, a desire he cannot name.

He says a prayer. He thanks God for it all, all this that has been waiting here for him, season after season. He asks God what he should do about the aggressive woman who has taken up residence here without explanation. What is his obligation to her? How can he not be angry that she has fouled the simplicity of his new life? *Has she become his responsibility? Will she be another reason he can't leave?*

Theodore stands and shakes off the debris on his clothing and in his hair. Cooper has given him a list. There's much that needs doing.

ZAIMA

I am intoxicated with the beauty
of the carpet of petals beneath the fruit trees
it's as if fragments of heaven
have floated down to earth

how can this be the same planet?
how can the sunsets be so similar?
one over desert and desperation
the other over the bodies of small children
playing in shallow lake water
both sunsets spilling rose orange
even magenta
into my starving eyes

so this is spring
what it looks and feels like
what it smells and sounds like
when not scented with car and truck exhalations
or the hum of the camp's generators
just the hush of new growth

seeds cracking open
everywhere life breaking from the soil
like the dead rising
from winter's grave

I like the sound of my boots
sharp and sure on LaCore Road
how the sound is different
going and coming
I like the way my arms swing
in this unfamiliar exaggerated way
like I am dancing my way somewhere

I can see myself here
as an old woman
again and again
experiencing spring
as if for the first time

I feel change in me
as if I were a dandelion
sprouting over a grave site
as if the face of God
has turned back to me
not with forgiveness in His eyes
but a willingness to forget

BRIGID

There's been a new guy coming by Brigid's bar. He's flirtatious, a little grungy, and sometimes mildly amusing. He hails from Saugatuck, an artsy town south of Holland. Says he's a writer, working on his first novel, which just about anybody could say. He has rented an apartment above the antique store two blocks from the bar, just for the summer, he says, "unless he has a reason to stay."

He goes by the pretentious name of Hemingway, whom he claims to emulate. Brigid asked him what his novel was about.

"Life," he said. "As opposed to every other work of fiction?" she had asked.

He brings her little gifts, some sweet, some useless. It could be a book of poetry (she does not like poetry at all), precious but common shells from the beach, and once an old, musty map of the Leelanau Peninsula. That she liked and tacked to the wall. A few weeks ago, when it was a cool late-April evening, Brigid was adding wood to the fire. Hemingway knelt beside her and handed her an oversized hunk of wood she didn't need. Obliging his attempt to help, she shoved it in the stove. He then wrapped his arm around her waist, intending to lift her to her feet, as if she were unable to do that on her own. When both were standing and his other arm began to encircle her, both Cooper Boyd and another farmer slammed down their beer glasses and stood up, ready to pounce on the future author. Brigid gently pushed him away, saying loudly, "If I want to be in your novel, I'll let you know."

That, however, did not deter his efforts and he is in the bar almost every night. He hasn't dared to touch her again, but his eyes are usually on her. He likes to say meaningless, corny things like, "If I were to fall for a girl, it would be a girl like you." *What the hell does that mean?* Once it was, "If I should fall into those green eyes of yours, I'd surely drown from love." She hopes for his sake that his writing is better than those lines of crap.

She knows people around here are making as much fun of him as he likely is of them. He may not have anticipated that a lot of folks here have read Hemingway. She's heard her patrons refer to him as the Young Man and the Sea, Kilimanjaro, and simply Ernest. And these people who he probably considers *hicks* may well know that the real Hemingway wrote a short story called "Up in Michigan," a salacious little tale which takes place in nearby Charlevoix. There is a large bookcase near the woodstove packed with some mighty fine examples of the written word, including a 1972 edition of Hemingway's short stories. In the past, long winter nights have featured Nathaniel or Cooper reading from that wheat-colored volume to a small group comfortably seated around the stove. The stories are short and easy to digest without a great deal of thought or conversation. Nathaniel also favored and read from Thurber, Flannery O'Connor, and Kipling, while Cooper was more of an Updike or Vonnegut kind of guy. It didn't matter the author, people just seemed to like being read to, especially in front of a warm fire with a cold beer in hand. Nathaniel's rich, deep voice was like a heavy dessert and some might doze through a few pages.

Nobody's been reading since Nathaniel passed. Maybe next winter.

Now well into spring the would-be reincarnation of Heming-way sits at the end of the bar farthest from the front door. He's scribbling in his weathered leather notebook, which was probably worn when he bought it. Perhaps inspiration has just struck or there is a keen observation to capture or, more likely, he is secretly play-ing sudoku. He runs his fingers through his tousled, dirty blond hair and over his three-day stubble, cultivating the look of the obsessed artist with no time for proper hygiene.

But he seems not to be a poor artist. Hemingway leaves embar-rassingly large tips or buys drinks for groups of strangers. Maybe, Brigid surmises, this is penitence for his pompous behavior, being consistently self-referential with zero listening skills. She imagines his ego is like a rotten walnut, hard-shelled with little inside. But no matter, she can always busy herself away from him, keeping their conversations short. Any good barkeep would know how to do that.

Who hasn't been around much at all is Theodore Dash. He's still up here; she knows that from Cooper. He had seemed a nervous, awkward stranger at Easter. Maybe the dress had been too much for him, because after his warm welcome, she somehow became the plague and he kept his distance. He dropped by a couple weeks after that, but only to unload more cash, which this time she refused. He had another larger envelope that he said he found under Nathaniel's bed along with some *Playboy* magazines. This discovery seemed to dismay him, but not her. Probably most men of Nathaniel's genera-tion appreciated that sort of light porn. She wished Theodore would spend a little time with one of those magazines. She didn't say that, of course, but she felt it might bring him into the real world just a few tiny steps.

Theodore wanted her to keep the envelope, which he said con-tained personal letters. He had read only one, an undated love letter to Nathaniel from Marie. She was free to read them or burn them; he didn't care which. He had no desire to do either and apologized for laying it on her.

Brigid did not want this envelope or the responsibility for its future. Maybe Isabelle might want them, but she doubted that. The whole thing should be burned. It was Nathaniel's private correspondence and it should stay private. But she couldn't bring herself to destroy it, so she punted. It came to live safely in her bedroom closet on a high shelf next to a shoebox of mementos she had found in her mother's dresser after she died.

Now on this May evening, it's raining hard and Theodore joins Hemingway as her only patrons, both perhaps escaping the loneliness and nostalgia that unceasing rain can weigh upon the soul. They sit at opposite ends of the bar. She coaxes Theodore into a glass of an expensive Bordeaux she's opened to celebrate the fact that the Nathaniel Dash Memorial Roof has decommissioned the pots under the leaks in her apartment. When she tells him this, he produces a smile so fast and small it might have been an itchy upper lip. Hemingway is drinking scotch, of course, and declines to share the wine with them. His eyes dart from alleged manuscript to the competition. He's heard of this fellow.

"There's a woman living in my barn," Theodore announces to Brigid, who is midway between the two men.

"If she's good-looking, I can put her up," Hemingway quips.

Brigid prickles at the predictable comment. He seems like he's from an earlier generation, maybe Ernest Hemingway's, when women inspired in men adjectives, never nouns. He probably has *Playboy*s under his bed too. She moves closer to Theodore. "Is this woman someone you know?"

"Never saw her before I found her sleeping in the back of the barn," he says. "She made herself a nice little room with stuff she pilfered from the house, pulled out of garbage bags and the pantry."

"Jesus, man," pipes in Hemingway, uninvited. "You should call the cops."

"She's not hurting anybody. Mac likes her, I guess," Theodore says, pushing his empty glass toward Brigid. "Please?"

"What does she look like? Young? Old?" Brigid asks.

"Hot? Not?" inquires the unpublished author.

"Who is this guy?" Theodore flips his thumb toward the other end of the bar. "Kind of early for seasonals."

"Hey! Brigid told me this is a friendly town," Hemingway shoots back.

She ignores the exchange. "You were saying, Teddy? Tell me about your barn dweller."

"Well, she's tall. Black short hair. Looks like she cuts it herself, you know, choppy. Exotic looking. Pakistani? Maybe Egyptian."

"I saw her!" Brigid says. "Easter Sunday, outside the bar. I tried to talk to her but she took off. Gorgeous woman."

Hemingway is frantically writing in his notebook. Maybe he's found some of the *life* he was looking for.

"I can't remember if she said anything to me. Does she speak English?" Brigid asks.

"Pretty much like any Midwesterner, I guess. Wants to fix the tractor, clean my grandfather's rifle."

"What rifle?" Brigid says, watching Hemingway behave like an old-time court stenographer.

"I didn't know who I'd find hiding out. I was armed."

"Hard to picture, Teddy, but adorable," Brigid says. "Your grand-dad would be proud."

"I doubt it," he says. "It wasn't even loaded. I'll tell you, she was kind of heartbreaking to look at. Something's happened to her. She's on the run. I told her she could stay around for a while."

"The Christian thing to do, right?" Brigid assesses, without sarcasm. "Want me to come by and talk to her, see what's going on?"

"I can do that," Hemingway interrupts again. "I can channel Christian. Love my neighbor and all," he says with a lecherous leer.

"Wait awhile," Theodore tells Brigid. "She may not stick around for long."

"I'll give it time," she says, "but I need to know that you're safe. Lock your door at night."

"Birdie, c'mon. What is she, a murderer? A terrorist?"

"Profiling! From the Middle East so hence a terrorist!" Hemingway shouts. "Not an appropriate thing to hear from a brother's lips."

Theodore's eyes meet Brigid's. "Sorry, Teddy," she says. "I just mentioned a couple of things about you, that's all. Just about Nathaniel's passing and you working on his place, well, *your* place."

"Oh, she talks about you all the time, man," Hemingway gripes. "It's kind of a drag."

Theodore pushes his glass away and slaps a twenty on the bar. "See you around," he says and leaves.

She's growing tired of tiptoeing around him. He's like a young birch in a windstorm, swaying back and forth, always in danger of snapping.

"Sorry," Hemingway says in a decent imitation of meaning it.

She takes a hard look at him, feeling in equal measure attraction and repulsion. "Don't worry about it," she tells him. Unlike Theodore, Hemingway is easy to understand. She knows that if she asked him to hang around until closing, he would. If she invited him to come upstairs for a nightcap, he would accept. And if she led him into her bedroom and ripped off his bohemian, shabby chic clothes, he'd let her. Then if she stripped, pushed him onto his back on her unmade bed and mounted him and her breasts bounced in his hands and her hair came loose and fell into her half-closed, green eyes as she proceeded to blow his scotch-saturated mind, he'd have plenty to write about. It would be an uncomplicated, satisfying, carnal carnival.

And she'd never get rid of him.

BRIGID

A COUPLE OF DAYS LATER

She hates running. Whatever hormonal high you're supposed to get
is nothing she's ever experienced, but she needs the exercise. This
is free and self-scheduling. There's no high- or even low-end fit-
ness center here or anywhere nearby, just miles and miles of hiking
trails, bike paths, and endless beach. So she slathers on the sun-
screen, throws on a T-shirt and her tight, black, stretchy shorts.
Those shorts are intended for biking, given the padded crotch and
butt, but they work fine for this too. The only thing she spent any
money on at all is footgear from a running store in Traverse City.
The shoes weigh nothing and they're a bright orange and an electric
blue not found in nature.

The day is warm and overcast. She drives on Dune Highway
farther up north (and yes, they do say it that way in Michigan).
If you live in Saginaw and want to get to a completely different,
calmer, less populated locale, you go *up north* (or all the way south
to Florida in colder months).

Brigid pulls her old Honda Civic west once she reaches Little
Glen Lake and parks near the picnic area. With her reused plastic
water bottle tucked unstylishly behind her into the waistband of her
shorts, she takes off on the Cottonwood Trail. When she reaches the

northernmost point, she leaves the trail and heads due west, up over the dunes to the big lake. The dunes are a bitch to climb but a trip to run down, and this time she loses her footing in the deep sand and ends up at the bottom coated in fine sand. So before running south along the shoreline, Brigid decides to strip down to her sports bra and skivvies for a cleansing dip. The lake is still cold and she's back on the beach in under a minute.

She's sitting on a sun-bleached log letting the wind dry her body when *shit,* she had hoped to have the beach to herself, but someone is running at her from the south. She fears it might be some horny teenage boy until the figure gets closer. No, it's a barefooted woman in a flapping shirt and cut-off jeans. She's running full out, so light and effortlessly that she barely disturbs the sand or gentle surf beneath her.

Now Brigid could struggle into her sweaty shirt and shorts over her wet body, but it wouldn't be pretty. *And why bother?* It's just the lake and the two of them, *womano a womano.* She sits up and crosses her legs as if she were a woman of leisure, sunning herself on a cloudy day. But once the stranger is close, she stops short, and behold, the stranger is not a complete unknown. It is the lamb lover, the perhaps Egyptian, the troubled one who sleeps with animals.

"Hey," the woman says, not even out of breath.

"Hey," Brigid replies. It's the way their generation greets each other. It could mean simply *Hello* or *Do I know you?* or *Friend or Foe?* In this context, it's more likely *I'm acknowledging your existence here, but this is not the beginning of a conversation.*

Brigid is too curious to leave it at that and decides to explain her lack of wardrobe. "I was hot and didn't have a suit."

"No worries," the woman says, still planted in the sand. Brigid knows that this *no worries* is also part of their shared lexicon and can mean anything from *you're welcome* to *I don't give a shit.* Here she chooses it to mean *nice underwear.*

"Want to take a breather?" Brigid asks.

"We've met?" the woman says, coming closer.

Brigid feels uncomfortable, but in a good, titillating way. This girl has got some serious male energy, direct and commanding with no words wasted. Her looks are unsettling as well. She could be a model, whether it be as a woman or a man.

"Yeah, we enjoyed a nanosecond together near my bar in town," she answers, then wonders why she put it so lamely.

It's not cold out, just in the low seventies, but the wind delivers a visible chill on Brigid's wet body, her jaw suddenly jumpy. Immediately her companion does something that in its gallantry suggests her upbringing. She removes her denim shirt and drapes it over Brigid's shoulders. The thing is damp with sweat and smells of rural life, but it stops Brigid's chattering. This leaves the woman in only her short, loose T-shirt and cutoffs, which are undone and ride low on her hips below her pudgy midsection. Brigid can't help but stare at her in wonder. She's performed this intimate gesture, shedding clothing for another in need, leaving her own body exposed and vulnerable.

"I'm Brigid, Brigid Birdsey. Townie. And you are?"

"Zaima. From out of town."

"I hear you know Theodore Dash." *There, got that in there.*

"No, we don't know each other. Not at all," Zaima answers.

Brigid stands, removes the shirt and hands it back to this enigmatic and elegant creature. "But you're staying with him, or on his property anyway, right?"

"He doesn't want me there, not even in his barn," Zaima says, walking past her and then turning back. "He's willing to tolerate me. He's a good Christian. He can't *not* help me."

Brigid yanks on her shirt and climbs back into her shorts. "Where's home for you?"

"Wherever I am."

"Right," Brigid says dismissively. "Well, if you decide to make this your home for a while, stop by my bar and maybe we can have an actual conversation." Admittedly a little snarky, so she adds, "That was sweet of you to lend me your shirt. Let me thank you with food. I love to cook. I'll make you anything you like."

"You probably couldn't cook what I like," Zaima says.

"Try me."

"All right. My parents are from Iraq. How are you at making masgouf?"

"Ah yes, a big favorite at the Bird's Eye. I'm not quite sure how you spell it though . . . in case I want to advertise."

Zaima spells it.

"I'll need a few days to buy the ingredients. How about you stop by Monday at six?"

"Will you be inviting Theodore?" Zaima asks.

"No . . . no. Just us girls," Brigid says. "I'll close the bar. I could use a night off. Come upstairs."

"All right. I'll come."

"Awesome," Brigid says. She ties her shoes together, slings them over her shoulder, and runs barefoot down the beach. Zaima picks up the water bottle Brigid left behind, downs the contents, and heads off in the opposite direction.

BRIGID

She's done her research. FoodsofIraq.com supplied the masgouf recipe as well as enticing, simple side dishes of basmati rice with pine nuts and a yogurt salad. The Fish House in Traverse City did not have carp for the masgouf so she substituted a whole catfish, which they butterflied for her. She makes a marinade of olive oil, coarse salt, tamarind (not so easy to find), and ground turmeric. That she slathers on the flesh of the fish and grills it in a wire basket.

Brigid is as nervous as Brigid gets, which is more like a mild agitation. She has never had a female as a close friend, has always felt more comfortable in the company of boys and then men. She promises herself that she will not get too attached to this beautiful, enigmatic gypsy.

It's only five and she's showered, dressed with some thought, and now needs a little something to take the edge off. There are three bottles of a New Zealand sauvignon blanc in her fridge. She also digs up a dusty bottle of ouzo that was Mediterraneanish, so close enough to Iraq. She does a shot of that and because she likes the anise-infused jolt, has another.

The apartment is tidy if not clean. She can only go so far. There is no dining room so they will eat in the kitchen, bathed in the luscious, late afternoon sun.

As she sits on the back deck, she waits for Zaima and wonders about the woman's connection to Theodore. There has to be a reason for her being here, for living like a stowaway in his barn. He said nothing, really, about her. Felt obligated to help, like she's a charity. That's it.

Six o'clock comes and goes. At seven she opens a bottle of the wine and pours herself a healthy glassful. The fish is still on the grill but with the propane shut off. At seven thirty, Brigid is pulling the catfish off the grill when Zaima climbs the steps toward her.

"I apologize for being late," Zaima says formally. "I got a late start and then I tripped on a break in the sidewalk." She points to her left knee, which is badly scraped and bleeding down her bare leg.

"Shit," Brigid says and walks her into the apartment. "Sit here. Let me clean that up for you."

"I can do it," Zaima says. "It's nothing really."

Brigid returns with a wet washcloth, antiseptic, gauze, and tape. "C'mon, be a brave girl and I'll give you some cold fish." As Brigid kneels and works on her, she absorbs all the information she can from this stranger. Her skin is the color of coffee with cream. She does not shave her legs. Her calves are like dense fish bellies. She wears dreadful nylon athletic shorts and her white T-shirt smells like Ivory soap.

When Brigid is finishing with her knee, Zaima does the oddest thing. She gently touches Brigid's hair, fingering individual curls. "My grandmother had hair this color. It came from a bottle. It got a lot of talk, and none of it flattering."

"A bit of a rebel, maybe like her granddaughter?" Brigid asks, looking up at her.

"I'm no rebel. Quite the opposite," Zaima says, standing.

"Are you hungry? I can pop a plate into the microwave for you."

"No need," Zaima says. "Let's just have it the way it is."

And they do, hovering over the spread, picking up chunks of fish with their fingers, scooping up the rice and yogurt salad with spoons right out of the serving dishes.

"This is refreshing," Brigid says, wiping her hands on a cloth napkin. "Oh, I forgot. Would you like a glass of wine or should we just swig it from the bottle?"

Zaima smiles and it is such a tender smile—like one reserved for a close relative—it unnerves Brigid and she looks away.

"I don't drink," Zaima answers.

"Friend of Bill?"

"Pardon?" Zaima says.

"I mean, are you in a program? No big deal. I have cranberry juice."

"I'm Muslim, but not practicing," Zaima explains. "It's the world I grew up in. My parents drink alcohol. I just never have. But please, go ahead."

So Brigid does have another glass of wine and watches Zaima eat. She has always enjoyed seeing people consume food with enthusiasm and abandon and Zaima does not disappoint. Once almost everything Brigid had prepared is gone, she slaps down the bottle of ouzo. Zaima shakes her head.

"I'll just nurse a shot," Brigid says. "Let's stretch out in the living room."

They sit on opposite ends of the old couch, sinking into it comfortably.

"Where did you grow up?" Brigid asks innocently. "If you don't mind my asking."

"Dearborn."

"How old are you?" Brigid thinks this conversation is already winding down.

"Early twenties."

Don't give too much away, Brigid wants to say. "Well, I'm well past high school myself. Most of the people I grew up with have left Empire, you know, for larger, more glamorous places like Grand Rapids or Ann Arbor. I see them in the summer sometimes, but they soon disappear again."

Brigid takes a sip of the ouzo, then expels a tiny burp. Zaima is just sitting there. She could be watching television; she seems that detached.

"I always get the same feeling when they leave," Brigid says. "You know what that is?"

"Sad?"

"More than that. Left behind. Stuck," Brigid says. "I mean I love it here and I own this entire building. Still I've never been out of the state. Pitiful, right? Have you traveled? I mean more than coming up here."

"Yes, I've been overseas. Not for pleasure." Zaima is looking like she wants to split, so Brigid changes tactics.

"Even Theodore. I think he feels sorry for me too. God, I hate that more than just about anything."

"I hate that too. I find it arrogant," Zaima says.

Brigid is wondering if Zaima is calculating just how much conversation she must bear to repay her for the meal.

"Teddy's not arrogant, he's just mortally empathetic," Brigid says frankly. "You know we go way back. He summered here with his grandparents. We were inseparable. His mother insisted he go to college, but I don't believe his heart was in it. She's a real drill sergeant of a mother, that Isabelle. Her father, Nathaniel, who I adored, died a few months ago and Isabelle got totally hammered after the funeral. She could barely focus, but was still barking out orders, running the show. Insisted Theodore sell the farm and go back to the seminary."

"But he hasn't," Zaima says, showing some interest.

"Nope, too busy pitying me. Poor Birdie. No man. No future. Dead parents. Lives above a bar."

"I saw the way he looked at you in that green dress on Easter. Didn't look anything like pity," Zaima comments. "So, is Theodore an only child?"

She saw us? How? "No, he has a brother in the service. In Iraq."

"What's he like?" Zaima asks.

"I honestly don't know him," Brigid says. "Seriously good-looking though. You have siblings?"

"Just a younger sister."

"I have no family," Brigid says. "Just my pub family, people I really do care about. I feed them. I get them drunk when they need it, cut them off when they don't. Laugh with them, listen to the story of their lives. And cry with them too. This whole town was devastated when Nathaniel died. Such a good soul. I probably miss him more than anybody else does, with the exception of Teddy, of course, and Cooper."

"Cooper is the man who lives with John?"

"Man, they are *so* married. Cooper and Nathaniel were like brothers . . . helping each other out, hunting together, fighting with each other. Years ago they got so pissed with each other, they didn't speak for almost a year. If one of them was in the bar talking to me and the other came in, he'd just walk right back out. Heavy drama. Went through a whole growing season. Finally, Marie, that's Nathaniel's wife, and John got them back together. Those two were not fans of each other, more like rivals. The whole town was relieved. Nobody ever knew what the whole thing was about. Maybe John or Marie did, but they never said as much. For as much as this town loves gossip, nobody knew."

"My community is like that too," Zaima adds. "I never fit in. I didn't care. I just left as soon as I could get out."

"Well, I say I don't care what people say, but some part of me does care. Good luck having a private life around here. Not to shock you, but a few years ago I got pregnant, a result of some random recreational sex with someone I wouldn't even go to the movies with, let alone raise a kid. I was drinking too much then and not taking care of myself, not even good about contraception. Stupid and messed up over losing my parents. You ever been in a deep hole like that?"

"Not like that, but in a deep hole of my own."

"Then you know," Brigid says. "This idiot dude had a big mouth. I never should have told him. Tongues were wagging. Anyway I got an abortion as soon as I could. Nathaniel helped me even though he was totally against abortion. Somebody once said if men could get pregnant, abortion would be a sacrament . . ."

"May I taste that wine, please?" Zaima interrupts.

"What! Are you sure, girl? You're like a virgin and I don't want to be the one to pop your cherry."

"I'm not sure what you're talking about," Zaima says, heading for the kitchen. "I just want to taste it."

"All right then, a half glass," Brigid says, following her. "You'll probably get totally schnockered. This could be fun."

Brigid finds her glass and gets one for her new drinking buddy. She puts them both on a clean, white cloth napkin. "Now, in your faith, is this a venial or a mortal sin, if you know what I mean?"

"It would be, I think, minor, compared to others I have committed. Our God is forgiving. He knows we are weak."

"Hard to think of you as weak," Brigid says as she pours. "You've committed major sins?"

Zaima does not sip the wine, but bolts it down. Pushes her glass back to Brigid.

"I'm not going to ask you if you liked it because you didn't even have time to taste it," Brigid observes.

"I have harmed innocents," Zaima says. "That is against all religions."

Brigid refills her glass. *Harmed innocents? Should she ask another question?*

"After my abortion, I got three things," the barkeep says flatly. "Flowers from John, a nasty note thumbtacked to my front door, and a knot in the fibers of my heart that has never eased. What I never considered in getting past this pregnancy, which I thought was just a burp in my life, was that this was *my* child too. My child who would be near kindergarten age now, the grandchild of my parents. An anchor. A reason to have health insurance and a savings account. I guess I harmed an innocent too."

Zaima sips daintily from her glass. Smiles. "I'm pregnant now."

"Oh." Brigid draws that one word out into a full sentence. "Tell me it's not Theodore's."

"No, no. Not him. I was raped."

Brigid reaches a hand toward her, but Zaima flashes a palm to stop her. "No pity, please. Remember, we hate that."

"You're going ahead with the pregnancy?" Brigid asks.

"Enough harming of innocents."

Brigid knocks back her wine and sees the empty bottle between them. Zaima's eyes are on fire and directed at her, daring her to say more.

"But you were the victim, you were innocent," Brigid says firmly.

"It was someone I knew. I believed we were friends. He forced himself on me."

"Did you report it?"

"He would only say it was consensual. I had no proof. It would have made matters worse. I ran away as soon as I could. It's what I do."

"What about your family? Do they know where you are? Do they know you're pregnant?" Brigid asks.

Zaima looks away. "Too many questions."

"Do you want me to drive you home, Zaima. You look ready."

"I prefer to walk. The meal was delicious and so thoughtful."
And she leaves.

Brigid wonders if she should follow her in her car from a distance. Then she quickly concedes that she herself should not be driving. *Why did she drink so much? What was she afraid of?* Probably not the best decision either to pour alcohol down the throat of a pregnant Muslim. Still, she asked for it.

ZAIMA

Behind the barn, there's an outdoor shower. Only cold water is available and there are a few raised slats of wood to stand on. There's a nail for a towel, a rusty iron soap dish, and the only privacy afforded is the side of the barn itself. The shower was probably intended for bathing a dog or rinsing muck boots, tools, or feed buckets.

Even though Theodore knows she's in residence, Zaima still chooses to shower here than bathe indoors. The view is exceptional, nothing but orchards and sky. A year ago, this freedom and safety would have been unimaginable for her.

It's in the midseventies with only a modest breeze and she doesn't mind the cold water at all. By late afternoon, she's usually in desperate need of cleansing and cooling. She's been weeding and adding to the raised beds, working into the soil the composted horse manure from the burlap sacks that periodically appear. Along with these came young vegetable and herb plants to be planted, and colorful packets of seeds to be sown.

Theodore is seldom around. He's likely out in the orchards, at Cooper's, or in town. She's been caring for Levi and the chickens, and doing some cooking whenever food magically appears in the fridge or on the countertop. Fortunately she found a worn copy of *The Joy of Cooking* in the pantry that was full of scribbled recipe changes, as well as the dates foods were prepared and who was at the table. Once Theodore left a labeled bag of fresh walleye in the fridge that, with the help of that invaluable book, she scaled with a dull knife, removed the guts, cut into fillets, then coated and pan-fried. The next morning, a grateful Theodore left two singles tucked under his clean plate, probably a tip.

They never eat together, but she has food on the table for him at seven thirty most evenings, while her meals are taken in her room in the barn or outside somewhere. Just last night, she watched him from a distance as he ate his dinner sitting on the porch steps with the blood-orange light of the setting sun splashed on his bearded face. Once finished, he put down his plate and extended both arms toward the sunset as his lips moved in what she thought must be a prayer.

The fact that they have no direct contact with each other seems to suit them both. This avoidance stems not from any animosity, but from respect for the other's privacy and recovery from their immediate pasts. They appear to others to be content, if not happy, and to be staying in place at least for now. There is no for-sale sign in front of the farmhouse; and Zaima's wardrobe, with Father McGurley's help, has new diversity and depth.

Theodore has been kind to her, she realizes now as the water curves around her breasts and swelling belly. The kindest thing is simply letting her alone, letting her be without questioning. There is no need for conversation. No need for lies.

From the dish, she takes the lavender soap that someone put there for her. Other things have suddenly appeared. In the kitchen, a box of couscous, which she hates. Garden gloves in a detestable floral pattern.

Zaima turns off the water and reaches for her towel just as Theodore comes around the corner, moving from the intense low sun into the barn's vast shadow. When he sees her, he stops and stares. She does not cover her body and he does not look away. It's a theatrical, dramatic moment and with neither moving, it lingers. She fears he may approach her, want to touch her. If she covers herself, it may suggest shame. Weakness. Vulnerability. With so many people knowing she is pregnant, how could he not? From the look on his face, and where his eyes travel, she sees that he did not know.

"I'm sorry," he says in just a whisper. *What is he sorry for? It could be for so many things. The rifle in her face, pretending she doesn't exist, the couscous?*

"For what?" she asks, grabbing her towel, but still not covering her body.

"Invading your privacy," he says, but does not leave or even look away.

"And?" Zaima asks. "Is there something else?"

His shoulders drop and he takes a deep breath. "Why didn't you tell me?" he stammers. "Why didn't you tell me that you're pregnant?"

"Like during one of our many conversations?" she says as she casually dries her body and wraps the towel around her. He walks slowly toward her, his intent unclear. "This changes . . ."

"Nothing," she says, cutting him off, and then walks in the opposite direction.

"You should move into the house," he calls out.

"I'm fine where I am," she shouts back, not turning around.

ZAIMA

MID-JUNE

Cooper has come by late in the morning looking for Theodore, who is nowhere to be found. Cooper shows no interest in being around Zaima and quickly explains why he is there. June drop is on, he tells her. That's when the apple trees naturally drop fruit. Time to start thinning the fruit. He then walks toward the orchard, motioning for her to follow.

"It's easy," he shouts. "Anyone can do it."

Okay, insult taken. She wonders why he treats her with such disdain. *Is this about her friendship with John?* She doesn't care.

"Just show me," she shouts back. "I'm a fast learner."

"See this here cluster?" Cooper tells her once they're in the orchard. "Use your thumbnail to pinch off these two and leave the big one. Take off anything that's too close to the others. Should be about eight inches separating them. And take off any that don't look healthy.

"Makes for bigger apples. Ripens sooner. Limbs won't break. And you'll get more flower buds next year. All the little fruit gets tossed into the compost pile. I can send over some help tomorrow. Think you can tell all that to Theodore?"

He has crossed a line with her. "You have a problem with me?"

"Don't want to. Just can't say I trust you. You came outta nowhere and sure looks like you're fittin' in just fine."

"I work for Theodore and I'll do some of this. I'm not a criminal."

"Well, how would we know that?" he asks. After he walks a few yards, he turns back. "Two things, young lady. First, don't you dare harm that boy. Second, keep off the ladder. Just get the stuff you can reach."

After he's off the property, she gathers some five-gallon buckets and a couple of stakes to mark her progress. She has finished the bottom two-thirds of an entire row when Brigid shows up. She carries two bulging paper bags.

"Here you are," the barkeep says. "Thought you might drop by again. Since you didn't here I am."

Zaima walks to her and, surprising even herself, kisses her on both cheeks. "Why does Cooper despise me?"

Brigid puts down her bags and crosses her arms. "Thinning, huh? Just focus on one tree at a time and don't look down the row. Years of your life could pass before you finish."

"Cooper is sending help."

"Hmm, Cooper," Brigid says. "First off, he ain't over losing his best friend and he feels responsible for Nathaniel's property, and his grandson. Also he's cranky and territorial. Different from John, who is sweet and territorial. Love them both though. Give it time."

"We're both vets. We've both seen a lot of different types of people."

"Okay, that's another bombshell," Brigid says, catching her breath. "Not as powerful as the other, though. Afghanistan?"

"Iraq. Home of my ancestors."

"Wow. Zaima, you are full of breaking news. Is that where, you know . . ."

"Yes. That is where, you know."

"Holy shit. Now I get why you didn't report it."

"I was just going up to the house to get some water," Zaima says, exiting the conversation. "Come with me."

At the kitchen table, Brigid starts emptying her bags. "I went to Traverse yesterday. Man, I had a blast. If any of this is too awful, tell me."

One bag is just for Zaima. There are drawstring pants, large T-shirts and sweatshirts, and a mac jacket. "Seasons change fast up here. I didn't get you anything that screams maternity."

Zaima smiles. "Thank you. I like them all."

Then Brigid just pushes the second bag toward Zaima. "This is for later. Check it out when you feel like it. I don't believe in baby color-coding so it's a real rainbow. Just some basics."

"I need to tell you something. It's hard to say. I'm hoping maternal instincts are something that just materialize when you give birth." Zaima hesitates and then adds, "I feel no connection to this fetus."

"Then why did you choose to keep it?"

"I chose not to kill it. Those are two different things."

Brigid has no response. She had no problem with making that decision, and in her case the act had been consensual.

"Is that wrong?" Zaima asks.

"No. No, it's not wrong. It was a brave decision. I admire you for it."

"Your friendship means a lot to me," Zaima says, lowering her eyes. "It's new for me."

"Me too. But before we both get misty-eyed, let's get into that orchard and abort those unwanted little apples. I've got a couple hours to burn."

"Where is this compost pile Cooper referred to?" Zaima asks.

"I have no idea. Maybe off near the woods."

"Theodore will know."

"Yes," Brigid says. "He's learned a great deal. Let's hope he stays."

"He doesn't know about how I got pregnant."

"Really? Well then, *mink chaps*," Brigid says.

"*Mink chaps?*"

"Oh, funny story. As a kid, I once walked unannounced into Bill Brooder's barn. He was standing there in, I swear, a pair of riding chaps *made of mink!* I tried not to laugh, but I couldn't help it. Bill made me swear I'd never tell anyone. I never did until he died a couple years later. Anyway, *mink chaps* means that it's a potentially embarrassing bit of information that is not to be shared. You'll hear it used at the bar. Just in good fun. We want it to go global, like if Bush was asked about his true intentions in Iraq and he says, 'Sorry, that information is mink chaps.'"

"A rape seems more than embarrassing," Zaima points out.

"Okay then, *moose chaps*. But honey, everybody, even Theodore, is going to learn the truth at some point."

THE MUSINGS OF JOHN QUIMBY

EARLY JULY

I worry about these twenty-somethings. It's not that I'm afraid they're lost. I think they're not looking. The very way they talk can be devoid of meaning. Everything is "like" (as in "I was like so messed up") or "whatever." Reaction time to just about anything is slow and minimal. I just want to take them by the shoulders and shake them hard.

Just ran into Teddy at Deering's. No time for conversation. Too busy. And he is busy, a regular spinning top. He spends the bulk of each day either with Cooper or doing whatever Cooper tells him to do. I should have that much time with Cooper. But has the boy made any decisions about his future? Is he still going to pursue his alleged religious calling? Is it "like" even still important to him? Never talks about it. But doesn't leave either. The farm is not up for sale. As far as I know, Zaima is still living in the barn and she's evidently still pregnant. Another nondecision. "Whatever." Every time I suggest we go to the clinic, offer to pay—although she must get veterans benefits, which would require her applying for them—every time she is, like Teddy, too busy. There's the weeding and the chickens to tend and she's painting somewhere. What is this, a century ago when women just kept on doing whatever they were doing with no time to care for themselves or the child they're carrying? Will she just one day wander out into the orchard and squat when her time comes?

And Brigid? I worry about her more than anyone. What's her plan? She might as well marry the Bird's Eye and all the characters who call it their second home. Doesn't she want a husband? An actual family? And that idiot Hemingway. Just sits at the bar trying to look brilliant and better than everybody else, staring at the poor girl. Yet another without a plan. He's an author with a ripped-off name and no book. Where are the fruits of his labors? Probably on his computer, typed in verbatim from his scribblings, all his stream-of-consciousness drivel, all unedited, unscrutinized, and sent to some poor publisher who will dispose of it after reading the first page. You'd think if he really had the hots for the bartender, he'd do something crazy like ask her out to dinner. No, he'd rather stare and sulk. Pathetic.

Oh, but the worst of it, the most shameful and disheartening, is all the buried angst and denial that lurks in the tortured heart of our boy, Teddy. I am aware of what happened to him in Detroit. I know how and why he ended up at that seminary. I got a letter from Nate after he heard from his mother that Theodore was still up here and nothing was happening with the farm. Nate told me about Teddy's problems. Isabelle wanted Nate to talk some sense into him, but Nate confessed that Teddy never listens to him. He didn't care what Teddy did, as long as he didn't hurt himself. Nate asked me to keep an eye on him. As if Coop and me wouldn't.

But that's not what worries me most about Theodore. It's that he's like an emotional time bomb, quietly ticking away, so much inside, building up. I can feel it in him because I was the same way. He's on remote, doing one thing after the other. You become like an engine with a faulty valve. Everything is fine enough until the whole apparatus fails. What is all this angst of his about? I don't know. I just know it's right there below the overly busy, thin surface. Maybe it springs from his mother not providing a father's lasting presence. Maybe it is about that missing male figure. Or maybe it's about Nate, the favored son—or so Teddy thinks. Maybe he's angry with God. Or angry with himself for what he sees as his failures.

I think he needs to get laid. Is that crude? Simplistic? No and here's why. The first time Cooper and I lay naked next to each other on an army cot freed in me not just my true sexuality, but this huge chunk of my identity.

The suppression of this side of me, what I thought was an ugly, disgusting, sinful side of me, fueled a rage of self-loathing and deep denial. But once I was on that cot with this beautiful man who wanted me the same way I wanted him, it became something outside myself, something real and not imagined that I had to deal with.

Let's be honest here. Sex isn't just about interacting, romantically or not, with another person. It's about that other person, sure, but also a lot about just you. About releasing demons, clogged emotions, inhibitions, lies. Orgasm can be transformative. Especially for someone like Teddy the Time Bomb. And especially if it involves someone he really cares about. I don't know if he's a virgin or not. I doubt he is. But I bet he's never had any great, transformative sex. And he should!

I'm no philosopher or shrink. I don't like telling anybody what to do, with the exception of Coop. I don't profess to know if some steamy, mind-blowing diddling will save Teddy or help him at all. But I do know that apple blossoms raining down on his upturned face, pruning lessons, spraying chemicals, or even a magical, bountiful harvest won't do it. Gazing at sunsets or gorging on splashy sunrises over the evergreens, they won't do it either. How do they say it . . . get some skin in the game? Pun intended.

Right now, I'm going over to LaCore Road and find Zaima, and once again try and coax her to go to that clinic with me. I will fail. But maybe she'll let me rest these arthritic old hands on her bulging belly and sense that little amphibian that grows inside her. And because I'm very perceptive, practically psychic, I may well ascertain the creature's full parentage. Or maybe because I think I already know. I pay attention. I put things together. I did with Nathaniel and Maureen, too, when nobody else suspected a thing.

None of that matters now. Today I'll help her if she lets me. Take her blood pressure, ask her questions about how she's feeling that she'll hate answering, but she will. I'll present her with some elastic-waist pants I found for her and a bottle of vitamins that all she'll have to do is swallow. I'll tell her that I've delivered babies, which I haven't, but I could. Nature does most of the work anyway. You can do it in a taxi cab, for God's sake.

ZAIMA

his kindness
the ease of it
feels to me like
weakness

he shows
too much,
is easily read

so pure of spirit
he's translucent
proudly defenseless

I feel I could so easily
harm him

he looks toward me now
with sugary compassion
is all forgiveness
without even knowing
the sin

which renders his forgiveness
a sin itself

Christlike
he forgets that Christ could be
an angry man

I see he tries to be
not of this world
strange
as this is a world
he appears to so deeply
love

I see him
caress the young fruit as if
the warmth in his hands
could convey his hopes and aspirations
for it
as to a child saying
"I believe in you"

I see him
in the early morning
watch the sun
unveil the landscape
each leaf and
each glint on every form of water
all for him to savor
with prayerlike
reverence

his kindness
is inexplicable and random
he casually throws it about
like candy from a parade's passing float
well intentioned
but uncaring
about whose hands
or lives
it reaches

he sat with Cooper Boyd
yesterday
after they shared a simple evening meal I prepared
sat not on the ancient porch
but in the silence
of the small weedy lawn out front
the old man easing down
with of course
his showy assistance
and soon both were
flat-backed on the ground
filling their eyes
with evening sky
like children
past their bedtime, capturing
every stolen moment
every small tinging, slapping,
wind-seduced sound

the younger in love with his new perfect life
the older with his past

why is it that
we hate what is
too pure?
is it envy?
is it cynicism?
lack of trust?
or are we just naturally drawn more
toward darkness
and the comfort of all it
hides?

ISABELLE DASH

LATE JULY • CHICAGO

She sips coffee from a paper cup. Her deli brings it piping hot along with an unbuttered, toasted sesame bagel every weekday morning at exactly six thirty, accompanied by the *Tribune* and the *New York Times.* Isabelle appreciates the best of everything, except for coffee. She does not like overpriced, overly strong signature brews. She grew up drinking ground, canned coffee with her parents from the age of thirteen and has not matured in that habit. Isabelle swears at this very moment that the paper cup adds authenticity to its contents, simple and unpretentious, like a good-looking man in Jockey briefs. This makes her think of poor César, already gone by the wayside. Having a man around for too long is for her akin to a year of Christmases. It just isn't special when every day you open the same gift.

Isabelle sits at her desk in the corner of the massive living room that travels the entire width of her condominium. Windows everywhere display the best views of the Gold Coast, including Oak Street Beach, both East and North Lake Shore drives, and the big lake stretching to the horizon. She pushes aside the stack of papers in front of her and looks north. On this same lake hundreds of miles north Theodore remains, locked in a world of nostalgia and inertia.

How can she get him back at Wayne State? He was only an average student, but if he found something that captivated him, she believes he has the aptitude to excel. *But what would that be?* Well, he'll have to figure that out. He can't just stay up there stranded in that dead-end place she couldn't wait to leave. Forget that seminary misstep. After he had disappeared for many, many months in Detroit, how did he resume contact? She got a pathetic little note written on a holy card letting her know he was all right now. *When was he not all right?* Not for Mom to know, she assumes. She's just a checkbook mother and now that he has money and property, will he even need her? She's asked Nate to attempt to pry Theodore loose from his latest dodge, but will he even contact his brother? They've always lived in different worlds, now more so than ever.

She's phoned him herself many times, dialing that old familiar number that was her parents'. *Oh God, was it even her number growing up?* Teddy used to have a cell phone. What happened to that? The priests probably made him give it up, tool of the devil and all. There used to be an answering machine. He must have tossed it like every other modern convenience. *Is he cooking over an open fire? Does the man shower? Did he shave that dreadful beard or does he even comb his hair?*

She's only caught him at the farmhouse once and their conversation was brief and vague. Her son talked about a night he had slept in the orchard at the top of the hill, under the stars with only a dog to keep him company. *What could she possible say to that?* It seems he has reverted to being the Boy Scout he never was.

Isabelle finishes her coffee, but has no appetite for the bagel. It is a luscious morning with the sun painting the lake a glimmering purple. It's wasted on her though; she feels distracted and unenthusiastic about the packed day before her. She lays her hand on Nate's letter, which came only yesterday. His tour is up next month and she prays he won't sign on to another. He included a photograph of himself. He was his handsome, rugged self, but in his eyes she sees things only a mother could see, a weariness, a resignation, a vulnerability that is new. He looks so much like his grandfather, it's unnerving. Nate's personality also has unsettling similarities to that of her father, a man he barely knew, their contact always so abbreviated, her fault as much as his. They both have the same brio, lust for life, and overblown self-confidence. Both with that chiseled masculinity women are always drawn to.

Nate was built for the military; he could never have farmed, or sold shoes or stocks. War for him is probably the ultimate high. For her as a mother, the ultimate fear trap. When he does return, she'll have something to say about what he does with his civilian life.

From observing the organized chaos of the world below her, and the people who attend the same parties and events, all the operas and fund-raisers that she does, nobody would guess we are at war. More accurately, we are now stuck in the middle of a civil war. Who in her circle of close friends, even business acquaintances, has family over there? Go to another neighborhood and it's a different story, she's quite certain. Somebody besides her is shouldering the weight of this misadventure. Somebody has to be suffering the losses.

How many Americans have died over there now, there in Iraq, once Mesopotamia, the cradle of civilization? So many losses to so many families. She guesses that the number is around twenty-five hundred. How many Iraqis? A hundred thousand? More?

God willing, Nate will be back in Chicago soon. She will provide options for him. And she will send Teddy the printed fall schedule from Wayne State because, Lord knows, he has no computer to find it online.

Isabelle still has plenty of time before her bitch of a day begins. She dials the number. Should she just send him another cell phone? *Even John Quimby has one!*

"Hello? Teddy?"

"Hi, Mom. How are you?"

"How are things progressing up there? Any offers yet?"

"Ah, no," he answers. "It's not ready, or maybe I'm not ready."

"What does that mean? *Why not?* It's prime time! Let me help."

"I can handle it, Mom. There's a lot to running this place. We can't risk losing the harvest."

"Losing the harvest? The trees have been there forever. They'll be just fine." She didn't mean to shout that.

"Mom, you know how much work is involved. You lived on this farm."

"Theodore, my father hired Mexicans to do that labor, anything beyond what he could handle. Do you think I was out there on some flimsy ladder picking goddamned apples?"

"Didn't those goddamned apples send you to law school?"

Isabelle is silent for a few seconds. There's no point in mentioning the mountain of student debt she had to pay. "What is keeping you up there? What about the seminary? What about school? What about the rest of your life?"

"I'm trying to live in the moment."

"Good God almighty, Theodore. You know that's just another way of saying I have no plans."

"I have no plans," he says flatly.

"Your brother will be back soon. I'm sending him up there."

"Great. I could use the help."

———————— • ————————

Of course, she's disappointed. She has this killer day ahead of her and she'll have to drag this communication failure around with her through it. She showers, does her hair and makeup, and dresses. Time is tight but she won't rush. They all can wait. No money or property can change hands without her in the room and they know it. On her way out, she has a quick, warm smile for her doorman.

"Good morning, Mrs. Dash. Will you be needing a taxi today?" he asks, swinging open the heavy, brass-and-glass door.

Always with the *Mrs.* and she never corrects him. He has known her two sons forever, so for him, it's a given she's been married. "No, Arnoldo. I need to walk for a bit," she answers. "But I'll be back shortly, thank you."

East Lake Shore Drive is, as usual, pretty quiet and she crosses easily. Then she strolls through the shabby little park that separates her street from North Lake Shore Drive. There's a lot of litter in the park of the usual variety and much of it is accumulating near the half-empty garbage receptacle. The grass is patchy and the shrubs sad and inadequately watered. Still there's greenery and relief from concrete. North Lake Shore Drive is the predictable wall of traffic, four lanes in both directions pulsing along at well above the ignored speed limit. Isabelle stands at the park's edge and stares forward, not at the blur of cars, but at the blue bowl of fresh water beyond that, which connects her to Theodore. The water is choppier now as if agitated by the congestion on land. She misses her son in an ancient, aching sort of way, and feels that mythical connection between a brooding mother and her wayward son. She yearns for Theodore, his body in her arms. He was the affectionate one, who never squirmed away when she chose to express her fondness for him. She realizes at that moment that she sought out physical affection from the often distant elder son, and was put off by Theodore's need for it. She was always enough for Nate, but not for Theodore. She knew it then as now. *What's blocking her expression of affection for Theodore?* Then she wonders whether it's just the hormonal roller coaster of menopause that's making her overemotional.

A car sounds its horn and Isabelle gasps. She's somehow stepped over the rusted guardrail without intending to and is perched on the broken cement curb of the busy roadway. Then she has that sensation, that inexplicable urge. *Do others feel this?* Say you're standing on a sheer mountain ledge, and you are tempted to jump. She remembers it while high on the Eiffel Tower and on the rim of the Grand Canyon. Again on both the Brooklyn and the Golden Gate bridges. It's not that you want to or will. It's just there, something you could do so easily. Maybe some people commit suicide in this way, succumbing to this urge, unplanned, alluring.

Isabelle turns and steps back over the guardrail. Even if she wanted to kill herself, it would be unfair to the unsuspecting driver who would carry the weight of her death and the harm it might cause him or his vehicle. And that, she realizes, is the most civic-minded thought she has entertained in some time.

The little park seems brighter now, less depressing, like it might after a near-death experience. She feels more positive. There is nothing happening with her sons that can't be improved. Once Nate is back, maybe they'll both go to Empire to see Teddy and not hound him. She'd like simply to touch Teddy, the tip of his soft ear or the scar on his forehead from a sledding mishap.

She's at East Lake Shore now and sees the majesty of her vintage building, the perfect potted ferns standing guard, the hideous but colorful begonias packed into the window boxes. And there's Arnoldo and his friendly, appropriate wave.

What happens in the next fifteen seconds is a chain of loosely related events, slapstick in nature, but with a dark outcome. A middle-aged man in oversized sweatpants, the bottoms of which are ragged, torn, and dragging on the pavement, loses control of a large dog. The dog is young, poorly trained, and uncomfortable in his new city home. The leash has slipped from the man's hands and the dog is running toward East Lake Shore, so his owner lunges to retrieve control of the leash and trips on his shoddy attire. He is momentarily airborne with all 227 pounds of him directed, with right hand outstretched, smack into the mid-back of Isabelle Dash. She is standing where a parked car could have been when she is hit hard by the human projectile, which causes her to be pushed face-first into the street. As she struggles to get up, knees bent and pushing up from her bruised palms, she looks to her left and finds she is in the path of an oncoming car. The unlucky driver of the 2004 Lexus is an older man, running late, doing forty in the heavily populated area. Reaching for his coffee, he does not see her, but feels his bumper slam into her thorax, breaking her ribs, which then puncture her lungs and her heart. He swerves and hits his brakes hard, but his passenger-side rear tire crushes her pelvis before he comes to a complete stop.

The dog suddenly reappears, safely crosses the road, and races toward Arnoldo. At the same moment Isabelle, less than a minute after first impact, races into the unknown, erasing all the glints of optimism she so recently felt. The man in the sweatpants is soon at her side, pulling his phone from his deep pocket, shaking his head at the already impressive amount of blood that pours freely from her femoral artery.

Arnoldo pushes him away and throws his uniform jacket over her torso. He checks for a pulse. The doorman is sobbing, having seen the whole bizarre thing unfold so randomly. Soon there are sirens, police, and then an ambulance. The first impact was likely enough to kill her, Arnoldo hears an EMT say, and he hopes this is true. They carefully cover her body and carry it into the ambulance, but the vehicle does not pull away. Latecomers to the scene are talking into their phones, shaking their heads at the bloody spot in the street. No one takes a photo.

The dog has disappeared in the chaos, but a police officer will not allow the owner to search for him. She assigns another officer to do this and he reluctantly obliges.

Poor Arnoldo—likely the last to speak with Isabelle—is a mess. He tries to reconstruct it all for the police, struggling to form words that are accurate and in the right order. He knows the scene will forever be with him, will inform his conduct when walking with his two young children. It will replay in his mind and dreams, the flat sound of the car striking her as she was trying to get up, the guttural screams of the dog owner, the dog running playfully toward him.

It is a crime with no villain. Not the dog or his owner. Not the man who reached for his coffee. Certainly not Arnoldo who would have prevented it if only he could. *Should he not have waved?* Did that distract her for the few seconds that allowed every other thing to fall into its fateful place?

The police question the building's superintendent about Isabelle's family. He can provide little personal information and explains that Arnoldo knows her much better. Still composing himself, Arnoldo tells them he's never met her husband. There are two sons, grown, and yes, he knows their names and roughly where they are—one up north in Michigan, the other in the army, in Iraq. Isabelle had a friend who was a constant, first name Faye. She often stays for a few days. Friendly. Maybe her sister?

They soon find Isabelle's purse in a low evergreen in the small park, near the scene. There is no wallet, no phone, only cosmetics, cough drops, a compact, and comb. Evidently they were not the first to find it.

The super tells Arnoldo to take the rest of the day off. He refuses. He would love to hold his wife, bring his children into his arms. Still his job is here right now. He feels he must stay on, speak with those who knew her. She had many friends in the building.

Then the super takes two officers up to her penthouse. They look around, check recent calls on her landline. There is the Empire number, the last she dialed. Later they will call that number a dozen times before, finally, a woman will answer.

Ironically, Nate was easier to find and contact. He is with the Army National Guard, stationed at Camp Speicher near Tikrit. An officer will be assigned to tell him in person about the death of his mother.

A STRANGER NAMED AIDEN

A LITTLE LATER

Tomorrow he will not be here. This brightly lit, chilly, impersonal room will have a new master of ceremonies and he will be retired. As he enters what he refers to as his office, it may well be for the last time.

He does not want to retire, hates the thought. He wonders how his skills will translate in a life of leisure. He's a mere sixty-six and within throwing distance of perfect health, challenged only by severe nearsightedness and the pesky floaters in his vitreous humor that wander like semitranslucent animal crackers through his line of vision. Blood pressure, cholesterol levels, BMI are all exemplary. Only minor arthritis and possibly too keen a love for good Irish whiskey (which both he and his wife monitor).

It's his wife who wants him to leave the job that he—and likely few others—loves. She wants to travel *(costly, unsafe, unfamiliar)* and to spend more time with the daughter, the son-in-law, the three grandchildren *(needy, spoiled rotten, speak to him as if equals)*. They live in Brooklyn. He hates flying *(especially landing at LaGuardia with its short runways and water dangers)* and long car trips. And once in Brooklyn *(foreign country)*, he always seems to get stuck entertaining the two youngest while the rest go shopping or to lunch. He can never wait to go home.

He prefers building birdhouses in his basement and fishing with his buddies, but not every day. He currently likes the way the week is divided between workdays and weekends. Not working will feel like suffering summer all year long without hope of ever seeing the clear winter sun. *What's next? Florida?*

Here on his final day, he looks at the figure on the metal table before him. "Good afternoon," he begins and then glances down at the chart in his hands, "Mrs. Dash. Mrs. Isabelle Dash. I like that name Isabelle very much. You know it was my blessed mother's name, as well." *(Untrue)*

He pulls a metal chair next to her body and sits for a moment. She's wrapped loosely in a plastic sheet, her arms at her sides, her legs extended straight down. There's a pillow under her exposed head and a rolled towel supports her jaw.

He removes his thick glasses and cleans them on his lab coat. He examines what he generally examines first, that of most interest, the face. She's an attractive woman, but her skin is now mottled with red patches and her eyes and mouth are closed and sunken. All to be expected. Beyond that, there are touches of blood on some of the tips of her light hair and only minor abrasions just below her chin.

"Mrs. Dash, and perhaps I can call you Isabelle given the intimacy of the circumstances, my name is Aiden. You are a person to me who has been a victim of tragic circumstances beyond your control. I will treat what's left of you with the utmost respect. I apologize that I, a stranger, will be tending to your body and that it is not a loved one caring for you in this way."

Aiden rises and approaches a table equipped with items not normally found in a prep room—a CD player with two compact speakers and a stack of about thirty CDs.

"Guessing from your age, which is probably older than you look . . . and you're welcome . . . I'm thinking either Gershwin or Michael Bublé, a favorite of my wife's. It could also be Springsteen or Debussy. Well, if you're not going to tell me, and since I have no Springsteen and can't tolerate Mr. Bublé, let's go with a Gershwin collection."

When *An American in Paris* begins with its street noise and honking, he immediately knows it's a bad choice, given the details of the death. He makes a quick adjustment and the more appropriate *Rhapsody in Blue* fills the room.

But now there is work to be done and he dons his gloves and gown. "Please forgive the gloves," he says. "It's just protocol, nothing personal."

Aiden removes the plastic covering and the pads placed beneath her and disposes of them. Rigor mortis isn't as much of a problem as the amount of blood she lost and he must cut away most of her clothing. Damage to the body was primarily to the internal organs and bones, and nothing that an onlooker would notice once she is in her shroud. Isabelle is already tagged on wrist and toe, so he proceeds to wash and disinfect, keeping as much of her body draped as possible. This is as unusual as it is unnecessary, but it has always been his practice to treat every body as if it belonged to a relative.

As he is chattering away, explaining to Isabelle his dislike for his grandchildren and his subsequent shame and remorse, the phone rings. He removes his gloves and listens, jotting down a few things on her chart.

"Good news, Isabelle. You're slated for cremation so there'll be no nasty embalming fluids for you. We'll just keep you fresh and cool until one of your family arrives."

Lastly Aiden washes and combs her hair. He gently applies a moisturizing lotion to the dehydrated skin of her face and then wraps her in a clean sheet that he lightly tapes closed.

He stands above her then, knowing he has done all he can. He thinks he sees something in her face—a lovely face he imagines many have examined for clues to the person within—something that he takes as gratitude.

"I don't know if you're a religious person, Isabelle Dash, but I am. It certainly wouldn't hurt for me to utter a brief prayer."

Aiden turns off the music and the lights. He moves slowly toward her and places his hand on her forehead. "All forgiving and loving Father, please take this fine woman into your care. And accompany those that soon will feel the weight of the crushing blow this world has so unfairly delivered. Please be with them all, Father. Amen."

It's a version of what he always comes up with on the spot, but then on this his final day, he throws in one more request.

"And with the wife and the hospital administration willing, God let me continue in this work at least part-time or I will go out of my bloody mind. You know how I hate babysitting."

ZAIMA

AROUND THE SAME TIME • EMPIRE

She knows where he is. She could easily walk through the orchards until she found Theodore. Where he was this morning, she wasn't sure; but now she thinks he was probably with Cooper, since all afternoon she's heard him mowing the clover and grass in the orchard rows with Cooper's small tractor and mowing attachment. She's been tinkering with the Farmall in the barn, but can't get it going. That tractor would be too big for mowing anyway.

Now well into her seventh month, Zaima feels energetic and focused, not like the aimless soul who arrived in Empire last April. She spent the morning repairing the walls in the downstairs rooms, using the lightweight spackle and sandpaper as John had shown her. Then with John's chop saw and the lumber Theodore had been instructed to purchase, she spent the afternoon hours cutting and replacing water-damaged windowsills and trim. John had hand sanded the one-by-fours to mimic the rounded edges of the old wood.

She never would have answered the phone except that it had been ringing a good part of the day, unnerving her consistently every thirty minutes or so.

When she finally picks it up, it is an Officer Darnell Washington from the Chicago Police Department. He asks to speak to either Theodore Dash or Nathaniel Dash. *Is he referring to the deceased or to his grandson?* Zaima answers that neither is available. The officer asks if she is related. She says no. He needs to speak with a family member. There has been an accident. He leaves a number to call as soon as possible when a family member returns.

She waits for him on the front porch. Then it is after eight and he is still not back. No need to search for him. Whatever this news is, it will hurt him and likely draw him away. Let him have these last few mindless, worry-free minutes in his new playground. She goes to sit at the table in the darkening kitchen. She's keeping a roasted chicken warm in the oven. It's very plain, only salt and pepper with an onion thrown in the cavity. There are fresh green beans in a pot on the stove and the first of the cherry tomatoes in a clear glass bowl on the table. His place is set, but he won't eat any of this. She already would have eaten if this were a normal night.

At almost nine, the phone rings again. This time a woman asks for Teddy. She adds that she must speak to him, it is urgent. She doesn't ask Zaima her name or question why she is there. The woman starts sobbing, the breathy, choking kind. In the course of her life Zaima has heard so many women crying that it doesn't elicit a reaction. She asks if she can take a message. "I'll call back," the woman replies and hangs up.

Zaima returns to the porch and the morose magenta sky. She had thought there was an abundance of safety here, that all changes would be incremental. That death was behind her for a while. *Was that woman his mother?* Why wouldn't she say so. And if the victim of the unnamed accident was Nate, why was the call coming from the Chicago police?

All this transports her back to Iraq. There's the familiar numbness that had allowed her to separate herself from her life there. If you shut down your emotions, your reactions to what was right in

front of you, you had a better chance of getting through it. Feeling
was not a luxury, it was an impediment. She doesn't see Theodore
approaching until he's almost at the porch's first step, where he
stops, surprised to see her there. He smiles. It's the drunken grin of
someone who has been in the orchards all day, breathing in unison
with the leaves and the wind. She hates to break this spell. He may
be thinking there has been a thaw in their relationship, that she may
invite him to sit with her and have dinner. *Would he even want that?*
She just stands there, spackle in her hair and sawdust on her boots.
She could throw her arms around him. Instead she shakes her head,
sits, and pats the spot next to her on the top step. Theodore takes
his seat. They have not been this close physically since he had a rifle
nesting on her cheek. Zaima hands him the scrap of paper with the
officer's name and number and the message, *a woman called asking
for you and will call back.*

Without a single word she has just placed the burden on his
shoulders. He has words in his open mouth that can't escape, so
he hurries inside. Zaima heads directly toward the barn. Hopefully
he will shut off the oven. The hysterical woman will or will not
call back.

Whatever this is, it is too much. She lies on the bed that Theodore had rebuilt for her after the shower incident. It is longer,
wider, with a real twin mattress, probably his. Actual sheets and
a nice feather pillow. More food is packed into her crates, and
recently, she discovered a better, bigger rug on the floor. He is like
a stranger on a bus, offering her a seat. He is randomly kind. Why
she mistrusts him, she's not sure.

Zaima curls her body protectively around her belly. This is the
first time she's felt connected to this child growing inside her daily.
It's not an entirely good feeling, just different than her usual apathy.
It's all exhausting and she falls asleep quickly. She will not know
when he left. It could have been within minutes or hours, but by
sunrise, man and truck are gone and Mac is on the front porch

waiting. She runs into the house to find the oven off and the chicken still inside. She rips off chunks of breast meat and drops them into Mac's bowl. He's not interested, so they both return to the porch and stare at the road.

It is well into the afternoon and there is still no news as to what has happened, so she heads over to John and Cooper's place.

COOPER BOYD

SOON AFTER

He sits on the edge of his chair, leaning forward with elbows on knees and chin in his hands. His low back feels like he's been smacked by a baseball bat, what with all that pruning he'd done yesterday. Tomorrow will be easier, he thinks, just selectively spraying the Phosmet.

Through the open kitchen door, he watches John and that girl he's so fond of. They're scrolling through John's contact list on his phone. They've already tried Isabelle's numbers and there were no pickups. Cooper believes that if this was all about Nate over there, it could have been Isabelle's hysterical voice on the phone trying to reach Teddy, but why was a cop calling too? He knows this is about Isabelle. It's just a question of how bad this accident was.

John has no one else to call so out comes his laptop. The Internet takes its own sweet time coming up so the two of them stare at the computer to speed it along. The girl, being of that generation, slides the laptop over in front of her and controls the keyboard as they search for the Chicago precinct in Isabelle's fancy neighborhood. Soon they have that and a phone number too. John dials and gets passed around a few times before someone knows who called Empire and why. First, the cop wants to know John's relationship to Isabelle Dash. He lies without thinking, her uncle.

John's face lengthens. He listens, shakes his head slowly and rhythmically. After a few minutes, he writes down a name and a number, then thanks the officer.

"It's Isabelle," John says, looking through the doorway at Cooper.

"Figured as much. How bad?"

"She was killed right in front of her building," John says, wiping away tears. "Accidentally pushed in front of a car. Some guy chasing his dog tripped and knocked her into the street. She's gone, Coop. He said both sons have been notified. I guess that's where Teddy went, you know, to see the body."

"Shit," Cooper says. "Following Nathaniel into the great abyss. Who could have predicted this?"

John wants to hold him, comfort him, but knows better.

"I'm going out for a smoke. And don't give me a hard time, John. It's just one thing out of a million that can kill you." He grabs his cigarettes from the pocket of his old denim jacket that always hangs by the back door.

"You want company?" John asks.

Cooper waves him off. "Probably not even a funeral to go to. Bet not even a memorial service. Selfish way to leave, I think. Not caring how everybody deals with it." He slams the back door on his way out.

"He doesn't mean that," John tells Zaima. "That's how he deals with loss. He gets pissed off."

Cooper *is* angry. He pulls hard on the cigarette. He doesn't believe in God, but if he is out there, there's blood on his white robe for letting this happen. "Isabelle, Isabelle, Isabelle," he mutters, trying to understand. She was a good, smart girl and he did love her. Top of her class and so popular. He didn't fault her for leaving Empire either. She was a free spirit and she did good for herself. Seemed like Nathaniel always looked at what she wasn't. What she wasn't was like *him*. He and Nathaniel had fought over this very thing more than once and they hardly ever fought. When Cooper would see her pulling up in a fine car, dressed the way she was, he knew she was something special, her own person, not to be defined by any man. If she'd been a man and lived her life exactly the same way, people would have praised her strength and independence.

Stupid way to die. He throws down the cigarette and grinds it into the dirt. He was just getting somewhere with Teddy. This is going to throw him into a tailspin. No getting around it.

IN THEODORE'S HEAD

MUCH EARLIER THAT SAME DAY • EN ROUTE TO CHICAGO

Pieces of me are disappearing. Now it's just Nate and me. Both of us orphaned. Never knew any father and now no mother. Abandoned. Again. How can this even be happening? Isabelle Dash. Indestructible. Even breast cancer couldn't keep its hands on her. We all bet on her. That was ten years ago.

How can she not be living and breathing, being the force of nature she was? Isabelle Dash. A personality like a tsunami, consuming smaller, weaker personalities in her path. This woman can't just die in a street. You can't take her out that easily. The car should have been totaled and she should have walked away. Laughing. I can't think of her defeated like that, bleeding out like a normal human being.

I love her. Why was that always so hard to say? Did I worry she wouldn't say it back? Worry she really didn't mean it if she did? It feels dangerous to live in a world without her. Like anything could happen. Nowhere is safe.

I'm afraid to see her body. Really afraid that she'll pull the life out of me. I'll touch her cold hand and I'll be cold because I am alone now. There are no grandparents for me. No mother. Maybe the son of a bitch masquerading as my father will be at the morgue. Beat me to identifying the body. Maybe that pale dead body of hers will be enough to kill him. I bet he's older than she is, maybe has a bad heart. But how would I know it's him?

I don't even know his name or what he looks like. Is he the selfish asshole Granddad said he was? Is he even still alive? Who cares? Not me.

I'll cry like a baby. I'll be blind with tears. They'll pull me out of the room, pity me. Or worse, I won't cry. I'll feel so much it will feel like nothing.

I've loved so few in my life. I'm really not good at it, but I've loved no one more than her. Not that she understood me. I wouldn't let her. I knew I wouldn't be enough. I'm not brilliant like she was. I'm not motivated or successful. I wandered. I wasted her money. I disappeared. Just as well I didn't know my father. More expectations.

She did love me. And Nate. Of course, Nate. He'll be a mess too. He'll cry, but in a manly, battlefront kind of way. A single, massive tear zigzagging down his bristly face. He'll cry only for her, not for himself. Not like me.

Weird, he's the one in constant danger. Roadside bombs. Mortar attacks. She died on fucking perfect East Lake Shore Drive, in front of her beautiful, perfect fortress of a building. Fucking unfair. Fuck. God, I remember Mom and Nate daring me to say that word. C'mon Teddy, say it! We were in our kitchen, as big and shiny as a restaurant's. I was around sixteen. Say it! Say fuck. C'mon, you can do it! I wouldn't and they laughed even harder. Finally she came over and hugged me. My good boy, she said. I wanted to get away from them both as fast as I could.

Fuck, fuck, fuck. Proud of me now, Mom?

She's gone. I won't see her again. Just at the morgue. This is all so unfair. So unnecessary. What's the point, God? You did it just because you can? If I pray and pray and pray, it'll make no difference. We prayed when she was fighting cancer. You just felt like listening then.

I think of all she's accumulated. Truckloads of money, stocks, expensive clothes and furniture, artwork. Busloads of lovers, mostly men but I always suspected that Faye was more than just her buddy. Clients, associates, people who waited on her, relied on her generosity to feed their kids slightly better food. Painters, decorators, plumbers, and electricians. Hairdressers, plastic surgeons. She could, on her own, keep the economy of a small country humming.

What happens to all that now? Let Nate deal with the things. All the lovers can fight with him over it. Keep me out of it. God, I may have been *the last one to talk with her. Why did she call me? I can't remember what her agenda was. Selling the farm, that's it. Why was it taking so long? Should I have told her the truth? Let's see, Mom, I have this pregnant woman that fell from space and landed in your father's barn. I saw her naked in the outdoor shower so that's how I found out about the baby. Mom, she looked so graceful and so lovely and she didn't seem to mind my staring. How about this, Mom? Your dad's best friend is my best friend. And I love the orchards and I swear I can watch the apples plumping up. I feel more at peace with myself there than in any place I've ever been, and sorry, I'm including growing up privileged and prodded, basically a sad little introvert. But there is one thing in my life right now that you would approve of. Brigid Birdsey. You'd be proud of my lascivious dreams about her, how I won't return the sweater she left behind on Easter, even though it was cold when she left and her dress was . . . let's say, not warm. The sweater hangs on my bedroom door, as if she would throw it on after she rose from our bed. All this terrifies me.*

I never mentioned any of that. What did I say to her? Oh yeah, something beyond lame. I am trying to live in the moment, like my life is a self-help book. What crap. Most of the time I'm pretty happy, either working in the orchard or jerking off thinking about Brigid. The rest of the time I'm trying hard not to remember the comforting burn of a needle and all the gorgeous fat emptiness that follows. That little friend will always be tagging behind me, begging me to play with him. In Chicago it would be so easy to find heroin. I know the perfect neighborhood. I could have it within minutes. Money's not an issue anymore. Hey, Granddad, look how I plan to spend your money! Still love me?

I'm not doing that. No. It won't bring her back. It'll eat up my life again. I don't know what I want, but I don't want that. Pray, Theodore. Even if you don't believe it will make a difference. Mouth the words. Pretend.

I will refuse to cry when I see her. I will touch her and tell her how much I love her. I'm going to tell her what's really going on with me. She won't judge me. She'll be proud of me for being so honest.

FAYE

THE NEXT DAY • CHICAGO

Theodore had called his mother's condo from outside the hospital. It was the only number he still had in the entire city. After driving through the night and then seeing Isabelle's cold body, he was lost about what to do next that wasn't self-destructive. He slept in his truck in the parking lot for he didn't know how long. He couldn't stay there and he didn't have the energy to drive back to Empire. The worst of it was that the money in his wallet was looking for another home.

Thankfully, Faye answered the phone and that familiar Texas drawl commanded honesty. No bullshit. He told her he was in trouble. He admitted without cushioning the fact that he was an addict. Heroin. He felt ashamed. He has been clean for two years. He needed somewhere to go, to be with someone who cared for him. The devil was on his tail, that's what he said.

She told him that she was that person and to come over immediately. She would tell Arnoldo to expect him. She warned Theodore that the doorman might attempt to hug him, that he'd been teary and emotional since the accident. It had happened only yesterday. Everyone seemed to be frozen in place, unsure of what to do next.

Faye had slept in Isabelle's bed. She, too, was a wreck, roaming the condo, touching things, smelling clothing. They'd known each other forever. It was impossible to believe. Isabelle would certainly open the door, laughing, at any moment. *Gotcha, Texas!*

But now Teddy is on his way. She showers. Screw makeup. She brushes her teeth with the toothbrush that always hangs next to Isabelle's. *Unfucking believable.*

From a living room window, she stares at the street below until she sees him pull up and park, not even twenty feet from where his mother died. He sits there in the truck for a good fifteen minutes. She knows that Arnoldo has hosed down the street, but she's guessing what is running through Teddy's mind.

Finally he opens his door, climbs out, and looks straight up toward the penthouse. She waves, but of course he can't see her.

Soon he is standing before her in the doorway, looking every bit like the eleven-year-old she had once driven to Empire that June so many years ago. They had talked and laughed and carried on pretty much the whole way, stopping often for pop and pork rinds, comic books, or to scout out anything that interested them. It took the entire day.

Now she sees in him a new vulnerability and innocence. Of course he was prime fodder for the street thugs who got him hooked on dope.

"Baby, get in here," Faye says, her heart breaking. She's a tall woman, broad-shouldered and commanding. "Give your Aunt Faye a good hug. We both need one." Once he's in her arms, she whispers, "You did the right thing coming here. You sensed I was here. You're safe."

She sits him down on the softest and most inviting of the four couches in the living room. She brings him a blanket and a pillow. "Listen, there are a few things I've got to run and do. I'll grab us some food. You are to stay here and sleep some if you can. You're a darling boy, but you look like shit. Teddy, do not leave. Promise me."

He shakes his head yes. "This is really happening, isn't it, Aunt Faye? I talked to her yesterday morning. I didn't know that . . ."

"Who could know, sweetheart?" she says, stroking his hair. "We argued the night before. I stormed out all mad. I was going to call her later, but I didn't. I went out with friends, went back to my place. Thought we'd patch it up in the morning."

"That sucks," he says.

"Oh, it's all right. Listen, Teddy, I'm not going to beat myself up over that silly argument. I wish it hadn't been our last words, but that was just one bad night. I knew your mother for well over twenty-five years. There were a lot of great nights. Whatever went down in those last conversations between you and your mom or me and her, honey, those are just a few bad grains of sand on a beach full of love."

He winces. "It's not that. It's all the things I didn't say."

"I'm not a mother, but I knew yours as well as anybody did. There was nothing your mom needed to know about you that she didn't know. She adored you, Teddy. *Especially* you."

Theodore pulls off his boots and stretches out on the huge couch. Faye covers him with the blanket and kisses his forehead. "You wrap yourself in that thought, baby. I'll be back before you wake up."

———— • ————

Hours later, she has hunted and gathered Isabelle's favorite takeout dinner—southern fried chicken, three-potato salad, Asian coleslaw, and given the occasion, three *(not just one)* bottles of good champagne. She gently wakes Theodore and they sit on his blanket on the floor and consume all of it except for one bottle of champagne. Then Faye gets up and pulls one of the smaller couches directly in front of a huge window so they can sit and watch the traffic snake along the big lake. Both rest their backs against the arms of the couch, facing each other and charting the sun's progress as it shuts down a very long day. They share stories of the past, many about Isabelle's discomfort with domestic life, her lack of interest in culinary or housekeeping activities. Faye tells him that as a parent, however, she was diligent, strict, and demanding, always safeguarding her boys in a city growing increasingly dangerous. The brothers never took public transportation or went out alone at night, even as teenagers. Later Faye turns off all the artificial lighting and sets candles around the room. They drink that last bottle.

Before heading to bed sometime around eleven, Faye sets her glass down ceremoniously and takes Theodore's hand. "I hope you don't mind my sharing this with you. You'll understand why soon enough. I'm sure you know I loved your mother, but she and I were also lovers. Never exclusively, but we had a physical relationship."

She lets that sink in for a moment. He isn't looking at her, but is staring at the lake and the clear night sky. He nods. He gets it. Remembers all those nights Faye never went home, as any visiting male would have. *Was he aware of where she slept? Does he care?*

"If you asked either of us," she continues, "we would have told you we were unthinkingly heterosexual. And we were. I just . . . well, I fell in love with Isabelle, with the person she was. I admired her so greatly. I had no desire, Teddy, to own or control her, or to be her only lover."

"I'm not surprised," Teddy says, head still turned. "Nate and I talked about her being bisexual. It's not something I wanted to think about. And no offense, Aunt Faye, but why do I need to know about it now?"

"Well, you don't, honey. I only mention it because it relates to your father."

"My father?" Now they're eye to eye.

"I'm guessing you'd like to know about him."

"Can we leave this for tomorrow? I can't think straight," he says.

"I'd be happy to, except I probably couldn't get it out if I was sober," Faye says. "Sit back and just listen."

He's too agitated to sit back. "Why didn't my mom tell me about him. Why all the damn secrets?"

"Honey, I could ask you the same thing. Why didn't you tell your mother your secrets? I can guess why. Because it wouldn't have changed anything. You just love a person sometimes and you don't need to know every little thing about her."

"The identity of my father is not a little thing," he says, having trouble with words over three syllables, *identity* here sounding more like *idembity.*

Faye has more experience with conversing while crocked. "Yes, of course, baby. I told your mom you should know about him. She had her reasons for not telling you or Nate. I'm just going to say it. Your father was my husband."

"Holy shit," Theodore says.

"Just listen to me, please. Michael and I got married really young, before either of us had a clue who we were. We were impulsive, obviously, and barely old enough to do it legally. It didn't last. We decided to stay legally married, stayed living together because it was easier financially and we got along so well. We granted each other complete freedom to see anybody we wanted, just not to bring that person home. Worked fine until we were at a party together, some boozy political thing, and we met Isabelle. She was beautiful, sexy, smart, already successful. Michael was, by that time, bisexual, but your mother snagged him good. I let him bring *her* home. And soon enough, I was drawn into their relationship . . . well, maybe that's enough said.

"I never wanted kids, but your mom did. She had everything but a child. She didn't want a husband. She was way too indepen-dent for that, as I'm sure you know. Michael gave her one, Nate. You were—sorry—an accident. A happy one, of course."

"Did my grandparents know all this?"

"God, no. They had grandchildren. That made them ecstatic. But Michael? They thought he was a gigolo, your grandfather's term. He wasn't that at all. A decent guy, sweet. He was not, however, interested in raising kids. He'd come around once in a while. There were expensive presents. He was dating a lot then, all men. One Christmas when you and Nate were both still under five, he told us he had AIDS. Your mom and I got tested multiple times after that. Always HIV negative, thank God. Michael pretty much disappeared after that revelation and died a few years later."

Faye leaves him for a few minutes. He doesn't look stunned, only confused. She blows out most of the candles and returns with a bottle of scotch and two glasses with ice. "There will be hell to pay for this tomorrow. I don't much care, do you?

"Teddy, I'm sure this surprises you. You asked me about your father a number of times growing up. Do you remember that?"

Theodore shakes his head. "I don't. I think I grew to believe he was some random sperm donor."

"Sorry, honey, but Michael kinda was."

He sips his scotch. "Why didn't she ever settle down? With you? With anybody? Why the parade of men?"

"Yep, there were many. Can't say I wasn't ever jealous. She liked variety. She picked interesting men and not always the best-looking ones. That last guy, César? Sure, he looked like a total player. He was actually a social worker, a counselor. He worked with recovering addicts. Your mom fixed him up, dressed him, gave him expensive gifts. That reminds me. There's one other little thing you should know about your mom."

The look on his face makes her pause. It's been a truckload to throw at him, but she's on a roll.

"I'll tell you this because you're going to find out soon enough. Your mother was a successful attorney. She was also not restrained in her spending. She was basically broke. And in debt. There is no inheritance. She borrowed money, as much as she could, against this condo. It will have to be sold. I've read her will. I helped her write it. The contents of this place are all she can give you and your brother."

"Nate can have it all," Theodore says.

"Yes, Teddy, I thought you'd feel that way. Your mom told me about your reaction to Nathaniel's will. She wanted you to go back to school, you know that. I think she was coming around to at least accepting your decision to stay up there."

"I like it there. I wake up with a purpose. How long I'll stay I don't know," he tells her. "I feel needed. I can't remember anyone ever needing me."

"Who needs you? That old horse?"

"No. Yes, Levi does. But . . ."

"A woman? C'mon, spill it to old Aunt Faye."

"Yes, it's a woman, but it's not what you think. She's in trouble and not easy to help.

"Mac and I sometimes go down to the beach to watch the sunset . . . I have my bare feet buried in the warm sand and the sky changes color every second and . . ."

"Who is Mac?" Faye asks.

"He's a great dog. I never had a dog."

Okay, mission accomplished. Faye stands and pulls on his arm ineffectually, trying to get him upright. "All right, nature boy. Help me out here. You okay on the big couch?"

Finally standing, Theodore stumbles over and falls into it. "I'm fine."

"Listen, tomorrow, let's look around the place. There are photos, paintings, clothes, all kinds of stuff you should at least look at. I know I can find at least one photo of your father . . ."

"Please don't call him that," he says, eyes already closed.

"We need to talk about a memorial service," she adds, tucking a blanket around him. "What to do with the ashes. Nate should be arriving soon, from what I hear."

"I'm going home tomorrow. Scatter Mom over the lake here. She hated Empire."

——————— • ———————

Faye removes all her clothes and buries herself in the familiar bed. She's out of tears. All that's left is this vast wasteland of yearning for the person she can no longer touch, no longer vent to about her day, no longer fall asleep with after making love. No more jealousy, no more fights, no more disappointments either. *There . . . an upside.*

She closes her stinging eyes. Already Isabelle's face is harder to conjure. The voice though, that's as clear as if she were lying there right next to her. *Gotcha, Texas!*

In the morning, she'll coax the boy into the shower. She'll get a razor and some Barbasol. She'll cut his hair, because he needs it and she's a hairdresser. It's what she does. She knows that under that hillbilly, northern Michigan thing he's got going on, there's a fine-looking young man, not her son, though certainly family.

THEODORE

THE NEXT DAY • EN ROUTE TO EMPIRE

He has more than three hundred miles to replace the image of his mother, a lifeless body on a metal gurney, with what the rest of his life is going to look like. There are a box of photographs, two small paintings, and a suitcase of clothes from an earlier life next to him on the seat. Theodore's heart isn't broken. It feels enlarged and surprisingly open. If someone were to ask him at this point about the nature of love, he would have no words other than names. Isabelle. Nate. Nathaniel. Marie. That nameless nun in the ruins who saved him. And Faye. She had always been around and now he knows why. His mother was loved. Faye was in love with her. Amazingly, Isabelle loved her back. She was not alone. His father was a real person, not a cardboard villain. He was a free-loving man who was infected with HIV, a condition that now is basically manageable. He wonders about this unsettling, yet intriguing threesome as he drives north on 94 toward Benton Harbor. Were they radicals? Nonconformists? Or just three people who loved each other outside the confines of normal relationships. *And why not?* He is, he realizes, sort of related to Faye. He likes that.

On the familiar slog along the lake he feels relief. His mother had known some happiness. Had sustained a lasting relationship. She was more than her successful career and accumulation of wealth, things, men. Faye has delivered a pretty huge revelation and confirmed that Isabelle Dash had always made her own reality. Yes, she was often the school-yard bully, set on getting her way. Great for a lawyer, but maybe not so much as a parent. But that wasn't all there was to her.

Is there any part of him that feels relieved that she was broke? Does it make her more human, more accessible, even now? Theodore realizes right then, driving his grandfather's reliable old pickup, that the direction he's traveling is toward a life free of the expectations of others, especially her expectations. He also must admit, if he were a stronger man, he could have come to this realization without her death.

When Faye sells the condo, if there is anything left, he wants her to keep it. She is a widow without credentials, only the horrible loss.

He takes with him a new respect for his mother. And he is going home. The priests and brothers at Saint Anthony's had saved his life. Now it's up to Theodore Dash to make something out of it.

BRIGID

The bar is packed. The Cherry Festival in Traverse City, with its cherry-pit spitting contest, outdoor concerts, and air show, has passed. The crowds still linger to enjoy the pies, the beaches, and the potters. All the summer rentals were snatched up months ago. Deering's Market and all of Front Street are packed with sunburned faces, smeared with ice cream and smiles.

Brigid loves the July panic. She'd hauled her propane grill down to the front sidewalk and had poor, reluctant Hemingway hawking hot dogs and sausages from noon until dusk. These weren't free, but they were reasonably priced and of good quality. The condiments alone were worth the price—three types of spicy mustards (including one with jalapeños), local sweet relish, grilled raw onions with caraway seeds, and the special Birdsey touch, kettle-cooked potato chips to be tucked in next to the bun. *And ketchup? Never.*

Brigid offered to pay Hemingway. He declined, preferring to barter for scotch. They agreed on two fingers per hour, to be consumed at a later date. She had to admit, Hemingway had become easier to tolerate as he gradually melded into the local ways. He seemed less pretentious, more relaxed, and the visiting college women found him a handsome distraction. He had even left the bar with one or two of them, making sure Brigid took note of his amorous adventures.

It's now nine and the sun is sitting fat and pretty on the surface of the big lake. Brigid hired a downstate bluegrass band that was still hanging around from the festival. They're set up on one side of the room, and tables have been cleared away so folks can dance if they like. There's a new cocktail on the board in honor of the recent harvest, the Cherry Bomb. It contains a little ice, some cherry juice, plenty of vodka, a splash of cognac, and is served as a frozen mash. Sweet and powerful, it's a big hit. Brigid herself has enjoyed two already.

She's just left the dance floor after a quick jig with Hemingway, who has finished his day's work out front. Brigid's face has a glossy sheen of perspiration and her hair has mostly fallen from its arrangement on the top of her head. She has stripped down to a bright green tank top and shorts and is barefoot, which is not permitted at the Bird's Eye. People are lined up at the bar and she serves up more Cherry Bombs and plenty of draft beer, the local favorites being Right Brain Brown Ale and the tasty June Bug from North Peak.

The place is buzzing with music and laughter when she catches sight of Theodore and freezes. He stands there motionless returning her stare, holding a framed object under one arm.

It's an awkwardly romantic moment. The band finishes a tune and the applause breaks their inertia. Hemingway, uncharacteristically thoughtful, jumps behind the bar to free up Brigid. *C'mon, the man's mother has just died.* "I got this. Just go," he tells Brigid, even though he's never tended bar before.

She moves slowly to this newly orphaned man who is smiling at her. His beard and mustache are gone and have been replaced by an eerie white half-circle of skin beneath his nose. His hair has been cut, and dare she think it, styled. This transformation causes his dark eyebrows to look glued on, but his eyes are what they have always been, lethal for her.

Now she's around the bar and soon standing squarely in front of him. She takes the framed object from him and leans it gently against the wall. His arms are now dangling without purpose so she takes them and wraps them around her waist. Theodore lowers his head and she whispers in his ear, "Who are you and what have you done with Theodore Dash?" Then she gently kisses his mouth. This generates some hoots and clapping from the crowd, but the two ignore this. "I'm so, so sorry, Teddy," she says, holding his face in her hands.

"It's okay. I'm all right," he tells her.

"You can't be, but good show," she says, taking him by the hand and retrieving the framed picture. "Get in here. Let me get you something to eat. Come sit near me behind the bar." There is a stool there and he takes it.

The music is loud and everyone seems to be screaming. "I've been serving drinks as best I can," Hemingway tells them. "I made up prices and the money is next to the cash register, which wouldn't open for me." Then to Theodore, "Sorry about your mom, man. That really sucks big time." Brigid screws up her face. *Okay, he still needs work.*

Theodore doesn't mind his blunt remark. "Yeah, it really does suck. A stupid, random accident."

The hot dogs and sausages are gone, but Brigid always has something in her upstairs fridge. "Hemingway, take the helm one more time, will you? Drafts are three bucks. Tell them that's all we got for a few minutes unless they want a shot of something. Charge four for those." She opens the cash register drawer. "Don't bother ringing anything up."

Upstairs, she has baked ham and yams. She heats up a plate in the microwave and then adds a slice of cherry pie.

When she returns she finds Theodore pouring shots for a young couple at one end of the bar and Hemingway at the other end serving up drafts that are half foam. "Good job, boys," she shouts, putting the plate of food next to Theodore. "I'll take it from here."

"Okay, Birdwoman," Hemingway shouts back. He pulls two more frothy drafts and then joins Theodore.

Time passes much as this, the two drinking, laughing, and shooting eyewinks to the bartender. They are at one point invited to dance by what looks like a mother and daughter, both healthy looking and attractive. The older favors Theodore, the other, the scruffy author. What Hemingway does on the dance floor more resembles a seizure than dancing, while poor Theodore is at a total loss and is soon abandoned by his partner for an older, hipper guy. Brigid scoots over and takes mom's place, her hands resting on his hips. As her shoulders and hips sway, so do his. Folks smile at them like they would at puppies tumbling over one another in play. It's all good fun; and if not for the recent losses in the Dash family, a normal midsummer night at the Bird's Eye.

It's only near closing that Brigid thinks of Zaima. She imagines her sitting on the front porch with Mac, staring down the road. Maybe she's cooked something up for him. Maybe she's rehearsed what she'll say when he walks up to her, broken. Maybe one or both of her parents have died and she understands how it changes you. You have to experience it to know. It doesn't break your heart, it hollows it out. The only saving grace is that you know you loved someone enough to feel that bad. Losing both of her parents so suddenly had turned Brigid into a zombie, all stiff-legged and looking for something, anything to make her feel alive again. People tend to make bad decisions in that state of mind. She sure did.

But then as she wipes down the bar, Brigid realizes that Zaima has something neither she nor Teddy has. Zaima has new life inside her. She will have a child and through her parenting of that child, she'll grow a love big and powerful enough to fill even the emptiest, most bruised heart. Or so Brigid imagines.

Almost everyone has left the Bird's Eye. Hemingway may be a salacious, cornball romantic, but he is also a realist. He leaves with the supposed mother and daughter, each on an arm, and sends an air kiss to Brigid as they pass. "I want graphic details," he says, and Brigid smiles. "I don't," she tells him.

When only the two of them are left in a room that is now ear-piercingly quiet, Theodore retrieves the framed artwork. He holds it in front of him like a waiter revealing an ostentatious wine list. "It's a watercolor of Lake Michigan, looking north from Oak Beach near our home in Chicago. It was my mom's. The lake connected us. It's for you."

"Beautiful, Teddy. The painting and your words."

"I want to stay with you tonight."

"Shit," she says, then covers her mouth. "Nice romantic reply, right? Sorry. It's just that my place is a mess. I'm a mess."

"Maybe a mess is just what I want. And look at me, Birdie. I'm a farmer in T-shirt, jeans, and work boots. I have a two-tone face and someone else's hair."

"Yeah, what's up with that? Is that product in there?"

"Faye gave me a makeover before I left. You don't know her, but you will. She was my mom's best friend. No, that is not the truth. She was my mom's long-time lover. Her husband . . ."

"Wow, go Isabelle!" Brigid interrupts. "Who would've thought? What about her husband?"

"We're getting off track. We were talking about us."

"I'm really nervous, Teddy. We've got a lot on the line here."

"I'm nervous too."

"What if this changes us?" she asks.

"We need changing. I'm tired of our teenage romance."

"And the seminary?"

"Not an issue," he says.

"Just like that?"

"No, it took awhile for me to know that," he says. "I've found something else just as meaningful."

"And Zaima?" That was not easy for her to get out.

"I stopped home first. She's okay."

She locks the door and they climb together up the back steps. As soon as she closes the apartment door behind them, Theodore pulls her to him and kisses her. It's a good, honest second kiss. *Does he care that she's been with so many other men?* She feels like a prostitute with a teenage boy.

"Tell me, Teddy dear, that I am not your first," she ventures.

"You are not my first."

"How about a nice shower?" she asks, already leading him down the hall. In the bathroom, she lights a candle and turns off the harsh overhead light. The shower is a simple, tiled square, not a bathtub. They undress quickly and she adjusts the water's temperature. Brigid leads him in, placing him in front of her, letting the water fall over his upturned face. She presses her body against his and wraps her arms around him. This all would be easier if this was just another man, not Teddy. Just a body, a body in pain, needing healing. But he is the mythical boy she shared her past with, kissed first, has always longed for. *Too much thinking, Brigid, just be here with him.*

She begins to wash Theodore's body, his back, his buttocks. On her knees, she lathers his legs. Rising again she turns him, presses her body into his, allows him to lift her, come inside her while she holds on to him. Why they don't fall in a heap on the shower floor is a tribute to his strength, but not his stamina. It is quickly over.

It wasn't the best sex she's ever enjoyed, due partly to the limited space and shower spray in her face. It does, however, take an emotional toll on them both. They crawl naked into her bed. The night has turned more humid and the temperature has dropped only slightly from the peak heat of the day. She becomes all the cover he needs, lying next to him, holding him, rocking him to sleep.

Sometime before dawn, they make love again; this time more intentionally, more intensely. Then he tells her about the man who was his father, about his freakish twenty minutes at the morgue with his mother's body, how she did and didn't look like herself, how her hair was brushed back so drastically and her coloring gone. Theodore tells her about Faye, how kind she was to him when she had to be feeling equally bad, how she patiently answered questions again in the morning that he had probably asked the night before.

The last thing he shares concerns Nate. He should have stayed until his brother got into town. Something in him did not want to see his brother or come anywhere near his pain. He didn't want to know if Nate knew about Michael, if there had been a pact between his mother and Nate to keep it from him. If there was this little secret between them, and there were probably others, let them die with her.

As he stares out the open window near the bed, Brigid gets up and brings back glasses of cold water. Then she pulls a thin sheet over them both and kisses him one more time. She knows she is not falling in love with Theodore Dash. She has loved him most of her life. She has always enjoyed the nervous energy she feels around him, whether she'd seen him yesterday or two years ago. "I love you, Teddy," she whispers, more to herself than to him. "I pray we haven't screwed things up."

ZAIMA

She is naked in front of the full-length mirror that is screwed into the inside of Theodore's closet door. A single table lamp illuminates her changed body. The body she sees does not delight or disgust her. It might as well be someone else's.

She's been trained in this tactic, strengthening mind over body. Weeks of sleep deprivation, persistent humiliation, and extreme fatigue made her more machine than woman. Every demand on her body made her mind even stronger, impervious to pain or defeat in any form. So now the back pain, the crippling leg cramps, the heartburn, and the constipation are merely annoyances, nothing pronounced enough to keep her from doing what she needs to do.

She examines the woman in the mirror. How does she differ from the soldier she once was? Now she has courser, wavier hair. Her eyes look disproportionately large and the skin around them is puffy. The center line of the nose sports a jagged cut that has mysteriously appeared. Teeth still good, but the lips are chapped and peeling. Shoulders are unnaturally slung back to compensate for the changing center of gravity. Skin on the breasts is taut like the skin on an overripe tomato. Nipples are the color of wet hard sand. The midsection is distended and elongated, as if a wild creature has

233

crawled inside, which is quite accurate. Hips appear to be missing. The legs look fine except for some extra thigh meat. Ankles slightly swollen and feet are feet.

The morning sickness is long over and she feels healthy. It is tiring at times, lugging around the extra weight. It's nothing compared to sixty or more pounds of gear.

John counts the months, she does not. He asks so many questions, she's starting to dread his appearance. He tells her he has a friend at the firehouse with a free crib. That's nice, but the baby will sleep with her. A woodstove would be more valuable to her. She wonders why people make it all so complicated. Would a homeless and pregnant Iraqi woman be worried about these silly minor details?

Zaima turns away from the mirror and dresses. She has no underwear that fits so she wears none. She puts on a shirt and pair of pants that Brigid gave her. John has offered clothing, too, many made for obese women in patterns better suited for tablecloths. He has apologized for not supplying intimate articles like bras and panties, but will gladly take her shopping. She hates that word, *panties.* The military would never use it and neither should he.

When she was at the library last week tracking down a Farmall manual, she looked through a couple of books on childbirth. It seemed like a pretty straightforward affair, just pain and gravity. Her body's been through worse.

Theodore said he won't be back tonight. With no explanation. He had a gift for her though. He had brought it back from his boyhood bedroom in Chicago. He held it out to her, a framed illustration from a 1928 first edition of *The House at Pooh Corner.* Christopher Robin, Piglet, and Winnie-the-Pooh (with a honey pot stuck on his head) are all sitting on the floor together confabulating. Theodore told her it was for the baby's room, like that was a defined place. Then he left, without Mac or any supper. Zaima hung the illustration above her bed; *that* was the baby's room.

What he didn't know was that there were more books in her family's home than just the Qur'an. Her mother read chapters about that lovable bear's escapades to her and her sister not at bedtime, but on Saturday mornings when more fortunate children were allowed to watch cartoons—hours of them—on television. Her parents distrusted television and its constant, annoying commercials. Pooh Bear had better, more Muslim-like values, preferring nature, friendship, and traditional foods.

Theodore said nothing about his mother, about his trip, his state of mind. He looked so different without his beard and shaggy hair. In her religion, beards serve as protection and are also a symbol of piety. *Trim closely the mustache and let the beard flow.* Though Theodore does not follow the prophet Muhammad, the last thing he needs is increased vulnerability.

Now hours have passed with only insects and domesticated animals to distract her from the creeping loneliness. She's sitting at the kitchen table picking at cheese and olives when she hears someone pull up out front. She finds John hobbling up the steps as she opens the screen door.

"Teddy's not back yet? I got this god-awful fruit basket from the church ladies. Does anyone actually eat kiwis?"

"I'll help you," Zaima says when she notices the disassembled gift in his back seat. "What happened to it?"

"Oh, some deer crossed right in front of me. Had to swerve."

There are melons, apples, peaches, and cherries scattered on the seat and floor. "The ladies claim it's all homegrown, but these melons must be from down south," John says, as they gather it all up in the basket. "So where is our boy?"

"He's back, but not here. Should be home in the morning."

"Well, where the hell did he go overnight?" he asks. "He's not with us."

"Not my business," Zaima says. "I could guess."

"Yah, I can too. You shouldn't be staying here all by yourself. How about a little TV and a good night's sleep on a real bed?"

"I'm all right here," she says. "What's going to happen to me out here?"

"Suit yourself, honey. Tell Teddy I came by. Poor kid."

——————— • ———————

The sun has long been up when Christopher Robin appears. That's how the former fuzzy Pooh Bear looks to Zaima in the light of day with his beardless face and messy, little boy haircut. She also thinks his spry steps and silly smile are not congruous with what has just happened in Chicago.

They walk together to the kitchen. It's neutral ground. She starts. "I didn't say this before. I should have. I'm sorry you lost your mother. If you want to talk . . ."

"Thank you, no. I just need some time." He lowers himself into a chair at the table. "It's been a surreal couple of days. It's good to be home."

She sits across from him, and assesses the changes. Not only are they conversing in a stiff, somewhat normal way, but this is now officially home. "We need to talk," she announces.

In the history of time, it's likely that no man has ever heard those words escape a woman's lips without an instant jolt of dread. She knows that. When her mother dropped those unnerving four words on her father, he always looked like a man on his way to a vasectomy. Theodore is certainly no different.

"Is it about last night?" he asks, squirming in his seat.

She is not enjoying this, but asks anyway. "Were you with Brigid?"

"What if I was?"

Why so defensive? "If you were . . . if you are again, could she just come here? You could get a bigger bed. I just don't like being here alone." Her belly reaches the tabletop and her hands are tucked beneath. She despises the weakness in her voice, in her words. Is it the pregnancy? *Does that strip away your independence? Your self-reliance?*

His shoulders relax and he says softly to her, "Of course. I wasn't thinking. I left you here on your own for three nights to take care of everything. I'm sure Cooper would have . . ."

"It's not the work. And John did invite me over. I wanted to be here, just not alone at night."

"Of course. No problem. I like knowing you're here too. If that does happen again . . ."

"You should get a decent bed anyway," she interrupts. "You gave me *your* mattress. You know, there's a nice iron bed in the back of the barn behind the apple bins. A little sanding, some paint, a nice mattress."

"You're right. I'm sticking around. The place should reflect that. And you need to think about leaving the barn."

Is he kicking me out or inviting me in? "I'm not sure what I'm doing," she says. "I plan tomorrow and that's as far as I go."

"What about our little visitor?"

Does he mean the little visitor inside her body? "It'll work out," she says.

"A little planning might be a good idea. Is there someone . . . we never talk so I haven't asked . . . but the father of this baby, is he going to just show up at some point?"

Shit, she hopes not. "Doubtful," is all she says.

"How pregnant are you?"

"Ask John."

"You must know."

"Around seven months."

"Have you seen a doctor?" he asks.

"John's been keeping an eye on me. I want to have the baby here. I hate hospitals."

"Then we need a midwife."

"That's John," she says. "He's done it before."

Theodore stands and looks out the kitchen window. "Pretty unconventional," he says. "Shall we also place a manger in the barn?"

"John has a crib. Brigid gave me a bag of paraphernalia. You know, for the baby."

"Pick a room," he says, turning to face her.

"What?"

"Pick a room. It can be the living room for all I care. Next month, you will move into this house. There will be new life in this house and I'm not going to just wing it!"

Zaima stands and walks toward him. Before she has a chance to speak, he places his palm on her abdomen. Then he stoops and whispers to the child within, "Pick a room."

"The pantry," Zaima says.

"Seriously?"

"It's the perfect size and near the kitchen and the bathroom. If we take out some of the shelves, there's room for my bed, the crib, a small dresser. And I'd like a desk under the window."

"All right. We have to get on this soon. Looks like we'll start picking next week. Hector is bringing in his crew."

"I can pick," Zaima says.

"Oh, you will be. Everybody will be picking, even Mac if I can figure out a way. No lifting for you though."

"You don't have to coddle me," she says.

He ignores that comment. "Nice work with the walls and trim."

"I need paint, brushes. What's in the barn is no good. I need parts for the tractor too."

"There isn't a business around here where my grandfather doesn't have an account. Just tell them to send a bill. Can you drive my truck?"

"Of course."

"Take it when you need it."

ZAIMA

Just past dawn, the tree swallows' rhythmic squeaking is broken by the sound of the Farmall tractor as she maneuvers it full throttle from the barn. The engine's loud, irregular ticking indicates that the patient is not well. A dirty gray cloud is choked out of the manifold and then exhaled from the vertical muffler.

She shuts off the engine. First, she drains the oil, and then removes and cracks open the carburetor. It needs a good cleaning. She'll have breakfast and then borrow the truck.

At Phil's Tractor Supply in Burdickville, she procures oil, an oil filter, coolant, spark plugs, a distributor cap, and five gallons of fuel. She opts for the carb kit, too, as it's just twenty-eight bucks. Phil recognizes Nathaniel's old truck and after a little questioning, decides to throw in a cup of bad coffee, plenty of free advice, and the loan of a compression gauge.

By early afternoon, the patient's status has improved and the doctor is grateful to feel more her former, self-reliant self. She has military training and her finicky father to thank as well.

JOHN QUIMBY

A COUPLE OF DAYS LATER

Everyone in Empire seems to know about the pregnant woman who fell from the sky to come and live among them. Like a loose beach ball blown down M-22, she still jogs regularly, and uses her library card often. She hauls ass in Teddy's truck, although a day will come soon when she no longer fits behind the wheel. She has favorite haunts, like the rectory, the lumberyard, the beach, and the tractor supply store. She's set up a table right on the highway and sells vegetables she's grown at Teddy's place. No one would say she is particularly friendly, but she is always polite, if reserved. Brigid likes her and that means a lot around here.

That's all well and good, to John's thinking. There is, however, the elephant in the womb. He knows she trusts he'll get it out and that thought terrifies him. Sure, if everything goes smoothly, it's not that complicated. But what if it doesn't? It's not like the hospital is right here in town, it's a good hike to Traverse. So as stubborn as she is about going all natural and doing it right there at Teddy's, he's putting his foot down. There will be a qualified midwife there, and when she shows up it won't be the first time they'll have met.

Finding one is the easy part. There are three listed in the Yellow Pages and one is a woman he knows, Grace Aylsworth, the science teacher at the high school. Of course, it is not uncommon for locals to have more than one gig, if for no other reason than to pay the escalating property taxes. He calls and leaves a message.

The following Saturday, John and the midwife arrive at the farm and spend a good ten minutes hunting down Zaima. She is pulling a cart full of vegetables from the garden to the barn with the Farmall.

"You get off that thing immediately," Grace hollers to Zaima. "And keep off it. You are one major rut away from some serious complications."

Zaima climbs down and approaches them, her hand outstretched to John. "Is she military too?" she asks him.

"This is Grace Aylsworth. She's a certified midwife. How many babies have you escorted into this world, Grace?"

"I have no idea. Dozens, for sure," she answers.

"John, I thought you were going to handle this. Why do we need her?" Zaima asks.

"Oh, I'm in. Grace here is my little insurance policy. She can do things I can't," he tells her.

"John's right. What's your name?"

"Zaima," she says coldly.

"Zaima, I should check you out now and let's hope everything will go smoothly. I will monitor both you and the baby during labor. I'll have a few things with me that we may or may not need. I will work with you, not against you. So drop the attitude."

"I don't want any drugs," Zaima says.

"Yes, that is what you are saying now," Grace says dismissively. "And you should know that I am a stand-up-and-deliver proponent. I will encourage you to move around. You will need someone to support you, physically and emotionally."

"What is the cost?" Zaima asks.

"All business. I like that. I work on a sliding scale. John and I have worked it out. All you have to do is follow my instructions. Believe me, you don't want a wimpy midwife."

Zaima asks to speak privately with John, and Grace agrees. "I'd like to talk to Theodore. Where is he?" the midwife asks as she leaves them. "Don't worry, not about you. We're old buddies . . . from high school."

John asks Zaima why she is so resistant to Grace's help. She doesn't answer, so he explains that he will be there to make sure it all goes the way Zaima wants. Should he ask Brigid to be there as well?

"She practically lives here now, but I only see her nights," Zaima says. "So if it's during the day, yes, I'd like her with me. And John, no drugs. Promise me. I've been through way worse than this."

"No drugs. Now, please let her examine you, okay? It'll make me feel better."

"All right. But I'm still riding that tractor."

"We won't tell her," he says with a wink.

BRIGID

AS TIME PASSES

Most every night he shows up at her bar after dinner and brings her back to the farmhouse once she closes up. She rarely bumps into Zaima there but it is never strained when she does. They speak only of small, comfortable things, such as weather or plans for the day. A few nights, Zaima even cooked for them all. It's a contented web of interdependence that allows individual privacy while they wait out the harvest and the birth of Zaima's baby.

Brigid and Theodore become as they were as kids, exploring again, but now with their bodies the limitless mechanics of pleasure. They make love often, sometimes on a lunch break upstairs at Brigid's, once in the orchard, but mostly in the fine iron bed that Zaima has restored for them. That magnificent bed, the color of dusk, is topped with an expensive mattress, a gift from his grandfather's estate. The bed, a shared dresser, two bedside tables, and Isabelle's watercolor of the big lake are the only items in the freshly painted yellow room. The closet has equal parts his and her clothing, and also the heavy brown robe he wore into town last February. One night, she had begged him to wear it one more time so that she might seduce him out of it and into their bed. He obliged and fittingly, God's name was invoked many times that night.

This new toy, this intimacy, has dissolved other barriers as well. Late into the night, they have shared the sometimes ugly or difficult details of their pasts. She has told him about her abortion, about the shallowness of her previous relationships with men, how she used them, discarded them. She has talked about the crushing loss of her parents, how sudden and complete it was, how it felt like entering a different world where everything was unfamiliar; how she understood his loss and its many reverberations.

Theodore admitted his past addiction and how utterly lost he was at the time. He shared his academic failures, his emotional distance from his brother, and he hated saying this, but from his mother as well. He felt that their last conversation was emblematic of their relationship, her desire to mold him into someone he was not interested in becoming. Her disappointment in him was lovingly conveyed, but always there. Theodore then solemnly told Brigid that he was all that she could see. Nothing more. There were no hidden layers. He proclaimed himself to be only a simple man with simple needs. She had a simple response. "That, my love, is exactly what I'm looking for. I never wanted more than just you."

As the weeks passed, they also talked about their expectations of each other. He mentioned marriage. She thought it way too soon.

There was, however, one thing Brigid chose not to share, and with good reason. She had grown tired of the clutter in her living space. The Bird's Eye was always clean and well organized, while her apartment above was a chaotic mess. What time she spent there now, cooking or napping, she wanted to be soothing and pleasant. She washed windows that had never been washed. She scrubbed floors and went through closets. She purged and reorganized.

The bedroom closet came under attack and clothes to be donated were piled high on the floor. Then came the upper shelf, crammed with relics of her past—photographs, birthday cards, her senior year high school yearbook. She tossed some of the cards and tucked the rest of it into a single small box. Then there was the shoebox of her mother's personal things, which she dusted and returned to the shelf unopened. She still wasn't ready to go there.

The final item was the envelope of Nathaniel's love letters from Marie. Theodore had asked her to either cherish or destroy them, he didn't care which. Now she herself was lost in love's euphoric stupor, a state which prompted her to seek solace in the words of another woman similarly stricken. She would read just the one on top and then destroy them all.

> *Dearest Nathaniel,*
>
> *It was such a joy spending time with you the other day. We get so little time together. Often it's just the back of your head I see at church or your truck as it races out of town. So when your hands, as rough and work-weary as they are, are upon my face or stroking the nape of my neck, well . . .*
>
> *I shall not go on. Suffice it to say that these thoughts of you keep me going. Even the simplest task becomes quite the labor of love.*
> *M*

How lovely. But why would Marie be looking at the back of his head at church? When was this written? Before they were married? Brigid supposed that being a farmer would keep a man out of the house for long stretches of the day. Still there is something else there, a yearning for something unattainable. Brigid grew uncomfortable. She examined the flowing, flawless script with all its embellishments, the happy little curlicues on the *y*s and *g*s. The paper was a pale blue and scented. This was not a scrawled note. It was like a line drawing, perfectly positioned on the page. And the signature, the *M*, why not *Marie?*

And then she knew. It was not from Marie. She dumped the trash bag she'd been filling and found a birthday card, her sixteenth birthday. And there it was in the same fanciful script, *Happy Birthday, Dear. Love, Mom and Dad.* Mom being Maureen. *M.*

She thought of Nathaniel after the accident, how deeply he mourned with her. It wasn't empathy. He was grieving the loss of whatever her mother had been to him. *And what was that?* Was it a harmless infatuation or a full-blown, motel-at-midday affair? She can't imagine her mother doing that, sneaking off to thump Marie's husband, then scurrying off to her church group or grocery shopping or poring over her daughter's homework while cooking yet another bland meal.

She went down to the bar and made a small fire in the woodstove. She burned every one of Nathaniel's letters and every piece of correspondence from her mother's shoebox. She saved the photographs, the inexpensive jewelry, and her mother's birth and baptismal certificates. Also saved from destruction was a small, framed photograph of her parents on their wedding day. The couple was running down the wide front steps of the house in Monroeville, Ohio, where they lived with her grandparents in the early days of their marriage and where Brigid spent the first two years of her life *(thank God not in Empire, which would beget another horrible question).* In the photograph her mother wore a pretty hat with a half veil over her green eyes, and a toothy grin. She was thin and lovely in a dark suit and pumps. Her father was a step behind her, smiling shyly as he so often did, staring at the beautiful Irish girl he could call his own.

Did they love each other, she wonders as she feeds the last of the letters into the fire? Her parents were not demonstrative people. The affection they showed was mechanical, the peck on the cheek as one left the house, the predictable gifts. What happened behind the bedroom door could have been completely different, but she doubts it.

Brigid thinks then of Theodore. She yearns to talk to him about this supposed betrayal. Then she knows she can't. Why diminish the mythical hero Nathaniel must be to him? And based on what? One letter? Her overactive imagination?

Her silence on this would be her gift to them all.

BRIGID

She's tackled many things in her life, but never before has been asked to tear apart a pantry and repurpose it as a bedroom and nursery. Zaima had pulled up in the truck and knocked on her upstairs door, asking for help in this project. Since housecleaning was what Brigid was busy avoiding at the time, she accepted the challenge.

While Zaima waits for her now on the deck, Brigid scans her wardrobe for the appropriate clothing. She digs out some baggy jeans that she pairs with a tight, lime-green T-shirt (for Teddy's benefit, should he be on the crew). She has some sturdy hiking boots that were left in the corner of the bar after a night of live music.

"Do I need tools?" she asks Zaima. "I have a hammer and a good crowbar that might come in handy."

"Bring them," Zaima says.

"Girl, you are as big as a barn," Brigid observes, standing back to take her all in. "How are you feeling?"

"I have issues, but they won't kill me."

"What a trouper," Brigid says. "Hey, let me grab some beer and a radio. This kind of work calls for suds and cornball country music."

"I like country music. It seems honest to me."

"Can't stand it myself," Brigid admits. "Too much whining."

Theodore's truck has been loaded up with some lumber, and cans of primer and paint. Brigid throws the cooler and her supplies back there and climbs in.

"This is one cool truck," Brigid says as Zaima squeezes behind the steering wheel. "I think Teddy looks so sexy tearing down the road in it."

"You'd think he looked sexy if he was driving a school bus," Zaima says, pulling onto M-22.

"Especially driving a school bus," Brigid says. "What's hotter than that?"

When they get to the farmhouse, they finish clearing out what remains of the food and cooking gear still in the pantry. Then they rip out all of the shelving except for one upper section in the middle of the south wall, which will be Zaima's bookshelf.

Once Brigid has piled all of the debris in the front yard, they stand back and admire what now looks like a decent-sized room. Through the open double-hung window in the east wall, they can see Zaima's vegetable garden and the barn beyond. There are also two threesomes of square windows in the upper part of the walls, north and south. They repair all the trim on these windows and around the door, as well as the badly damaged walls. Sanding and priming are left for after lunch, which John has prepared and delivered. He's brought hardy sandwiches, thick with meats and cheeses, and a large bag of Lay's potato chips. It's a cold beer for Brigid and John, and for Zaima, Vernors, known locally as the champagne of ginger ales. Then John has other things to do and leaves the women to their work.

The early afternoon brings coats of a fast-drying primer, a butter-yellow paint for the trim, and the lavender blue of catmint for the walls. Between coats, the warm pine floor is washed by Brigid with the Murphy Oil Soap she found beneath the kitchen sink. It is what her own mother always used, and its unique, tea-like scent is more endearing and evocative than her mother's perfume.

"Did your mom use this stuff?" she asks Zaima as she works it into the old flooring.

"We were a carpet and linoleum family, so no. I do use it on Levi's tack."

"What's your mom like?" Brigid asks innocently.

Zaima is at the kitchen sink, washing the putty knives. She does not want to answer this question because there is no short answer. Her mother is as complicated as her mother's country is. She is of two worlds, here and back there. She is of two separate times, now and back then. She lives in her adopted country and still longs for her beloved homeland. She favors sometimes the new ways and sometimes the old. She is enamored with the things of this world, the easy comforts, but also the traditions. She loves the prepared foods and also those that take most of the day to make. She is deeply religious, but not showy in it. Everything is always black and white for her. She distrusts the gray, amorphous areas. It is yes or no. Stay or go. Good or bad. Her mother could never understand someone like her own daughter, someone confined to the gray areas. Someone who can no longer make decisions. Someone who coasts.

"She is a wonderful cook," Zaima tells Brigid's backside.

"And?"

"And I love her very much."

"She doesn't know about the baby, does she?" Brigid asks, standing now in the doorway.

"No."

"Will you tell her after the birth?" Brigid asks.

"Why would I?"

Brigid can't answer that. "You edge and I'll roller," she says. "I think your family should know."

"I think it's not my family's business," Zaima says, picking up a paintbrush. "We all prefer it this way."

At around four in the afternoon, the room is finished and Theodore arrives in Cooper's truck. Cooper hauls in an old cherry rocker taken from his own living room.

"This is from John," he barks to Zaima, "and I wouldn't mind having it back when you're done with it."

She is growing to respect his dislike for her, the way he doesn't attempt to mask it. "Of course," Zaima answers. "I won't need it for long."

Also hauled from the bed of the truck is a three-drawer, white dresser and a simple pine table and chair. There's a swiveling wall light, and from the extra bedroom upstairs, Theodore's childhood twin bed. Brigid and Cooper bring in the mattress from her room in the barn. The Pooh Bear illustration is hung by Theodore with great care above the space in the corner where the crib will be. They all stare and smile at the empty spot as though it were an omen of future happiness. Except Zaima. She has her back turned to them as she makes up her bed.

"Wow," Theodore says when everything is in place. "Makes the rest of the house look a little shabby." He slips an arm around Brigid's waist and pulls her close. "Nice job, Birdie."

A light bulb is starting to flicker in Cooper's head. Maybe it wasn't the sweetness of summer or all the time and schooling Cooper has so willingly shared with the boy that has kept him from leaving. And to Cooper, this is as it should be. Brigid will make a good wife, will balance his seriousness. *But this Zaima, where does she fit into all of this?*

"I've got to get back to my poor, neglected bar," Brigid announces, and she quickly kisses both Theodore and Zaima on the cheek. "Maybe this old grizzly bear will give me a ride back," she adds, pointing at Cooper. "And I've got cold chicken and potato salad if anybody's interested."

And everyone does meet there later, except Zaima. She hangs back, cloistered in her new room, stacking her things on the shelves, burying the baby clothes in the dresser. She stares out at the barn until it disappears into the night. She tries to write but little can penetrate the fog she inhabits.

ZAIMA

INTO THE NIGHT

I am a farmer's rusting pail
I am a torn paper shopping bag
I am an empty suitcase
I am the trunk of a car
I am a duffel bag
I am a churning stomach
I am my mother's purse
I am my father's wallet
I am the apple picker's bag
I am the church's collection box
I am the box for the bullets
I am a hijacker's jet
I am a hand cupped for water

I am a means of conveyance

ISABELLE MARIE DASH • POSTMORTEM

EARLY SEPTEMBER • EMPIRE BEACH

In the late-afternoon sun, the sand looks like the pocked surface of the moon, a blazing gold. I see the creamy fat crests of small waves roll onto the shoreline and my big great lake is a surreal greenish blue, making the water resemble a flawless golf course. I loved to golf, by the way, and was very good at it, often scoring lower than my male companions.

The Birdsey girl is singing in a lovely, spirited, but off-key way the predictable "Amazing Grace." I like how Theodore is watching her with a little tenderness, a little lust. *Encouraging.*

After what feels like a lifetime, it is finally over. Then John Quimby straightens his back and reads this odd little passage:

"What is life but time's sweet passing. What marks our time here in any lasting way? We become like a Sears catalog in the Internet age. Youth laughs at our antiquated ways and technical inadequacies, as though we were not built for this age. All our favorite foods will become extinct. Who will eat the little red-and-white swirled hard candies? The liver and onions? Drink the cheap canned beer?

"What then is life beyond time's sweet passing? Is it a dark and meaningless void that follows this folly? Is legacy more than a car model? Is honor just not getting caught? Why do we pray the dead rest in peace? They're not resting and peace is an illusion. It's like the public room we enter for the purpose of defecation is called a restroom. Same thing. Denial in a floral print.

"So farewell, sweet Isabelle. You are wiser than we are now. If you are laughing at us, please do so lovingly."

And I must laugh. Evidently John authored this himself. There are only five other people present and they look at each other, smirking and shaking their heads, baffled as to its meaning and pertinence. I see the Birdsey girl mouth to Theodore, "What the fuck?" *I get it though. I think he did a good job of it. These dreary rituals can be so histrionic.*

There's a beautiful, very pregnant woman standing off to the side many feet away. She's resting her crossed arms on her belly. Theodore keeps shooting looks her way, either to reassure her or keep her in place. *I bet there's a story there. Is that baby related to me?*

Then together Father McGurley and Faye in stylized, dramatic gestures place the small vase of what must be my ashes *(it can't be them all!)* in the sand. Faye is wearing the bright pink linen suit that I bought for her last spring. *Nice touch.* And thank God, not the ostrich cowgirl boots that set me back five hundred bucks.

McGurley blesses the scrawny vase again and again with the sign of the cross, mumbling something about God's loving arms. Cooper has his arm around John's waist. Too bad they've had to hide their feelings for so many years. They probably have the healthiest relationship of all. My parents' marriage was like play acting as far as I could tell. I'm pretty sure he cheated on her. Maybe she knew or maybe she didn't want to know. *Denial in a floral print, for sure.*

Theodore's beautiful, droopy eyes look so solemn and a little lost. I'm so glad he shaved and did something with his hair.

He's taking a piece of folded paper from his back pocket. *This is going to kill me.*

"Isabelle Dash was not a conventional mother," he reads. "Everything that was done for my brother and me was done by her. Paid for by her. She had no help from my father, but that wasn't entirely his fault." And then from his other back pocket he pulls out a color snapshot of Michael and holds it up for all to see.

"Here he is, my father," Theodore announces. "I look a lot like him, don't you think? My mother loved him, as you did, Faye."

At this, Texas smiles and nods. "I loved them both," she says. *Touching.*

"He died of AIDS when I was very young. I don't remember him. But I like knowing that he loved my mother." *Cat's out of the bag. I just never could say it. Felt like a failure on so many levels.*

The photo and the paper go back into his pockets. He picks up my ashes and walks to the water's edge. The others follow. Theodore shakes my remains into his hands and throws them toward the water and into the wind, allowing them to fall back onto his body. He puts a silly grin on his face and they all hold hands, lined up at the shoreline, like I was off on a pleasure cruise.

"I know you are safe, Mom. I wish I could tell you one more time, slowly and intentionally, how much I love you."

There, Teddy. There, you just did.

ZAIMA

SEPTEMBER • EMPIRE

Dear Abbi, Sweet Ummi,

The heavy, throbbing rain is battering this old farmhouse and my resolve to stay clear of you. My mood is dark and my not sleeping well is partially to blame. These things will pass soon enough.

You have done nothing to deserve the worry and fear my sudden disappearance has likely caused you. I haven't written sooner to allay these feelings because I had nothing to tell you that would in any way make you proud of me. It is quite the opposite.

You saw how I was when I returned from Iraq. You had so many questions. I gave you very little about myself in that country that means so much to you. Abbi, I remember you saying the nightly news had more warmth in its words than his older daughter.

It was a mistake, my enlistment, my tour there, and I fear even the war itself. Someday I will tell you about Iraq. I believe we will leave it more broken than we found it in 2003. But your people are strong, I saw that as well. They defied death threats and mortar rounds to turn out in huge numbers to vote in the country's first free elections in fifty years. But you know this.

The war did not change me. It merely reinforced my negative traits . . . my quick, reflexive anger, my introversion, my bad habit of not facing difficult things, the constant running away.

255

I am fine. I am the healthiest in body and mind that I've been in a long time. Ummi, you would be proud of what I have grown in a modest garden. Abbi, I brought an old farm tractor back to life with the skills and confidence you taught me.

I pray for you every evening, and for Jamila. She may hate me for abandoning her. Or she may not care. I have never really been there for her. We have nothing in common but blood.

I pray for your forgiveness. And that you are healthy and will enjoy a long life. And that when friends ask you what became of me, you will not feel shame.

You will see me when I am there.

All my love,

Zaima

JOHN QUIMBY

THE NEXT DAY

John is an honest man, almost annoyingly so. If a cashier returns too much change or undercharges him for an item, he points it out. "I'd complain if I paid too much," he'd say. "What's the difference?" Even regarding Marie's coveted recipe box, he had never taken a peek inside, even when alone in the room. Once when riding in the ambulance with a seriously injured accident victim, the patient asked if he was going to die. "I couldn't tell you," John told the man bluntly, "but I'll do all I can." Ever since he had denied his relationship with Cooper for so many years and did eventually leave his wife more than four decades ago, he has vowed to tell the truth, whatever the cost.

But now he has a dilemma. Early this morning Zaima showed up with a letter. She entrusted him with the delivery of that letter, asking that it be mailed from Traverse City. Driving Theodore's truck was getting more and more difficult, she explained. The envelope was addressed to two members of the al-Aziz family, undoubtedly her parents. The Traverse City postmark is intended, he's quite certain, to make finding her less likely. *And what has she confided to them?* Probably not much.

John agreed. He wanted to make that trip soon anyway, in need of a larger grocery store than Deering's. He promised he'd take care of it that very day.

Now he's purchased a stamp for her and is ready to drop it in the bronze slot. But he can't. Not yet. What he intends to do will be dishonest. It will violate a trust. *But what of the greater good?* He's sure her parents are worried about her. How could they not be? All that time in Iraq and then, *poof!* She's gone. Zaima is on the brink of delivering their grandchild. *Is that bit of news in the letter?* Probably not.

What he does next seems only the smallest betrayal. It's something any good, caring neighbor would do. He flips over the envelope and in small, neat printing, states a simple fact and adds his first name and phone number. He'd want to be informed if he were in their shoes. If she were his daughter, he'd thank someone who cared enough to get involved, to take the bold step which might bring the family close again.

John slides the envelope through the slot.

LULU AND MAHMOUD AL-AZIZ

The letter and its torn envelope lay on the Formica-top kitchen table in the sunny kitchen on Artesian Street. Lulu has read it three times; Mahmoud only once. Jamila has left for school and will not be shown the letter when she returns. She has forbidden her parents from speaking her sister's name and they have mostly respected that. It isn't worth the hormonal hurricane that might form after the utterance of a single word.

Their elder daughter had left their home without a good-bye or even a note. At first they welcomed the respite. Since her return from Iraq, she had been sullen and withdrawn, prone to angry outbursts over even the smallest thing. Often her food went untouched and there were days when she only left her room to use the bathroom. She was the hardest on Jamila, who seemed to irritate Zaima by her very existence.

Then they grew worried. Phone calls were placed and inquiries made, but nothing came of them. So they waited.

All of this they can forgive. Even her bland, vague words in the letter can be forgotten. She is alive and they are grateful for that. The message on the back of the envelope, however, this is another matter entirely. Six words, ten numbers. There for all to see, the postmaster, the mailman, anyone who cared to flip the envelope over.

SHE IS ALMOST NINE MONTHS PREGNANT
JOHN 231 376 4201

Lulu sips her cold coffee. All her tears have been spent. "How is this possible? For all the interest she has shown in the opposite sex, I feared she was homosexual."

"Looks like no," Mahmoud says. "This is apparently not the case." He repeatedly runs his fingers through his thinning black hair.

"But who? Who has done this?" Lulu wants to know.

"She has done this, aided by perhaps this John. Or some man in Iraq. How would I know?" he says angrily. "We are only her parents, what right to know do we have? She cares nothing for propriety, for what is acceptable in the eyes of her family or God."

"You encouraged this in her," Lulu says, pointing her finger at him. "You! You raised her like a boy, taught her things girls need not know. You stoked her anger against Saddam, against all injustice. You were secretly proud when she enlisted. I know you were. Now are you proud?"

"These things are not related, Lulu," he fires back. "Yes, I wanted her to be independent, to be strong. And yes, to fight to free the people of Iraq. I did not want her pregnant!"

"Yes, look at our country. How many hundreds of thousands have been murdered? It is worse than under Saddam. Voting has taken place, as Zaima wrote. Now al-Maliki can preside over a civil war. Where is this liberation we sent our daughter to secure?"

Mahmoud slams a palm against the table. "I cannot sit here and debate the future of Iraq. We must talk about Zaima. What is our response to this news from Traverse City? And why is she in Traverse City? To be the only Muslim? To stand out, pregnant and unmarried?"

"We don't know if she is married or not," Lulu says, hoping to calm him. "That is the smallest of our problems. We should go there and look for her."

"And then what? Even if we could find her, what do we say? She does not want to be found."

"Let's call this number," she offers. "Here is someone who knows exactly where she is."

"What do we say to him? Marry our daughter? Take away at least some of this shame?"

"Zaima may need our help, Mahmoud."

"She did not ask for it."

"She's pregnant!" Lulu says.

"This is not a life-threatening condition," he argues. "It will resolve itself soon enough."

"I am calling that number."

"I could tell you that I forbid it, but I know you will do as you please," Mahmoud tells his wife. "And you say she is more like me."

ZAIMA

SEPTEMBER • EMPIRE

When Zaima opens the screen door, curious to see who owns the new Jeep in the driveway, she sees the two brothers embracing. Hands are slapping backs, hair is tousled affectionately. They've only spoken on the phone since Isabelle's death and only legal matters were discussed. When they sense her presence, they disengage, and turn toward her still all smiles.

Nate's immediately vanishes as he gawks in disbelief at the big-bellied private first class.

"C'mon, Nate," Theodore says. "You've never seen a pregnant woman before? This is Zaima . . ."

"What the fuck!" Nate blurts.

Zaima holds his angry stare, fuels it, stokes it with her entire rigid body. "Exactly," she says to him, three syllables barked as one.

Theodore backs farther into the room and lowers himself to the couch. He watches as Nate steps toward Zaima, bringing both hands close to her face. He slowly counts with thumbs and fingers to eight.

"I like you better like this than in combat gear," he smirks.

She seethes with hate for his mocking tone, his hideous civilian clothes that suggest an urban cowboy. Hates his stale breath and his backhanded compliment.

Theodore joins the conversation. "Wait, you know her? Combat gear? What's going on?"

Nate speaks to his brother without turning away from her. "She never shared our fun and games in Iraq with you? We were both stationed at Speicher. Had a little Taco Bell romance. Did you know that we could eat Taco Bell over there? Subway too. But we preferred Taco Bell, right, Zaima? But as you can plainly see, fast food can make you fat."

Nate is close enough that she doesn't need to move much more than her left foot slightly forward and shift her weight back on her right to deliver a solid blow to his face. The flat of her fist lands in that perfect little nest so as to injure the cartilage and bones of the nose, eye, and cheek.

Nate reels back but quickly regains his balance and readies his body to fight. He twists and cocks back his right arm. Theodore lurches and wraps both arms around his brother's waist and brings them both to the floor.

Zaima has one hand on the arm of a chair and is shaking off the throbbing in the other hand. "There was no romance!" she shouts. "I thought you were a friend."

Nate stands and faces her again. "That ain't what your figure says," he whispers.

"You raped me. We both know that's what happened."

"That's your version of what happened," Nate says. "Why are you here? To seduce my brother too?"

Theodore steps between them, facing Nate. "You have to leave." He pauses, tries to slow his breathing. "I mean it. You have to go."

"You're gonna kick your poor orphaned brother out? Really? I don't know what she's doing here, but I'm family."

Theodore turns around but Zaima is gone. He opens the screen door but she's nowhere in sight.

"Help me out here," he says angrily to Nate. "I knew nothing about Iraq. Or about the two of you."

"I was her staff sergeant. She was a pretty little army grunt with a shaved head. She was a good soldier, did what was asked of her. She worked the checkpoints, ran in some convoys. She saw a lot. She never should have gone to Iraq. She was conflicted. I mean she's Iraqi. Her parents are from there. People didn't trust her."

"And what about you, Nate? Did you rape her?"

"No, little brother. That's her take on it."

"Could you be more evasive? Why did she come here?"

"Ask her," Nate answers.

"Is that baby yours? Is that what the finger counting was all about?"

"Got me. I don't know who she's been with. Could be yours for all I know."

"You know that's impossible," Theodore says.

"Listen, Teddy, I came here to see you. To see how you were doing. You never contacted me after that letter. Everything I heard about you came from Mom. I was relieved to hear about you going into the seminary. I was probably more worried about you than you were about me."

"I prayed for you. Always."

"Yeah, okay. Thanks. Mom wrote me that the old man left me ten grand and you pretty much everything else. I have no problem with that. I never liked it up here. A little slow, you know. If this was all mine, I'd sell it in a heartbeat. That's what Mom said you should do. Maybe you should honor her wishes. So if you want to pay me back with that . . ."

"You won't need it," Theodore stammers. "As soon as the contents of Mom's condo are sold, you'll have plenty. I don't want any of it."

"That's going to take some time. Her estate is a mess. I need some cash now," Nate explains calmly. "Listen, I'll turn my ass around and drive back to Chicago as soon as I get that ten grand. You and Zaima and the mystery baby can make your own little life on the farm here, but I wouldn't trust her, Teddy. You really don't know her."

"The bank is right in town, on 22. There's only one. There's an account in your name. Should be easy. He left you some other things too."

"Oh yeah, I forgot. Just hang on to those for me. Can't transport guns across state lines. Just give your poor brother a bag of ice for his face and he'll be on his way."

"Sorry you missed the memorial," Theodore says with a whiff of sarcasm.

"I did my own thing for Mom," Nate says. "We always kinda rolled on our own."

———————— • ————————

She sees Nate pressing the bag of ice against his face. The anger has left her and she stands there against the barn, indifferent as to whether he sees her or not. But he does, and pounds the hood of his Jeep and then heads directly for her.

Zaima crosses her arms and rests them upon the soft curve of the child inside her. *What can he do?* She knows him well enough to know not even he would strike a pregnant woman. He has only the power of his voice to attack her.

"That fuckin' hurt," Nate says.

"I meant it to."

"You gotta talk to me."

"You raped me. Violently, like an animal, you raped me," she says.

"Listen, you teased me."

"I turned you down, you mean. I had no feelings like that for you . . . or anyone. I barely had any feelings at all. I just wanted to get the hell out of Iraq."

"And you got pregnant to do it," he says.

"I got pregnant? As in, I intended this to happen? As in, it was anything I wanted?" She steps closer to him. "You know about the Depo-Provera they inject us with. With all the stress and weight loss, I hadn't had a period in months. I wasn't even thinking about getting knocked up."

"So why didn't you go and get an abortion?"

"Maybe that's something I couldn't do. Maybe your brother talked me out of it. You pick."

"My brother. The fuckin' saint. That *is* what you think, isn't it?" Nate says, and then hurries back to his Jeep and grabs something from the passenger seat.

"Here, read this," Nate says, pushing an envelope in her face. "I was just gonna give it back to him. Remind him he owes me."

Zaima takes the envelope, stares at the address.

"I love Theodore," Nate tells her. "I sent him money. What's happened between you and me is . . . unfortunate. Let me know if you need anything. I'll see what I can do."

———— • ————

Zaima goes behind the barn and sits straight-backed against the stone foundation. She holds the letter from Theodore addressed to their base in Iraq. She doesn't want to read it, doesn't know if it's right to do so. If Theodore read her poems it would be a huge violation of privacy. She could take it into the farmhouse right now and return it.

But she can't. She opens the letter and reads:

Dear Nate,

I don't know who else to write to. I am in a bad way and it's all my doing. No one forced me to make the decisions I have made.

Depression has dogged me for some years. I don't know where it comes from but it can immobilize me. I have tried various distractions but it's always there.

Maybe that's why psychology was an obvious choice for a major at Wayne State. To try to figure out what was wrong with me. I did a lot of menial work before that. Nowhere jobs that at least made me feel like I was doing something. I tried the student life, but in the second term things started to fall apart. I just gradually stopped going to classes, gained weight, and this woman I was seeing just abandoned me, declaring me "vacant." This provided another reason not to go to classes because she was in two of them.

I was well on my way to flunking out, I was underemployed, working one night a week at some hipster café on Woodward. That's when I fell in with this group of people who were just as aimless as I was, but unapologetic about it. There were two guys, Zachary and the other went by Spooky. And a woman, thin as a twig with ink black hair, Ophelia. She was intense, said she was a poet.

We ran into each other at the Detroit Institute of Art. I like going there. It's quiet and peaceful. I especially like that room filled with Rivera's murals of Detroit. They are like a love poem to manufacturing and labor, but sometimes a bitter one, too, him being a Marxist. The four of us are the only ones in there and suddenly this little dog bolts into the room, dragging his leash. The thing has four stubby legs, his belly is almost scraping the floor, and his long snout is sniffing around and I could guess why. He goes right over to the columns under a mural of rounded women with their grain and fruit, and takes a long piss on the base of one of the columns. A guard appears and tries to shoo the dog out but the little guy just starts running in circles all around the room. Now we're all crouched down on the floor laughing and then it gets better. An equally stubby Mexican woman runs in yelling, "Colima! Colima! Come to me!"

Maybe this doesn't seem all that hilarious to you. Maybe I'm boring you. But right there under the sacred images of fertility and birth, it just seemed ironic that a dog would relieve himself there and we all got it. We could not stop laughing. We and the dog were forced to leave.

Just like that we started spending time together, mostly just hanging out at their place on Burroughs Street. Nate, remember that wishing well we loved that was in the lobby of I can't remember where. You slipped a penny in at the top and it swirled around and around the sides until it disappeared. I was feeling like that penny. They became a safe place to land. To disappear. And we were all living in a city that seemed to be disappearing as well, because not far from the museums and the academic buildings was a lot of poverty and blight. The city seemed to be decaying from the inside, like a bad tooth.

They had all been students at Wayne State, but like me, none had lasted long. Zachary might be gay and Spooky was definitely into Ophelia. She played him and flirted with me too. I wasn't into any of that, but I lost some of my oppressive loneliness. I had a family.

Anyway, they were all addicts. At first they never did anything around me and then they did. Ophelia was the most dedicated user. I noticed that black sticky residue on her hands, on the bathroom light switch, even her face. She showed me how she heated up the heroin on a small piece of tinfoil over a flame and sucked up the fumes with a straw.

I moved in, slept on the couch. Zachary may have had a job as he was out of the apartment at predictable times. He never talked about it. Someone had some money though as there was always food, alcohol, and plenty of heroin, which they said was cheap and good quality.

I refused for weeks. They teased me but never pushed. But not doing it made me feel separate from them and they were all I had. We had spent so many hours talking about everything, the war, how screwed up politics was, and about the bad things that had happened to us. I remember thinking that we were like a nest of wounded birds, unable to fly away from each other.

Then one night we were all sitting on the living room floor together and Ophelia just handed me a bag, and without coaxing I did as she taught me.

Zachary had said once that you never want to try heroin, because if you do, nothing else will ever feel as good. Not alcohol, not sex, nothing.

It's impossible to describe. It brought me to a clear place of contentment. I was not lost. This place you go to is a place you want to go back to. Very quickly, my life soon had two purposes—doing drugs and getting more drugs. What money I had was soon gone. I picked up another night at the café. Sold anything I could. My life had a goal.

Zaima lowers the letter and concentrates on the rolling landscape behind the barn. The cherry trees look distraught without their fruit, empty nesters that even the birds ignore. It isn't Nate she's thinking about. He was as she imagined he would be, angry and judgmental, anxious to pass blame. It's Theodore she's focused on, a fuller, more interesting presence, imperfect, raw. And as if her thoughts have conjured the person in the flesh, there to her right stands Theodore, looking from her to the letter, and then back again.

"Why don't I read it to you?" he says. "I want you to know just how desperate I was."

"I should apologize," Zaima says.

"Why should you? It was in Nate's possession and he gave it to you. Now it's yours."

Theodore sits next to her and looks directly at her abdomen. "I'll read it to you both. Get to know the real Theodore."

He continues where her finger lands:

After a few months living like this, I started to see a different person looking back at me in the mirror, some sickly, haunted stranger.

Stopped shaving and rarely even washed my face.

The other three seemed to be able to function in their lives. Zachary continued to go off to his "job," Spooky left for a couple weeks to see some family up north, and Ophelia started back at Wayne State part-time. Or so she said.

But for me? I lost my apartment. Had to pack up every piece of clothing, every book, all I still owned that mattered to me. Nate, my life thus far fit into two plastic bags.

I need to get in rehab. It costs money. I'm really sick. I need help.

I haven't talked with Mom in a year now. The checks have stopped. She must sense what a bad investment I am. I thought of going up to Empire but I'm ashamed of how I look and what I've been doing with my life.

Can you help me? I promise that whatever money you send me I won't use for drugs. The return address on this envelope will find me. I don't know what will come of my sorry life, but it won't be this.

I hope you're all right. I haven't heard from you in a long time, but how would you even find me? I hope this address is still yours.

Your brother,

Teddy

"So you're human, that's all," Zaima says. "Are you clean now?"

"Spooky died two weeks after I wrote that letter . . . overdosed in his boyhood bedroom. That scared me. I signed up for my six days in hell and with Nate's help, I got clean and have stayed that way. He sent money regularly. No note."

"And where was your God in all of that?" Zaima asks flatly.

"In a nun in a decaying factory building. Then in the brother who ran my rehab program. He had been through it. He didn't push God on me, just told me I wasn't alone.

"I had to believe there was something bigger, because I was not in control of my life. I have always believed in God, but I had never needed him like this. God wasn't in a church anymore. He was smack in my day-to-day existence and survival."

She knows this about God. Prayer became a routine part of her life in Iraq. Everybody needed something to get through it. God for her was the healthiest choice.

"I was told that I had to establish some kind of routine," he says. "Like a job? School?"

"Neither of those worked for me in the past. I went to Saint Anthony's because I wanted to get away from myself, focus on other people. Busyness and prayer kept me clean."

"This child belongs only to me," Zaima announces. "This child would never take a breath if not for me and the sacrifices I've made. I had to leave my family. They don't even know where I am. That I am pregnant and unmarried would only bring shame upon them."

Theodore stands and extends a hand to help her, but she swats it away and uses the barn's stone foundation as leverage to push her way up.

"I need to know if it was Nate. Did he rape you? Or was it consensual?"

"Conception is a process in nature. Sperm fertilizes egg. How that happened is of no importance to me now."

"It *was* him, wasn't it? Did you love him? *Do* you love him?"

"What do you think? Did that look like love back there in your living room?"

He places a hand on her abdomen and she doesn't remove it.

"Then this child is related to me," he says quietly. "That's right, isn't it?"

She says nothing but stands there, glaring at him, challenging him to speak his next truth.

"Zaima, this child is a Dash."

No reply. She pushes away his hand.

"That's why you came here," Theodore states. "You came here to find me, to see if I was the same animal he was. To punish me for what he did. Because I do believe you. Nate has a history, not as a rapist, but as someone who treats women badly. My mother was the only woman I know of that he treated with any respect at all."

"You're a decent man, Theodore. I can't explain exactly why I came here, but it was never to harm you," Zaima says softly, and then adds with conviction, "and this child is not a Dash and will not be raised as such. That I do know."

NATE DASH

LEAVING EMPIRE

He leaves the bank. It has been the painfully slow, annoying experience that he imagines all small-town interactions to be, cloyingly familiar and touchy. Packed with double-checking and meaningless pleasantries. Now that the brother has been visited and the money withdrawn, Nate drives south in his Jeep, opting for the longer scenic route that hugs the water. He needs to think.

First to mind is a woman from his mother's firm. It had taken him six weeks to get her into bed and as soon as he did, she left him. *What did that mean?* She said he knew nothing about women. Well, he might just look her up again when he gets back to Chicago. Not that he believes in second chances; this would feel more like revenge.

The road has plenty of fun little hills and curves. He doesn't feel remorse at all about Zaima. He is pissed though about his brother taking her side. That whole scene had not gone down well. He was not prepared for that little shocker. *Was that baby his?* How the hell would he know? He couldn't very well follow her back to the states after she bailed. And why is she camped out with Teddy? That's no coincidence. How did she find him? He can't remember what they talked about really. He did like her; she was such a loner, an outcast. Opposite of him. He was not, however, hot for her. She looked like a pretty boy, not his type. His friends made fun of him for hanging out with her. They asked if he was gay! They joked that he was fraternizing with the enemy. She did sympathize with the hajis, questioned our being there. But, hey, she wasn't the only one.

There's some construction ahead and now nobody's moving in either direction. He cuts the engine and watches some kids horsing around in the water. He misses being in Iraq, misses his buddies. But he also saw a lot of things he'd like to forget. He lost two of his closest friends. All those images in his head have seemed so weird and out of place since he's been back. *It's like nobody here knows that we're in a fucking war.* Seeing Zaima is making those images, those losses, seem real again.

Two days before he and Zaima had sex, he'd been royally drunk. He ran into her at one of the fast-food traps there. They sat and talked a bit and he reached over and started playing with her hair. She freaked, said it made her uncomfortable, so he took off. He avoided her for a while, but then she just shows up and asks what's wrong. *Stupid bitch.* He told her that she hurt his feelings and she laughed at him. She didn't really hurt him at all, but she shouldn't have laughed at him. There was no one else in the room so he pulled her close and started kissing her. She didn't like it, but the more she protested, the more he wanted her.

The traffic is moving again, but Nate pulls off the road. He lights a cigarette. The images are flashing through his head like on a movie screen. She was struggling against him, trying to get enough distance to punch him. It wasn't that hard to contain her and he managed to get her pants down. There was a desk there and he turned her around and bent her over it. She had a great ass and he tried to get his hands on as much bare skin as he could. She was still fighting him. He wanted to think it was a game, that she was pretending not to want it. At least that's what he told himself later.

But right then, he felt crazy and out of control and he was inside her and what she was feeling he didn't know or care.

It was over fast. He just exploded and then she went totally limp, like he knows women do after an orgasm. He released her and as he was pulling up his pants, she flipped around and was able to knee him hard in his chest, even though her pants must have been around her ankles. He fell back and tried to grab her legs. She stumbled away from him. He yelled something after her, some smart-ass thing like, "You got what you asked for!" It was rough, yes, but it was not rape. Nobody would ever think that he'd have to force himself on a woman. Nobody would believe that. He had a reputation. Women went after *him*.

And there was blood. It was on his penis and on his leg. *It couldn't be her first time.* Maybe she was on the rag, he thought. He prayed she didn't have AIDS. He didn't see her again until today.

He drives on a few more miles and then sees a nice little pub. He could sure use a beer or two. Maybe a burger.

He sits at the bar and orders. As soon as a tall, beautiful beer is sitting in front of him, he's got company. A pretty young woman in short, cut-off jeans and a tight, sleeveless T-shirt sits next to him. She smiles as she raises his beer glass to her lips.

"Mind?" she asks coyly. She takes a dainty sip and wipes her mouth with his napkin. He feels like being alone and finds her flirtatiousness irritating.

"You want your own?" he asks, then takes a long slug of his beer. "Are you even old enough?"

"Of course I am," she answers. "In some states. I like your Jeep. Take me for a ride later?"

"You don't even know me," Nate says. "Didn't your mama teach you better than that?"

"You vacationing up here?" she wants to know. "This is a really small shithole of a town, and you kinda stand out."

Don't flirt with me, he thinks. All he needs right now is another tease. "I live in Chicago now. I'm moving to LA soon."

"Wow," she says, way too excitedly, like the silly schoolgirl she likely is. "I ain't been nowhere really. Just Grand Rapids once."

"Wow! Grand Rapids!" he mocks, but then softens. "It's a cool city. I'm sure you had fun there." He orders another beer and she again claims the first sip.

"It was my grandmother's funeral," she says. "It's okay. She was pretty old." And then she chuckles because, you know, old people dying is just so funny.

"Was she sick?" he asks, not really caring.

"She had a heart attack." Here a sad little pout erupts on her face like a pimple. "But she smoked like a chimney and drank all the time." Okay, she deserved it. "She was sixty-two."

"That's not that old," Nate says. "I'm sixty-one myself. Could go at any time."

"You are not," she teases back. "But I bet you're over twenty." Another keen observation.

"Listen, you seem like a sweet kid and I'm going to give you some free advice. Don't pick up strange guys in bars. It's naive and dangerous. I'm planning on eating the burger this nice gentleman is bringing over here and then I'm taking off. Alone."

"You don't need to be so mean. My boyfriend just broke up with me. That's him across the street laughing with his friends. I thought maybe, if he saw me with you, he'd get, you know, jealous."

Nate looks at the gaggle of scrawny guys across the street. "Which one is he?"

"The really cute one in the baseball cap."

"Yes, I see him. Cap turned around so handsomely," he says, suddenly feeling old. "Tell me, how old are you . . . honestly?"

"I'm eighteen. I just graduated last June. That's the truth. Look, here's my class ring."

Nate has a bite of his burger and then takes a look at the hand she's thrust at him. He examines the gaudy ring. Sure enough, 2006. "So what are your plans?"

"Who are you, my dad?"

"What are your plans?" He attacks the burger again and waits.

"I'm hoping to get a job," she says, "maybe at the state park."

"What do you like to do, I mean besides picking up men to make your boyfriend jealous?"

"You really are mean. There are lots of things I like to do."

"For example?" he asks.

"I like to draw. I draw a lot. Animals, the lakefront, and people too."

"What else?" He's paying his tab, leaving a nice tip.

"Read. I like biographies."

"I'm going to make you a deal. If you promise to check out one college, and there are plenty around here, in the infamous Grand Rapids and all over the western part of the state, north and south, pick out just one college you like . . . do you have a computer?"

"That's a dumb question."

"You do that, check it out and maybe even apply to get into an art or history or natural science program, you promise to do that and I'll walk outta here with you, hand in hand. When we see your dime-a-dozen, sorry-ass boyfriend, you turn to me and I'll give you a modest kiss. Nothing over the top, but he'll get the idea. Then we hop into my Jeep and I drive you home."

"One college? How will you know I did it?" she asks.

"Because you will promise me that you will do it."

"I promise," she says and they shake.

"Great. Let's go, girlfriend."

"You're a pretty nice guy," she tells him.

"You'll meet better and you'll meet worse," Nate says on the way out.

ZAIMA

LATE SEPTEMBER • EMPIRE

when I see this child of mine
I will be looking again
into your beautiful
bottomless
unrealistically
hopeful
eyes

I remember you so well
and that while passing by you
our eyes locked
did you hate me?
did you fear me?

I wanted to believe
that you needed me
like a child still needs an abusive parent
because you needed food
you wanted my MRE
and the water
I was forbidden to give you

The convoy stopped,
the tractor-trailers
that are stuffed with nothing
but invoices to the Pentagon
or perhaps toilet paper
or ammunition
and the five-ton gun trucks,
we all stopped and I climbed down
small, barefooted, defenseless you
a frightened, worried child
with a defiant, daring stare
small you
you who looked much like my child will look
your glossy dark hair
like lake water at midnight
your huge eyes
like targets

the yearning on your face
made me slightly nauseous
but more homesick

then came your words
shouted words delivered
in my parents' tongue
words foreign to me
but the rhythm in them familiar

forgive me, I want to beg
but children despise that in adults
because it reeks of weakness
and kills their hope
that you can protect them

or feed them
or provide safe, clean water
or return one small piece
of a parent's love
because maybe that parent
is now missing
maybe I am part
of the reason why

what if you had been my child
if you were
I would have disarmed
thrown off my flak jacket
and pulled your warm body
into mine
taken you to safety
we had the same skin
tea with coconut milk and honey
did you love that as I did?
we had the same searching eyes
the same love for Allah
the same tolerance for heat
children of Abraham
separated by wars
that are not ours

then you did the most shocking thing
you did not lob a hidden grenade
or a homemade bomb
but you allowed me to touch your hair
then your cheek
but then pushed my hand away
because I was not your mother

I was a soldier
who the other soldiers
were watching
with suspicion
I was one of them
the occupiers
who you hoped
would soon go home
to families who do not suffer
as yours does

when I do see this child of mine
I will be looking again
into your beautiful
bottomless
unrealistically
hopeful
eyes,
cha bibi

and what will this child
see in my eyes?
the eyes of the occupier
the eyes of a victim
peering back into the eyes
of the innocent

ZAIMA

Collateral damage. She finds the words, the concept, repulsive. For the supposed greater good, innocents are slaughtered. She looks at her hands, expecting to see blood. It feels as if the child inside her is punching the wall of her womb. It wants out. It, too, is collateral damage, but of a different sort.

She vomits. Drenched in sweat, she vomits again, producing nothing but an acidic, yellow slime. Zaima returns to her desk in her small, perfect room, the crib now positioned in the corner. With all its bars, the crib looks like a jail, as though an infant could escape without the ability to walk or even stand.

She tears the pages from her notebook, removing the ridiculous, hideous poem. She rips them into small pieces and flushes them down the toilet. *Words! How powerless they are.* A meaningless confession to no one but herself. Really, what good are they? *Does she feel better? Forgiven?* Vomiting was better therapy. That child she described so poetically could easily have ended up as collateral damage. How many breathing, loving, vital human beings innocently drawn into this violent chaos will end up the same? *Collateral* used to mean security on a loan. Now it means the murder of innocents.

She has now filled three notebooks. She gathers them and throws them into the trash bin beneath the kitchen sink. Opening the cupboards, she sees little jars of mashed organic food for her baby. Do they think the child will arrive hungry for solid food? Do the two of them, who right now are comfortably sleeping just above her, do they know anything at all about caring for the newly born? Maybe there's a manual on their nightstand that they consult each night before drifting off into their perfect misconceptions. There's another great word, misconception. *How apt.*

Her roiling anger had no outlet. She'd been bottling it up in these ineffectual poems, in her indifference, in her repetitive tasks around the farm. But it has surfaced now. The source of the anger is nebulous. It isn't just toward Nate or even the war itself. She's been a pawn. With a single sweep of her hand she clears the offensive infant food from the shelf and onto the kitchen floor. They don't break but scatter in all directions like roaches when the lights are flicked on. As she's ripping the neutral yellow sheet and blankets off the crib's mattress, she feels the fluid gush from between her legs. She opens her mouth to scream for them, but they are awake and already there. They say nothing. Zaima says nothing. They move toward her, arms outstretched, wearing sappy, sickening smiles. It's as if the circus has come to town. They lead her back to her room for some reason, as if she had only been sleepwalking.

"I'll call John," Theodore says to her. "We'll do this here, as you said. But if anything goes off," and here he struggles for the right word.

"Off normal, doesn't progress," Brigid finishes for him, "then we go to the clinic. It will be Grace's call. Zaima, you agree?"

"I can't do this," Zaima says, staring at her, looking half her age. "I can't."

"Honey, that was an option many months ago," Brigid says, stroking her hair. "We are going to have us a baby here. We won't leave you."

Those are, for Zaima, four of the most amazing words she's ever heard. They won't leave her. She is the leaver. She cuts out.

"You won't leave," she repeats to Brigid, just to be sure.

"Not if the pope told me to. Not if my dead mother told me to. Not if an angel of God dropped into this kitchen right this very second and told me to."

"Me neither," Theodore says, returning to the room. "John says this ain't the movies. It'll be many hours before we hear any screaming baby. He'll call Grace anyway and she may want to show up sooner than later. He wants us to call him back when the contractions bunch up."

"Said the EMT," Brigid adds. "Very professional."

"I need the bathroom," Zaima says. "And I don't need any help."

As the hours pass, Zaima is impossible to calm. She paces, eventually walking out into the yard without a coat or even shoes. She must be coaxed back in and wrapped in blankets to quell her shaking. Brigid puts on the radio and annoying, whining country music lyrics pour out. Zaima marches over and rips the radio's cord from the socket. When the midwife arrives, Zaima dismisses her, telling her she's not needed. Grace has seen this tantrum before and tells her flatly that she is not leaving and that there will soon come a time when Zaima will beg her to stay. From a stuffed gym bag, Grace extracts an array of tools for her trade, including a fetal heart monitor, belts, gels and lubricants, scissors and clamps, injectable Pitocin, a blue-bulb syringe, and sterile gloves. For herself, she's packed Luna bars, her phone and charger, water, and scrubs. She tells Zaima to keep moving and asks for a cup of hot tea.

——————— • ———————

It's now just before sunrise and still no birth. John is asleep in the living room and Cooper is parked out front in the EMS truck with oxygen tanks and masks at the ready or in case emergency transport is needed. Brigid and Theodore roam the house, either following Zaima or each other. Grace naps now and then, but keeps close tabs on Zaima and the progress of her labor.

For a while, Zaima is in the barn, moaning and stroking the side of Levi's massive head. The horse nods compassionately from time to time as she lowers in pain, her hands on her knees. Then, wrapped in a wool blanket and wearing Theodore's muck boots, she waits for the sun and screams at the near darkness. What she's saying, they can't hear, but Grace knows it's likely profanities.

When light finally fills the kitchen, Zaima returns, weak and submissive. She lies on her bed and allows Grace to reattach the fetal heart monitor and examine her. Her cervix is nearly fully dilated and Grace calls for Brigid and Theodore. Neither is trained to assist, but assist they must. Grace urges Zaima to her feet and strips her down to only a sleeveless undershirt. With Theodore supporting her from behind and Grace on her knees in front of her, they begin the slow process of delivery. Brigid brings whatever Grace barks for—pads, lubricants, the lollipop Zaima forcefully rejects. Brigid talks soothingly, reassuringly to Zaima, who grunts and howls, her eyes shut, her head tilted back.

Soon the crown of the baby's head is visible and Grace shouts commands that Zaima's body heeds. Then all of the head is in Grace's hands. She expertly twists out the entire body in a gush of amniotic fluid. An infant girl rests in the midwife's arms, as if she were a ripe, glossy apple falling perfectly into the picker's bag. Theodore stares at the child as he strokes Zaima's hair. Brigid is wide-eyed and speechless as she brings a soft, cotton blanket for the baby. The placenta is delivered, the cord is clamped and cut, and then the child is handed, screaming, to her mother.

"She is beautiful," Brigid says, gently touching the baby's toes. She wraps Zaima in a clean sheet and brings her and the child to her bed.

"Wow, you should have woke me up," John says, standing in the open doorway. "That's some beautiful kid, Zaima. Good job, Gracie."

"She did all the work," Grace says as she cleans up with Theodore. The exhausted, delirious Zaima stares at the creature in her arms. The infant's skin is moist and one size too large. She has puffy, red-rimmed eyes and a flattened nose. The head is misshapen, pointed at the top with strands of matted sandy hair. The infant stops screaming and releases a weak, contented whimper. She nuzzles and squirms like a worm on wet pavement.

She looks nothing at all like Zaima. She has *his* coloring, *his* squared-off jaw, *his* all-American plainness. She does not seem beautiful to her at all, more like a foreign object painfully removed from the body she has occupied. Zaima looks into her eyes, and they are an ominous, murky blue.

She had not foreseen this. She imagined a child with her features, her own mother's. Where is the lustrous, thick, black hair? Where is the beautiful skin the color of browning butter? Where are the dark eyes full of sensitivity and intelligence?

Instead she has merely been the vessel to deliver to the world yet another Dash. She will learn how to manipulate others, either through bullying or feigning compassion. She will take more than her share.

Zaima looks up to see that everyone is looking not at her, but at the infant, with tired, gratified smiles. They are talking, but she can't put meaning to the words.

"Lulu," Zaima announces. "Her name is Lulu."

"I love that name," Brigid bubbles. "Full of mischief."

"It's my mother's name," Zaima adds, stiffly holding the baby.

"Lulu Isabelle?" Theodore asks.

Zaima hears him. He did lose his mother only months ago. "Lulu Isabelle al-Aziz."

Brigid sees that Zaima is not taking to motherhood organically, and is probably exhausted beyond words. "Let's get Lulu cleaned up," she says to Grace. "I can't wait to get my hands on her."

COOPER BOYD

KNEE DEEP IN HARVEST

The Golden Delicious crop has been harvested and the Honey Crisp and Empire crops are half in. Next up will be the Northern Spy.

Often in the evenings, Hector's pickers and their families congregate at Cooper's farmhouse for communal dinners. It's always noisy and fun, with John's simple fare, never any alcohol. Theodore usually joins them and Brigid, too, when she's not at the bar. Hector Gonzales is thousands of miles from his home in San Luis Potosi in Mexico, but Cooper's accommodations are better than most. He has three decent trailers for families and a small cinder-block house that sleeps ten men.

Zaima helped pick before Lulu's birth, but now simply tends the baby at the Dash farmhouse. She has grown even more withdrawn, spending hours reading Nathaniel's volumes of Kipling's stories to the infant. She does care for the house and the shopping, too, when she can get out. She seems to be in wait mode.

All the apples are picked by hand, and the experienced men and women grab two or three apples at a time. They are dropped into their picking bags and then loaded into twenty-bushel bins. Hector often fills as many as twelve bins in a day, weighing in at around six tons. These bins are hauled away periodically to farm markets and packers.

Theodore is a slow and contemplative picker. From high on his ten-foot ladder, he stares out at the orchard and into the autumn sky. He marvels at the beauty of the fruit, placing each piece carefully into his bag. Cooper told him that each apple should be the right size to pick, close to two and three-quarters inches—so the young orchardist sometimes uses part of a finger to do the necessary measuring. Theodore also has been taught to look for apples that are half their ripened color; and that the ease with which the fruit lets go of the branch is another indication of readiness. Hector finds his methods amusing, but colossally unproductive. No matter though, as Theodore is not paid by the bin as he is, and after all, it is his first serious harvest. Let the boy revel in it.

Cooper knows this will be a bumper crop and he's rightly proud of all their efforts. Still, midway through the harvest, he swears as he often does recently, that this will be his last, that it is too hard on his body with both the physical labor and the stress. John tells him to back off and let Hector do his job. He never does.

ZAIMA

Zaima has lasted the two long months that transition autumn into winter. There already have been two significant snowfalls, and although her bedroom is the warmest room in the house, it never seems to be warm enough. The barn outside the rear window looms like a bulky memory of an easier life, one where she was responsible only for herself, for her own survival.

She stares at the shrieking baby in her crib. Lulu never sleeps for more than three or four hours, even at night. She is restless and seems constantly in need of some sort of attention—feeding, diaper changes, relief from some mysterious stomach distress. Zaima gave up on breastfeeding after only a few attempts and Lulu must be given formula, which she often just spittles back up, looking much the same as it did when it went down. Brigid and Theodore seem to love feeding her and that gives Zaima a chance to nap. She is exhausted in a deep, debilitating way.

She picks up Lulu and walks around the room with her. The baby screams on. She prepares her formula and sits with her in the rocker, hoping she'll quiet down and eat. And she finally does, her pouty lips encircling the nipple, her cheeks working like a calf's. She has such a mature face for an infant a couple of months old, or so it seems to Zaima, who sees more of the father in her day by day. She can't help but think of him and their last encounter, his lies, his mocking, his fingers in her face. Zaima doesn't hate him; she doesn't have the energy for it. Nate was just a lingering illness that she finally has gotten over.

Lulu has finished her bottle and now must be burped. Zaima slings the dish towel over her shoulder to catch the tiny stomach's overflow. She turns on the CD player Brigid has loaned her and plays the hauntingly beautiful vocals of Aida Nadeem, a gift to Lulu from Brigid. The squirrely rhythms and Aida's drifting, intense voice inspire Zaima with the desire to dance and to tell stories. She knows that Lulu's blood is Iraqi blood and will respond to this ancient ritual. As Zaima sways with the infant over her shoulder she talks. She tells her everything that comes to mind, about her own youth, the alienation she has felt as her constant companion, and in great detail about her parents. She describes them as complex, animated creatures who were loving and brave, but bewildered by Zaima. She tells Lulu about God, how to look for Him in everyday life, how to search for Him even though she has often failed at this herself. She admits that too. Keep looking, keep listening, she whispers, even when He seems distracted or completely absent. She tells her about Theodore and Brigid, and this monologue is the longest, stretching way past the moment when Lulu is asleep in her arms. Theodore and Brigid become fictional representations of themselves as she embellishes and imagines areas of their lives and relationship of which she knows little. It is vital that Lulu know and trust these two people.

As she lays the infant in her crib, she wishes she had not destroyed all of her poems. She would like to have read some of them to her daughter. She pulls her desk chair close to the crib and tells her the story behind one poem, about the young boy she encountered on that dusty road in Iraq, how she related to him and his desperation intimately. She tells Lulu how sorry she is for her participation in his pain and loss. Then bending over the crib, she whispers to the child that she has another family who will one day love her—grandparents, an aunt, and more family nearby as well as far away in an exotic and troubled land. Zaima begins to cry as she tells this fairy tale. In her sleep, Lulu waves tiny fingers upward, accidentally touching Zaima's wet face.

She turns and goes to her desk. There is a calendar from the tractor supply store. She sees that Lulu is already two months old. In one more month, near the middle and on Zaima's mother's birthday, she will leave Empire. She will leave Lulu. She stowed away most of what she arrived with, plenty of money to take her to a life that will feel more her own. She can imagine Lulu's questions for her if she could form them. "Why must you leave me? Why can't I come with you?" And she must honestly answer, "Because I am broken in pieces. Because I cannot provide what you need, what you deserve. But mostly, because you are more them than me."

Zaima believes that Theodore and Brigid expect her to leave, anticipate it as the days pass. She sees them try to fight their natural attachment to the child, forced to hold back just a little, thinking that when she does leave, they will lose Lulu. Still their love for her is obvious and growing and Zaima encourages it, offering them as much time with Lulu as their schedules allow.

The pieces are in place. It's time to cut the number of losses. She calculates how many lives can be saved here. *Lulu's? Her own?*

Could she grow to love this child? She worries that the resentment · and anger she feels will always block that sentiment. *Will she regret abandoning Lulu?* What John told her months ago about regret is true now as well. It is self-imposed misery that hurts you and helps no one. The only regret she might have is that she waited too long to make this decision.

THEODORE

AROUND THE SAME TIME

It is Theodore who is most smitten with Lulu. She adds more purpose to his life. His large hands are happiest when they are in her service, his heart open and receptive when her tiny body is pressed against his chest. All this comes naturally to him and the tenderness he exhibits reassures Brigid of his character and his capacity to love. They talk about having a child of their own, but it seems premature to them both.

Theodore does have unshared thoughts about Nate. If he knew exactly where he was, perhaps he would tell him about Lulu. *But would he want to know?* It seems unlikely that Nate would visit the child and her mother. He's quite certain that Faye knows where Nate has landed and Theodore speaks with her often. He never asks. In terms of paternity rights, he believes that Nate's were forfeited at the time of conception.

How this rift between brothers will ever be healed, Theodore has no idea. The relationship is broken and time alone won't mend it.

ZAIMA

TWO WEEKS LATER

Zaima has summoned them into the kitchen. It is snowing and has been for hours. Brigid has a roast in the oven. Lulu is napping.

"I want to thank you," Zaima begins once the three are seated at the table. "You have given me shelter, friendship . . . so much more. We brought a child into the world together. This has been as close to family as I have known for a long time."

"You're leaving," Brigid says for her.

"Yes. I didn't come to stay," Zaima answers. "I came to hide. Curiosity and necessity brought me here."

"You know you can stay," Theodore tells her, reaching a hand across the table toward her.

"No, I can't." Zaima puts her hands in her lap, out of reach.

"Where are you going? Back home?" Brigid asks.

"I'm not ready for that," Zaima says. "Neither are they. I'm going south, away from winter. Or maybe west to California."

"Do you need money?" Theodore asks.

"No. I have enough."

Then comes a long, silent, awkward pause. No one wants to ask the next lurking question. Zaima stands and looks out the kitchen window. The snow is falling so heavily it looks like dense fog.

"Lulu Isabelle," she says, not turning, "will you care for her for me?"

This they did not anticipate. Theodore's eyes are wide and questioning. "Are you sure?" he asks the back of Zaima's head.

No reply is given and he waits.

"If you are certain this is what you want, then yes, of course . . . if Brigid agrees." He looks at Brigid, but she looks stunned, says nothing.

"We would treat her as our own," he adds.

"Which she is," Zaima says, turning to face them. "Which she is. Think of me as a surrogate."

"I don't understand," Brigid stammers. "Theodore? What is she saying?"

"Oh, it's not his," Zaima says softly. "His brother is the father."

"What are you saying? Nate is the one who raped you?" Brigid stands and walks toward her. "Zaima, it was him, wasn't it? In Iraq. Oh, my God. Why didn't anyone tell me. Teddy, you knew, didn't you?"

"What difference does it make?" Zaima asks angrily. "Lulu is a Dash. Look at her!"

"I don't want you to leave," Brigid says. "Stay with us. You said we were like family. Please stay."

"Maybe I'll be back. I don't know when."

"You know where we are," Theodore says. "You know where we will be when you do."

And then, two weeks later, on a clear winter morning, Brigid takes a photo of Lulu in Zaima's arms, neither smiling nor crying. Theodore drives her to the bus stop, across the street from the very one she arrived at. She has plenty of food for the road and a new cell phone, which she did not want but accepted for their sake.

Zaima had named Theodore as the child's father on the birth certificate. That lie would make things easier for them all.

They let her go.

LULU ISABELLE AL-AZIZ

LATE SUMMER, FIVE YEARS LATER

She has seen the photograph so many times—there tacked above her bed—that she no longer notices it. She has no more interest in it than the water stain beside it. It is the Winnie-the-Pooh picture nearby that she cherishes. She knows Winnie-the-Pooh.

Lulu sleeps, she is told, in the same bed and in the same small room off the kitchen as did the woman with the flat, expressionless face in the photograph. And what's more amazing, she is the bundled baby in that stranger's arms. These historical details are all supplied by Brigid, whom she calls Bee, and Theodore—her papa for all intents and purposes.

Years ago, in a time she can only remember faintly, the parents of that strange woman came to visit. John brought them over. They seemed confused, as if they were expecting someone other than Lulu. They brought fancy dresses that she would never wear. They weren't hungry when offered food. They stayed for a short while and then went back to their own life.

Now before her is the face in the photograph with a whole body attached. She has soft, thick hair that Lulu is allowed to touch when the woman picks her up. She seems as strong as a man and squeezes Lulu just a bit too tightly. Her breath is sweet and fruity like a lollipop. Then the stranger cries silently for no reason, but just for a minute or so.

There are many fascinating things about this stranger, but it is her voice that Lulu likes best. She speaks as if she is singing when she talks directly to her. She uses a different voice just for her, quieter, sweeter, like she has known her all her life. Which, of course, she hasn't.

Then the woman is apologizing, but Lulu has no clue why. What has she done to her? She says she is the woman who birthed her. *Then who is Bee?* The stranger's name is like a fairy tale name—Zaima. Lulu remembers her papa and Bee telling her things about this Zaima. Those stories were just like other stories she was read from books. She wonders if Pooh Bear will show up someday too.

Zaima has brought a giant teddy bear for her and she can barely hold it without its touching the ground. It's not her birthday, but she's happy to have it. She also has books for her, more than the girl can carry. She loves books. *How did this Zaima know this?* No silly dresses from her, but colorful books about animals and trucks and faraway places. Lulu is only five, but she can read well, including much of her papa's farming manuals and nearly all of the words in Bee's cookbooks. Her favorite thing to read is not a book at all. It's that wooden box filled with yellow, stained cards that are filled with recipes, recorded in a perfect slanted writing that she had to learn again how to read. All the letters were connected, like it was in a secret code from long ago. The box belonged to Uncle John and when he died, it was given to her. She misses him and he won't be back, but at least he has Mac with him. Bee and papa told her where they thought he went but it made no sense to her. Father McGurley also talked about this peaceful place called heaven and it all seems hard to believe, like a fairy tale you know is made up to make you feel better about things.

Zaima reads her five whole books underneath the big birch tree. Then she says she'll stay for dinner, which turns out to be no ordinary dinner. Theodore goes out and gets walleye, fresh corn, and a big pie. Lulu is asked to beat the eggs and crush the saltines for the walleye. Brigid dips the fish into a special flour, then into the eggs, and rolls it in the crackers so it's ready to be pan-fried. Bee snags five bottles of wine from the bar, and Uncle Coop shows up with his famous potato salad that he adds pickles to. No one likes that except him, but everyone pretends to. Hemingway just shows up, bringing nothing to eat, only flowers for Bee.

At dusk, they all eat outside on two picnic tables shoved together. The still August night is perfect for lots of candles to keep away the mosquitoes. It seems Zaima likes wine. Lulu loses count of her glassfuls, but soon enough all five bottles are empty. When it's decided that Zaima shouldn't drive, Lulu offers to share her room. She tells Zaima that her bed has plenty of room for two.

Sometime during the night, when the room is flooded with the light of a full moon, Lulu wakes and snuggles close to Zaima. Why she feels so safe and familiar she does not know.

They wake early in the morning and decide to take a walk together through the orchards. Lulu is quiet and lets Zaima ramble on about where she lives, a magical city in California with a beautiful bridge that they will one day walk together. The child can already sense the woman's leaving.

Soon she prepares to do just that, before anyone else is even up. Zaima promises to come back, but can't say when. She stoops and takes Lulu into her arms and holds her again just a little too tightly, as if Lulu might run from her given the chance. She stands and hands Lulu a folded piece of white paper, then climbs into her old red pickup, and leaves a trail of dust on LaCore Road.

Lulu watches the last evidence of Zaima vanish as the road settles. Looking up, she sees that Theodore is standing on the porch, arms crossed, smiling and frowning at the same time as he often does.

"Why did she leave?"

"Oh, Lu, it has nothing to do with you. Zaima's looking for something. She couldn't stay because she hasn't found it yet."

"What does that mean?" Lulu asks impatiently.

Theodore has no easy answer to her simple question. He thinks of the many months he spent after returning to Empire, immobilized by inertia and doubt and his past failures, committing neither to staying nor leaving. *What had changed him? His mother's death? Brigid's love? Zaima's needing him? Lulu?*

"It means that sometimes the change you need comes from outside you," he says. "But something has to change inside you too. I think some people, like Bee, are just naturally happy. She doesn't think about it. She just feels it. Others, people like Zaima and even me, we have to search for it."

Lulu is satisfied with none of this. She squints her eyes, puts on a pouting frown, and throws the paper on the ground.

Theodore picks it up and takes her hand. He leads her to the porch step and they sit there close together, both watching the empty road. Theodore unfolds the note and wraps an arm around the child.

"Let's read what she wrote to you. Maybe that will help."

"I can read it myself," Lulu says. And she does.

Dearest Lulu,

I must seem strange to you, but you did curl up next to me last night. Maybe that's just your nature and how you sleep. Or maybe it's because we know each other in a special way.

I have no good excuse for not being here with you other than I knew I would fail you. I was not good enough, not whole enough, to provide all you would need and all you deserve.

I grew to love your papa and Bee and trusted them with the most valuable thing I've ever held in my arms. I trusted them with you. To be for you what I wasn't strong enough to be.

I used to write poems. I wrote them to understand what I was feeling. I don't write them anymore, but I will write one small one for you.

When you feel angry with me, and I know you will, please read these words again:

> know that there is love
> everywhere for you
> love close enough to touch
> and love so far away
> that you must use your imagination
> to feel it
> it is there
> and it is real

Zaima

IN THEODORE'S WORDS

LATER THAT DAY

I watch from the beach as they play in the warm waters of South Bar Lake. Brigid wears the red polka-dot two-piece that I just love. Lulu sports her Elmo swim trunks and T-shirt. She hates wearing anything tight, like a girly swimsuit.

The sun is high and intense, the dunes like rumpled, soft blankets.

Zaima took me aside last night at the end of our dinner. We were both pretty drunk and I was worried I wouldn't remember what she was about to tell me. But I do. She seemed agitated and asked me if I ever saw Nate. I told her only once and that it didn't go well, that my brother and I have lost something between us. Maybe it was never really there. She told me that she didn't hate him and hoped she wasn't the reason for the distance between us.

She also said she wasn't going back to California. She was headed to Dearborn instead. That's it. We hugged awkwardly and I think I held on to her a bit too long.

After Zaima left this morning, Lulu and I sat together on the porch step, just us two, for a long time. We both had questions, visible on our faces but trapped in our heads. We sat there, our bodies so close though not touching, staring straight ahead at everything and at nothing.

Eventually I suggested to her that she might say a prayer for Zaima. We sometimes cuddle in her bed at night and before she drifts off, she'll roll out an impromptu prayer in her perfect, simple words. It's usually only for one or two things, maybe gratitude for the night's homemade pizza or concern for the soul of a dead bird. She asks for nothing for herself.

But there on the porch she had nothing to say to me or to God. She stood, shoved Zaima's note into her pocket, and left me. God would have to wait.

I believe I'm no different than Zaima the day she landed in Empire, moving in a direction not self-determined. I'm not sure if it was her God or mine who piled mercy and grace on our troubled lives, but that doesn't matter. I just don't believe we did it. At least not alone.

And that's the best prayer I ever composed.

ACKNOWLEDGMENTS

THE AUTHOR WOULD LIKE TO THANK THE FOLLOWING FOR THEIR
HELP IN THE CREATION OF THIS BOOK:

JUDY AND MARTY SHEPARD, FOR THEIR BELIEF IN ME AND
WHAT I HAVE TO SAY

MIKKE AND GERALD KILTS, FOR THEIR INSPIRED
ASSISTANCE IN MY EXPLORATION OF THEIR LITTLE PIECE OF PARADISE,
EMPIRE, MICHIGAN

HANNAH FINDLING, FOR HER KNOWLEDGE OF ALL THINGS HORSES,
AND HER MOTHER, PAULA KILTS, MY WISE COUNSEL

CLINT AND GAYLA KILTS, FOR THEIR GENEROUS PROVISION OF WINTER
WRITING SPACE ON TODDY POND, PENOBSCOT, MAINE

REVEREND DIANNE RODRIGUEZ, FOR HER PUSHING, PUSHING, PUSHING
ME DEEPER INTO THE WHY OF THINGS, THE GOD IN THINGS

AND

RIVA PACKARD, MY DARLING DAUGHTER AND SOURCE
ON THE FASCINATING NATURE OF MILLENNIALS